What the critics are saying...

"A fast pace read that will keep you on the edge of your seat to find out what happens next. This intricate plot has a wonderful flow with many twists and turns... The sex scenes and ménage is beautifully done and extremely erotic... Pick this one up, you won't be disappointed!" ~Luisa, Cupid's Library Reviewers

"The characters are charming and very real. They are vulnerable, compassionate, and angry. Some are vengeful, mean or secretive. This is an intricate plot that will have you wondering what is going to happen next. Erik and Leila are a wonderful couple... I am surprised my computer didn't melt during most of the scenes." ~Oleta M. Blaylock, Just Erotic Romance Reviews

"I would recommend this story to you if you like the sex to be raw and up front. It is real, it is hot...and it is very much a major part of the action in this book. Ms. Kerce tells a good futuristic tale. You can practically see the planets and the ships flying through space." ~Jenn, Coffee Time Romance

"His Carnal Need is the next exhilarating story in Ruth D. Kerce's Xylon Warriors series and certainly lives up to its title... The sex is steamy, emotional, and highly explosive... There's blackmail, betrayal, and an unexpected twist thrown into the mix, keeping readers on their toes. Ms. Kerce writes a sensuous, erotic futuristic romance that will entice readers to turn page after page and discover the secrets hidden between the covers of His Carnal Need. ~Sinclair Reid, Romance Reviews Today

Ruth D. Kerce

His Carnal Need

XYLON WARRIORS II

ELLORA'S CAVE
ROMANTICA PUBLISHING

An Ellora's Cave Romantica Publication

www.ellorascave.com

His Carnal Need

ISBN # 1419953079
Edited by: Pamela Campbell
Cover art by: Syneca

Electronic book Publication: June, 2005
Trade paperback Publication: December, 2005

Excerpt from *Diamond Studs*

Warning:

The following material contains graphic sexual content meant for mature readers. *His Carnal Need* has been rated *E-rotic* by a minimum of three independent reviewers.

Ellora's Cave Publishing offers three levels of Romantica™ reading entertainment: S (S-ensuous), E (E-rotic), and X (X-treme).

S-ensuous love scenes are explicit and leave nothing to the imagination.

E-rotic love scenes are explicit, leave nothing to the imagination, and are high in volume per the overall word count. In addition, some E-rated titles might contain fantasy material that some readers find objectionable, such as bondage, submission, same sex encounters, forced seductions, etc. E-rated titles are the most graphic titles we carry; it is common, for instance, for an author to use words such as "fucking", "cock", "pussy", etc., within their work of literature.

X-treme titles differ from E-rated titles only in plot premise and storyline execution. Unlike E-rated titles, stories designated with the letter X tend to contain controversial subject matter not for the faint of heart.

Also by Ruth D. Kerce

His Carnal Need
Xylon Warriors

Prologue
The Sand Moon

Obscured by heavy, black clouds from an approaching storm, no stars or planets glittered in the eerie-looking night sky. She'd counted on the darkness and worsening weather to hide her presence and keep her safe. She'd counted wrong.

Josella's pulse raced, and her heart pounded against her ribs. She kicked out a half-broken window from the second story of the abandoned abode she was hiding in and crawled onto the outside ledge. Quiet did her little good now. She needed to escape.

She cut herself on a jagged piece of glass, and blood trickled down her arm. She winced, but ignored the wound...and the pain. She'd tend to it later.

The Egesa had found her!

Raised in another star system, the first time she'd seen the half-lizard, half-humanoid creatures with their bald heads, yellow eyes, long thin tongues, and claw-like hands, she'd screamed her head off. Her sister had warned her about the vile Slave Masters, but the warning didn't do the monsters justice.

She'd since learned the Egesa considered humanoid females a prime catch. On the Sand Moon, she was considered sexual currency among many of the gang-like groups.

As she swung onto the branch of a nearby tree, their foul stench filled her nostrils. The creatures lurked close by. Despite their attempt at stealth, she heard them moving through the building, trying to locate her.

Grateful she hadn't chosen a place in the flatlands to hide, she shimmied down the tree and ran into the hills. She knew of another place a few miles away. Only by moving from place to place had she survived so far. Her luck wouldn't last forever. She needed to find a way off the moon soon or find a protector.

Previously held captive on Marid, the main moon of Xylon, she'd stowed away on an orbiter, trying to escape the Egesa Slave Masters who had held her. On Marid, she'd been a mine worker, so she hadn't worried about sexual abuse, just torture. *Just.* She'd blocked out many of the memories for her own sanity. When she'd boarded the orbiter, she'd hoped they were headed to Xylon, where her sister lived — where she would be safe. But that had been wishful thinking.

If she'd known they were traveling to the Sand Moon, the most primitive of the Banishment Zones, she might have stayed put on Marid. She couldn't even remember the last time she'd eaten. She stopped to catch her breath.

A light breeze fluttered her long hair into her face. She pushed the tangled strands away, cringing at the gritty feel on her fingers. Sand. She hated the sand.

"Josella…" a voice rasped in the darkness.

Her heart leapt, and she took off running. She couldn't let them find her. *Please, Halah*, she begged silently to the sister she hadn't seen in years. Halah had cared for her after their parents died in an explosion. She was the only person Josella truly loved and trusted. *Please, rescue me.*

Chapter One
The Lair of Xylon

The crowd didn't deter him. He knew what he wanted, what he needed, what he intended to have. From across the room, he located her, a radiant beauty among women. He'd known she was here. He felt her energy.

Her easy grace, combined with strength, intelligence, and a sensual innateness drew him like no other. His heart rate accelerated, and his body went on sexual alert. *You belong to me!*

She attended the festivities only on official business. She never participated in the Joining Party rituals. He knew. Once his erotic visions of her had begun, he'd monitored her every move. "You are predestined as my mate, my beauty. I will allow no other male to claim you. Only me."

She'd dressed in the traditional female Joining colors of orchid and pink—instead of Warrior black and Medical white that reflected the status of a Xylon Warrior and Healer. He liked the feminine look. So did his cock, which stirred in anticipation of being gloved deep within her.

Soon, her body, along with her emotions, would belong to him. He intended to show her every decadent, physical pleasure she'd ever imagined, as well as some she'd probably never dared even in her fantasies.

Where her emotions were concerned, he knew her dark secrets. He understood what she needed, maybe better than she. The visions, explicit and detailed, revealed her deepest desires to him. He planned to give her every one of those desires for as long as life existed in his body—a body that throbbed with need as he watched her search the crowd, looking for signs of trouble.

The flowing, almost sheer pink skirt she wore hung down to her knees. Split on all four sides, the garment exposed a good amount of shapely thigh with each step she took. Underneath, she wore a translucent covering that barely hid her pussy from his view. His hands fisted at his sides. He wanted to rip away the material and plunge his fingers up inside her, until she cried out to him in ecstasy.

The orchid-colored sleeveless top, cut deep in front and narrow on the sides, allowed an enticing view of her full breasts. He itched to caress those mounds, brush his mouth along the soft-looking flesh, and suck the nipples he saw straining against the thin material.

The fact that other Warriors also saw her seductive assets made him crazy. A low growl rumbled from his throat. He wanted to hide her away from all others' eyes, make certain she craved what he alone offered — total emotional and sexual completion.

More than arrogance about the ability to satiate her fueled his thoughts and actions. He'd do anything to make her want and need him. Of her own free will, not from a sense of duty to Xylon and their society, or as a result of predestined visions, but because she couldn't live without him and what he could give her.

A sparkle, trailing along her satiny tresses, captured his attention. Her cinnamon-colored hair hung in a braid, woven with a golden ribbon, all the way down to her waist. He preferred her hair loose, and images of the long strands brushing across his naked body came to mind.

She sexually teased her lovers with great delight, or so he'd heard. She liked control. So did he. Regardless of her declared sexual tastes, he knew in reality she craved even more carnal, erotic experiences. He'd see that she got them.

Through him, she'd learn the pleasures of submission. Her body trapped beneath his, vulnerable, with her begging him to give her his cock, to take her to sexual heights she'd never known, was a fantasy he would fulfill.

She stepped clear of the crowd, and he eased closer. Even from this distance, her eyes drew him, identical in color to her hair, sparkling with intelligence and sensual secrets. With his view of her now unobstructed, he took in her gorgeous legs, toned and long, even though she wasn't a tall woman. He ached to feel those legs wrapped around his waist while he rode her hard.

Golden laces adorned her feet. Not close enough to see her toes, he imagined a soft pink covered the nails. He wondered how she'd react to his tongue grazing the soles of her delicate feet, lapping between each small digit.

The urge to claim her, now, hit him so hard he felt lightheaded. Because of her breeder status, many male Warriors wanted to Brand her as their own, but all had failed. He would not fail. She was his breeder-mate. The visions showed him the truth. *You've seen our future, as well, haven't you?*

"That's why you've refused all others," he said aloud.

A soft voice whispered, "Refuse? I would never refuse a Class 1 fuck, honey." A feminine tongue licked at his ear. "Come with me and my friends. We will pleasure your body."

He frowned and brushed aside the female seeking attention. "Find someone else." Other women paled in comparison to *her*. He stalked forward, never taking his eyes off the woman soon to be his.

Leila Abdera didn't see him, but she felt him stalking her, felt his sensual pull. In an attempt to evade him, she weaved through the throng of Xylon Warriors engaged in the Joining Party festivities.

Joining Parties, where Warriors indulged in sex acts while others watched, weren't a preference of hers. But as a Xylon Healer, she attended these events in case anyone overindulged and required treatment.

Their entire society revolved around the joining of bodies, and sometimes even minds, for true breeder-mates. Or so the legends told. The complete physical and mental connections kept them unified and strong. Until recently…

Due to constant attacks from the Egesa Slave Masters, determined to either enslave or extinguish Xylon's people, their society had suffered greatly. Xylon's new Warrior Leader, after taking control, had vowed to shift the balance of power and rebuild their fragile numbers so they could effectively fight their enemies once more.

The Joining Parties helped the Warriors relax after their intensive training sessions. These occasional festivities drew most, if not all, those inhabiting The Lair—the underground headquarters for the men and women commissioned to protect the planet.

Not to detract from the event tonight, she wore the female garb expected of participants, though she no longer indulged. Certainly, one less Warrior wouldn't make any difference.

But *he* was persistent, intense, determined. Carnal and raw in his needs. Her body craved him. Her mind would not allow it, other than in her fantasies.

The man was too dominant. A Class 1 Warrior. He would need to tame her, insist on submission. Submission was not an option for her. Only when she maintained sexual control did she allow herself to join with another. Abused in the past, she had long ago determined never again to put herself into a vulnerable situation. Still, the thought of allowing this one man control over her body, to experience the darker taste of complete sexual surrender, intrigued her.

She shook her head. The joining going on around her had affected her thinking and sensitized her body, making it difficult to resist her burgeoning needs. Giving in to her needs would only lead to disaster. Normally, she managed these events without incident. Tonight was different. She felt him touching her mentally, manipulating and changing the images in her head to something sexually wicked, each time her gaze flickered over an erotic coupling. "That's impossible. I know he can't do that."

Her nipples hardened and moisture gathered between her thighs. She often experienced erotic visions of them together. Not official breeder visions, she wouldn't accept the events as such, only powerful fantasies. Within the sensual thoughts, she gave him what he desired and enjoyed it. Tonight the decadent images, stronger than usual, ran wild and plagued her at every turn, screaming to be fulfilled. If he approached her now…

"No." She circled around a banquet table, seeking a distraction. Her stomach rumbled from the mixture of sweet, tangy, and spicy odors. Food would take her mind off her other, physical hunger.

Before she indulged, a particularly lusty threesome caught her attention. Pitch Pantera, a Class 2 Warrior, along with the Xylon Leader's two sisters, lay naked atop a low platform, among a pile of multicolored rugs and pillows. One woman hungrily sucked Pitch's cock, taking his full length down her throat. The other crawled along his body and straddled his face. She lowered her shaved pussy over his mouth. "Lick me," Leila heard the woman order in a tone that no lower-ranking Warrior would ever disobey. Both females held the highest-level Class 1 ranking and used their power unabashedly to fulfill their needs. Pitch spread her wet folds and tongued her lustily.

Though normally not averse to watching, Leila turned away. She felt too achy and on edge tonight. If she stayed here much longer, her body would force her to participate with someone, somehow, or she'd go mad with wanting.

She rushed forward and smashed into a broad chest. Masculine fingers wrapped around her forearms, restraining her. Her heart lurched, and a gasp caught in her throat.

Panicked, she tried to pull away. Her eyes snapped up to the face of the male holding her. "Oh." She breathed a sigh of relief and relaxed. "Kam." It wasn't *him*. Nor any other who might demand compliance. She glanced down at his hands on her. "What are you doing?"

"Looking for you." His voice deepened. "I need you, Leila."

Her heart skipped a beat. "Need me?" Someone bumped into her, pushing her closer to the Warrior's body. Her breasts grazed Kam Nextor's chest, and her nipples hardened so much they hurt. His muscular thigh pressed against her pussy. When he made no move to step away from the intimate contact, uneasiness crept up her spine. "Kam?"

She tried to pull back, but he held her tightly. The tall, blond-haired Warrior, with kind blue eyes, and half-brother to the mate of the Warrior Leader, had always made her feel safe in the past. Now, she wasn't so certain. Though in his arms, she remained protected from any other Warriors still seeking a joiner.

I'm on edge and paranoid. Kam was her friend and wanted nothing more from her than that. She trusted him. Her eyes rose to meet his. "You look pale." She cupped his cheek, checking his temperature against her palm. She was about to ask him if he felt ill, when she heard a low growl, not from him, but originating elsewhere. The vibration skittered along her ultra-sensitive nerves. She glanced over her shoulder. No one seemed to be paying them any special attention. Where had that sound come from?

Kam whispered in her ear. "I need a shot." His fingers tightened around her arms, almost painfully, drawing her attention back to him.

She pushed away the apprehensive feeling enveloping her, and her gaze returned to his. His request didn't surprise her. They'd been through this too often lately. "Kam… You've had enough." His addiction to the special formula created to treat him saddened her. She wished another, better, way existed to ease his pain. "Besides, I can't leave the party. You know that."

"Please." He rubbed his thigh along her pussy.

Oh! To avoid gasping at the incredible feel of his thigh between hers, she chewed at her bottom lip. His movement, no doubt on purpose to sway her, reminded her of how long she'd gone without an orgasm, even a small one.

"Three other Healers are here. Just one more shot to see me through for a while. We have a mission coming up. I need to stay strong."

The pleading look in his eyes softened her heart to his need, and compassion overruled better judgment. His headaches were steadily growing worse and more frequent. She knew he feared for his sanity. The shots helped, but they overstimulated his body, raising his heart rate and blood pressure. And lately the medicine made him more aggressive.

"Is the pain bad?"

"Not yet, but the throbbing started about an hour ago. I won't make it through the night." He moved his thigh away from her.

She almost groaned at the loss of contact. She needed to come badly.

"Please, Leila. Help me."

She couldn't refuse to ease his suffering. "Do you have your transport-connector?"

He relaxed, releasing his hold on her. "Yes." He unhooked the connector from his belt. "The lab?"

"My quarters." She kept a small supply of special drugs there, for running tests and experiments in private during off-hours. As a perk of being in charge of the medical facility, she'd arranged installation of custom equipment right into her assigned living space.

"Thanks, Leila." He leaned down and brushed a soft kiss across her cheek. In the next instant, the air shimmered, and he was gone.

She reached for the transport-connector on her woven belt of gold and black-colored material to follow.

A muscular arm snaked around her waist, pulling her roughly back against a body as hard as stone. Not only his chest and stomach, but she also felt iron thighs and an equally iron-hard cock pressing close. A spicy scent teased her nostrils. She didn't need to look. She knew who had her restrained. *Him.*

"Meeting Kam again?" the deep voice rasped.

Perspiration formed beneath her hair and down the center of her back. Her heart pounded painfully in her chest, and she couldn't seem to find her voice. He leaned closer, wrapping her completely within his body heat. His tongue traced the rim of her ear, achingly soft and slow. *Oh, my!* Her limbs trembled at the moist touch, which she felt all the way down to her toes. She tried hard to control her body, her reactions. She didn't want him to know how much he affected her.

"Are you letting Kam fuck you now, Leila?" he whispered, pressing his pelvis purposely against her. The fingers of his free hand grazed the outside of her right breast, moving back and forth in light, lazy strokes, easing beneath the material and inching toward her nipple.

His touch and voice were soft, but she felt his anger simmering right below the surface. Her sex life was nobody's business. And she didn't want him touching her intimately without permission, no matter how fantastic his hands and tongue felt. Not to mention his cock, which the uniform he wore did nothing to contain. She elbowed him in the ribs.

"Ow!" His arm dropped from her waist, and he stepped back. "Damn, Leila."

She spun around to face him—Erik Rhodes—a man too sexy for his own good and the second-highest ranking Warrior in The Lair. No woman refused Erik…except her. Maybe that's why he persisted so doggedly. "Why are you such a bastard?"

One side of his mouth quirked up into a grin. He raked his fingers through his thick, brown hair, while rubbing his side with his other hand. "I asked a question. No need to get violent, sweetheart."

Leila pressed her fists to her hips. "Don't call me that. I'm not your sweetheart. I'm a Warrior worthy of the same respect as any other Warrior. You enjoy getting a rise out of me too much, Erik. Go play with someone else."

He crowded her into a nearby corner, his green eyes glistening with mischief under the lights. "You've got that backwards. I'm the one who gets a rise out of you." His hand brushed his thigh. "And I'm not playing, Leila. I want you."

Her gaze dipped between his legs. The noticeable bulge shot her sensual cravings to painful proportions and brought back the image of his long, thick cock. Unknown to him, she'd seen him erect once on a video monitor, seen him *jacking off*, as the Earthlings called it, according to Alexa, the mate of the Warrior Leader, who had been born and raised on that planet.

She gave herself a mental shake, dislodging the erotic image, along with the sudden, unexpected desire to taste his cock, and know how deeply into her mouth she could suck its length. When he leaned closer and brushed her cheek with his, she trembled and tried to push him back.

He wouldn't budge.

"I'm not interested, Erik." Her voice shook just slightly, but enough to be noticeable — damn it.

"You're lying. You need a good fucking. By me."

She sucked in a sharp breath. The man was too arrogant and unfortunately intuitive for her best interests. She refused to let him rattle her, though. "I need to leave." Duty and friendship took precedence over desire, giving her the excuse she needed. "Keep your cock sheathed and under control. I already have plans."

His lighthearted grin faded. "To meet Kam? You two seem joined at the hip lately. What's going on? Am I going to have to challenge one of my best friends for you?"

"Don't be ridiculous. There's nothing physical between us." Why she even explained, she didn't know. With him towering over her, the spicy scent of his body, the sounds of sex surrounding them — she didn't know what she was doing or saying anymore. She should have simply said, "I'm not some prize to be fought over and won." And left it at that. But this wasn't her first encounter with Erik, by far, and tonight she didn't feel like parrying with him.

"Then you won't mind if I join you two."

She sighed. "Erik, stop stalking me."

He pressed his body along hers, crowding her even deeper into the corner. His hands roamed her hips and eased down toward her ass, gathering her skirt with his fingers at the same time. He caressed the bare skin of her thigh, then moved slowly toward her pussy.

His light touch felt good against her skin. He knew just how to touch her for the greatest sexual response. She couldn't stop herself from leaning into him and mewling.

"Mmm. That's right, baby." His lips touched the edge of her mouth. "I'm not stalking you, Leila. I'm seducing you." The vid-cell on his belt beeped, causing them both to jump at the unexpected interruption. He grumbled and stepped back, palming the communication device.

Leila breathed a sigh of relief. Probably for the best. She really didn't want to deal with him right now, not in these surroundings. He stimulated her senses too much, made her crave things that would only complicate her life. She took advantage of his distraction and activated her transport-connector.

Erik frowned when she dematerialized out. "Talk," he said into the cell. He barely paid attention to the voice on the other end, even though it belonged to Braden Koll, the Warrior Leader. His mind remained elsewhere.

Whenever he pressed his body closely against Leila's, he smelled her arousal. She desired more from him than friendship. He knew she did. She just hadn't admitted her need yet.

For himself, he wanted to rip off her clothes, drop to his knees, bury his mouth between her legs, and suck her essence inside him. On missions, they worked well together. He knew they'd burn hot as lovers, if she'd give him a chance to prove he wasn't really the bastard she often labeled him.

"What?" he asked, missing Braden's words.

The Marid Mission is a go, he was informed.

At the thought of a new mission, his heartbeat accelerated, and the blood raced through his veins in anticipation. Leila was essential to this particular mission's team. At least one Class 1 Warrior needed to accompany her to Marid, one of the five moons orbiting their planet. He'd already petitioned Braden to allow that Warrior to be him.

Although the Joining Party seemed crowded tonight, many of Xylon's Warriors had fled or abdicated to the side of the Slave Masters after the last uprising. Most believed The Lair would fall and decided to get out, align themselves with the stronger side, while they could.

The Lair hadn't fallen. But now, few remained in comparison to their previous numbers. With fewer Warriors available, Leila would have to comply with Braden's decision, whether she liked his team assignments or not.

"I'll be there," he answered, when instructed to materialize outside the Council Chamber for a special meeting. He disconnected the transmission and re-clipped the cell to his belt.

He stared back into the corner where he'd had Leila trapped. While touching her body and looking into her eyes, the need to fuck her had grown stronger than ever, making more than his dick hurt. Something deep inside him had turned over, making him feel raw and exposed.

He needed to know the details of the relationship between her and Kam. It bothered him that all of a sudden they were spending so much time together, and in secret.

Kam kept too many secrets, even from his close friends. Erik had never liked secrets.

He'd believed Leila when she'd said nothing physical was going on. He supposed. But she hadn't explained further. Why? He grabbed his transport-connector.

No matter what the mystery between Kam and Leila, he knew one indisputable truth. "That woman is *mine*."

* * * * *

Leila prepared the stimulant. "Drop your pants." If the Warrior Council—Xylon's governing body—found out about this, they'd both end up banished to one of the outer moons.

Kam's eyes widened. "Excuse me?"

"I'm going to inject the medicine into your hip this time." She tapped the three-pronged needle. "It'll be more effective. Lean over the back of the seating, there." She pointed to the red and blue stuffed lounger behind him. Usually, she tended to him in The Lair's Med Lab, but her quarters provided better privacy, especially since he needed the stimulant more often. From now on, she'd inject him here. That way, she could ensure no one discovered their secret.

"Are you all right?" He tugged at his belt.

"What do you mean?"

"You're flushed. I know it's not from the prospect of seeing my naked butt." He chuckled and waggled his eyebrows.

"Don't sell yourself short. I'm all aflutter." She batted her eyelashes, then laughed at the ridiculous action she'd witnessed once on an off-planet satellite feed. Even so, she recognized Kam as a strong, sexy man. A woman would have to be blind not to acknowledge that, even if uninterested in a relationship. His blond hair and pale, blue eyes often turned heads—both female and male. "After you dematerialized out, Erik showed up. It's nothing."

"Somehow, I doubt that." Kam pushed down his pants and leaned over. "Go easy on me. I'm not him. Remember that when you're sticking me."

She sterilized a spot on his hip, and slowly injected the stimulant. Kam's biology of half-Xylon, half-Tamarian caused his body to rebel on a regular basis. She pulled out the prongs, and waited for the three puncture wounds to self-heal, an ability most Warriors and breeders possessed. After only a matter of moments, the punctures closed and disappeared. Too bad he couldn't self-heal the rest of his body. The internal damage was too intricate and severe. The best he could do was hold his own, and not even that anymore without the stimulant. Unable to resist his submissive position, she caressed his butt cheek. Nice. Strong. Worthy of a woman's touch. She wondered how Erik's would compare.

He stiffened slightly, then chuckled. "You might not want to do that, unless you're prepared for the consequences."

Her pulse jumped, and she jerked her hand away. Touching a patient sexually during treatment went against Xylon's medical code of ethics. "Sorry." She stepped back. She obviously still needed a sexual release of some sort. Damn the party, and Erik's presence hadn't helped. "You're all done." She turned to dispose of the needle.

He slid his pants up. "Thanks. Have you told anyone about this?"

"About the injections? No."

"Braden would pull me from missions if he knew. He's already thinking about it, because of my headaches. I couldn't stand reassignment to research and training. You will keep our secret, won't you?"

"I don't have a choice. The Council wouldn't approve of the use of an experimental drug on a Warrior. They'd remove my ranking, if they found out."

Kam frowned. "I'm sorry. I put you in this situation. I know what you're doing could cost your authorization status. Let's arrange this situation where you're not involved anymore. Give me some prongs and formula. If caught, I'll say I stole the medicine and have been injecting myself."

"No one's going to believe you, given XT-66 isn't a drug we supply for general Warrior use. It's specific for your biology. I made the decision to create, administer, and test these injections, not you. I knew what I was involving myself in. It's getting harder to keep private though. Erik has already noticed we're spending a lot of time together."

"I didn't realize. What's he think we're doing?"

"Fucking."

At her response, Kam nearly choked. He coughed to clear his throat. "Sorry. I wasn't expecting you to say that." When she said nothing further, a concerned look entered his eyes. "I'll fix it."

"No need. It works in my favor, actually."

He cocked his head, then leaned back against the lounger and crossed his arms. "He wants you, Leila, and for more than just a fast fuck, unlike some others I've seen hovering around you lately."

"He wants any woman who will spread her legs. Sex is all he ever thinks about." As many Warriors did these days. Even though their society revolved around physical joinings, Xylon seemed overly obsessed with the activity, in her opinion.

"That's not true, and you know it. At least, he's not like that anymore. You can trust him. Erik sometimes speaks before he thinks." When she arched an eyebrow, he amended, "Well, more than just sometimes, but he's a good man. With a good heart."

She shook her head. "He's too aggressive." Even though that was exactly what she craved, deep down. "I couldn't relax with him. I need a different sort of man. Someone more like…you, maybe." Kam was such a gentle soul, most of the time. He never demanded more of her than she wanted to give. As such, she knew she could control him. She'd never be able to control Erik.

"Is that an invitation?" A smile tugged at his lips. "Is that why I got the extra special treatment here in your quarters?"

"Maybe. What do you think?" Mixing sex with friendship often drove a relationship right over the edge to destruction. She'd hate to lose Kam as a friend. *But I need sex.* She shifted uncomfortably.

He uncrossed his arms and glanced at the remote sensor strapped to his wrist. The small device displayed readings from the mood sensor clipped to his belt. "I think you just want Erik to think you're fucking someone on a regular basis, hoping he'll leave you alone." His eyes met hers. "Or maybe you're overstimulated from the party, and from Erik. And you're looking for someone to ease your sexual tension. A substitute." When she pulled her gaze from his, a slow smile crossed his face. "Or am I completely wrong on all points here, and you're finally seeking a breeder-mate?"

She turned her back. "I'm not interested in mating with anyone. Not to breed. Not yet." The thought of being bound to someone, especially someone who might expect submission made her shudder. However, she could never respect a man who allowed her to dominate. Bound forever to someone she didn't love or respect... An intolerable thought indeed.

Eventually, Xylon's Council would insist she mate for the good of their society, to help repopulate their numbers. Not many breeders remained. And predestined breeder-mates, those who experienced special, erotic visions of their future prior to being bound together, were even rarer. She feared her fantasies, those she refused to accept as anything else, were actually just that—those rare visions. If so, it meant she and Erik would eventually join and mate for life, no matter her wishes. She chewed on her thumbnail.

The Council had been patient and understanding with her up to now, but their patience wouldn't last forever. She needed to heal her damaged psyche, so she could move on with her life, minus this overwhelming, psychological weight she carried. Maybe then she could even indulge her true sexual desires without fear.

"I'm not what you need, Leila. Believe me. Erik cares about you. Give him a chance. He'd never hurt you. Not intentionally anyway. We both know what you've been through. Getting involved with a dominant male and having a good experience would help you get past things."

She spun back around, not believing how simply he presented the solution. "Get past things! I can't just get past things. And don't tell me what I need." The vehemence in her voice made her cringe. He'd hit too close to the truth, for her own thoughts had drifted in much the same direction lately. "Sorry." She lowered her tone. "What's done is done. I don't intend to cower in the corner and whine about it the rest of my life. But I have to deal with it in a way that doesn't make me crazy." She would decide when and how to move on, nobody else. "That's just the way it is, Kam."

He strode forward and wrapped her in his arms. "If I could change what happened to you, I would. Erik would, too. Your Initiation Rite should have been an erotic, satisfying experience. Not a time of torture and degradation."

Though a strong, caring, and probably a sexually safe man, Leila still stood stiffly against him, unable to totally accept his tender gesture. She couldn't give in to her emotions, any more than she could give in to her darkest desires. If she did, she feared she'd crumble completely.

The ceremony to prepare her body for breeding had scarred her for life, literally and figuratively. Nobody knew about her physical scars, except the trio who had caused them, along with Xylon's former leader. And only a handful knew about her emotional scars. Her team had found out about her atypical experience when a video recording of the rite had surfaced during a mission.

She'd learned to live with what had happened to her as best as she could. Consequently, she avoided sex, except when her need grew so great that she couldn't ignore the cravings. In those times, she chose a male who she could control and who would give her a mild release, just enough to quell the desire for more. Easy. Clean. And taken care of. Not overly satisfying, but better than nothing. She glanced up at Kam. He would fill that need perfectly. If only he were willing.

His eyes locked with hers. "I see your thoughts, Leila. I don't need my sensor to tell me what you're feeling right now.

You don't conceal your emotions well. Just because I'm a nice guy most of the time, doesn't mean I will let a woman control me. I know that's what you look for sexually."

Disbelief filled her, and she gaped at his words. "How did you know what I—"

"Warriors talk. At least some of them who've indulged you have."

Damn males. None of them could keep their mouths shut. A Warrior who took a submissive position during sex shouldn't brag about it. If she could satisfy herself, something she'd never been able to manage very well, she'd turn her back on the whole lot of them. "Certainly, you could submit with the right woman."

His hand drifted down to her ass, and he squeezed one fleshy mound through the barely there material. "Not a chance. Don't for a moment underestimate what I might demand from a woman. My needs might surprise and even shock you."

When Kam again squeezed her ass, and then glided his fingers down her crack while murmuring something in her ear about "a good ass fuck", she pushed his hand away and stepped back. Better not chance getting involved in something she wasn't yet ready to handle.

His vid-cell beeped, breaking the tension between them. Even so, he continued staring at her, his gaze raking her body, through the next three beeps, before he took the transmission. He disconnected after only a moment. "Braden wants me in the Council Chamber. You need to come, too."

"The mission to Marid?"

"Yes. He's ready to put together the team."

A mission. And an important one. She knew she rated as an automatic member this time. She looked forward to it. Anything was better than dwelling on personal matters that others couldn't even begin to understand, no matter how hard they tried. "Let's go."

* * * * *

Halah stared at the accommodations prepared for her soon-to-be prisoners. A communal bed, good enough for slaves, sat in the corner. Pillows and extra blankets covered the hard floor. A private area to bathe, more than most slaves enjoyed, was located conveniently through a side door.

They'd be captured within a few days, and become her responsibility. The place and time were set. She'd finally managed to attain enough credits to qualify for slave ownership, if she so wished for a personal stable. Still, she knew the Egesa Slave Masters watched her closely, not trusting her loyalty — the lowly creatures.

She hated what she'd gotten herself into, but changing the past wasn't possible. She had to live with her choices.

At least one woman would be among the captured. The Healer. Then, she suspected anywhere from one to three additional slaves. She wondered if the Class 2 Warrior she'd battled on Earth would be one of them. Since their encounter, she hadn't been able to get him out of her mind. She'd suggested his presence for this mission, knowing he and the Healer often worked together. She'd read the information in The Dome files. The massive amount of data Marid possessed about Xylon's personnel astounded her.

The blond-haired Warrior occupying her thoughts helped tie her to a bed, but hadn't taken advantage. So noble. Tying him up, stripping him bare, and fucking him mercilessly held appeal, and she intended to indulge. She had the right to get a little fun out of this deal. If he wasn't among the selected Warriors sent, perhaps she'd choose to play with another.

Getting to keep them as her slaves would be the challenge. They were considered enemies of Marid, more so than most Xylon Warriors. *If discovered, the Commanders will try to take them from me.* As their captor, keeping them was her right though. Even Marid's leader couldn't argue with his own law. She hoped.

Regardless, whoever ended up as her prisoners, she'd treat them as she wished, not as ordered. Her treatment of them would be better than the poor enslaved who toiled in the mines or those who served as experimental patients for research. They should consider themselves lucky. By agreeing to help, she was doing them a favor.

She'd need to see to their safety and eventual escape, too, whether she liked the prearranged plan or not. The Warrior Leader held too much control over her to defy him. Her hand curled into a fist, a nervous reaction. If Marid's Leader found out that she had betrayed The Dome, her life would be over. She planned to be extra careful.

After completing this assignment, she would, in turn, finally get what she'd searched for over the past few years. Then she'd disappear to another star system and leave this entire life behind her. Maybe she'd even return to Earth. The planet, still primitive in comparison to Xylon and its moons, involved a simpler lifestyle. And Earth was free.

For now…

* * * * *

Leila settled in at the Council Chamber's official table. Thirteen heavy chairs surrounded the large, wooden structure. Warriors occupied half the seats.

During the last uprising from the banishment zones, many Council members had vanished, including their former leader, Laszlo, who'd led the Warriors for as long as she could remember. After his disappearance, Braden had taken charge. And he didn't always do things as laid out by Council Law.

At the head of the table, he sat tall, looking strong and capable. His dark hair and violet eyes commanded attention. Alexa Sandor, his mate, now pregnant with twins, sat to his left. Erik sat to Braden's right. Torque Koll, Braden's brother, sat next to Erik.

Torque made her uncomfortable. His shoulder-length black hair, deep brown eyes that looked nearly black, and muscles that went on forever intimidated her to say the least. From the stories she'd heard, his badass looks went right along with a rebellious nature. They'd only worked together once, briefly, so she didn't really know him, or know what to expect from him.

Kam sat beside Alexa. Their blond hair and blue eyes weren't an identical match, but close enough. The half-Earth, half-Xylon woman was his half-sister, and the only super breeder remaining on Xylon. Leila sat next to Kam.

Tonight's meeting consisted of a mixture of select Warriors and friends. Braden called these types of meetings for sensitive issues or missions that had already received Council approval, if a problem or special circumstance arose.

Braden cleared his throat, as he always did to start a meeting. "You all know from Kam and Leila's research that a serious problem exists. The substance used in the first step of our Initiation Rite, to protect our people from poisons and diseases, is no longer effective. The Egesa somehow found a formula to combat the protective elements. Through sexual penetration, Marid Assassins, along with Commanders, can now sterilize our unbranded female breeders, which puts us in a vulnerable position."

Leila shuddered at the mere mention of the Egesa. The half-lizard, half-humanoid Slave Masters from Marid were cruel, disgusting creatures. Their Commanders and Assassins—former Warriors—were even crueler. They possessed the same high-level training as Xylon's protectors, along with inside knowledge of Lair society. Without their leadership and betrayal of their own people, Xylon could have easily defeated the Egesa long ago. Now, if Xylon's Warriors didn't defeat them soon, their kind would take over the planet and any other planet they could enslave.

"This mission," Braden continued, "involves taking an orbiter to Marid, getting inside The Dome, finding the compound they're using to override our protection, and retrieving it for analysis. All the details are in the folders in front of you. In addition, any information acquired about the Marid

Leader — Daegal — is to be brought back for study, so we can find ways to destroy him and the Egesa central headquarters in The Dome."

"I thought Daegal was to be neutralized on this mission, not further studied," Alexa replied.

"The odds of accomplishing an assassination without additional information are slim at this time. And we want to make sure we take out The Dome along with him, otherwise someone else may simply step in and take control."

"Like Laszlo," Erik stated bluntly.

"Laszlo will not betray us!" Kam responded without hesitation, his voice hard and unwavering. His hand curled into a fist on top of the table.

"So you say," Erik shot back.

By Kam's aggressiveness, Leila could tell the shot was beginning to adversely affect him. Beneath the table, she squeezed his thigh to let him know he needed to ease off.

He slumped slightly in the chair. The hand on the table pressed flat. His other hand brushed across the top of hers, under the table, in acknowledgement. When he continued, he lowered his voice. "Yes, Laszlo's disappeared. But he's working to help us, not working against us. I know he is."

"Either way," Braden interrupted, "it doesn't change what needs doing for the safety of our female breeders. With the approval of the Council, I've chosen a team."

Leila glanced around the table. Everyone in the room seemed to stop breathing in anticipation of the announcement. Equally anxious about his selection, she returned her attention to him and waited.

"Leila, you will be Research on this mission. You're the only one who can properly identify the substance we're seeking. Kam, you will be Consultant. Before Laszlo disappeared, he confided sensitive information to you about Daegal that might come in handy. You're to collect the additional data we need about him and The Dome. Team Leader is Erik."

Given the Warriors in attendance, Leila knew the leader would be Erik or Torque, since she doubted Braden would go himself — not while Alexa carried his unborn children. And now with his new position, the safety of The Lair Compound lay on his shoulders.

Torque, though Braden's brother, often acted unpredictable and wild, and was not really leader material, in her opinion. Erik, also wild, took his duty as a Warrior seriously. He was the logical choice. However, she wasn't the one doing the choosing, so the possibility had existed that Braden might have figured differently and picked family.

She and Erik always worked well together, as long as their focus remained on work. But an orbiter was a small craft. Being in such tight quarters might prove sexually difficult. At least Kam would be along to act as a buffer.

"How are they going to get inside The Dome?" Torque asked. "We should send someone to break through their defense system, so the team doesn't waste time trying to find entry. Let me go in first."

"That's not necessary. We have a double agent already in place." Braden flipped a switch. "Watch the monitor."

The expansive monitor on the wall behind him flashed white and gray, then a picture of a woman appeared. Erik and Kam groaned. Leila stared in disbelief, unable to make a sound.

"Are you shittin' me?" Erik finally asked.

"Not at all," Braden said. "After you land, she will capture you. As her slaves, you'll have access to the inside. She'll help you get what we need, then aid in your escape."

Leila stared at the female depicted on the screen. Dressed all in black, with short black hair, she looked the same as when they'd encountered her on their last Earth mission, where Braden had found and sexually initiated Alexa. The woman had spied for Daegal, passed along their whereabouts, and gotten them captured. Braden must be out of his mind.

"What's her name? What's her story?" Kam asked, not once taking his eyes off the screen.

The woman had done Kam some serious damage while on Earth. Leila was surprised he looked more intrigued, right now, than enraged. The electrical charge she'd hit him with had further damaged his already chemically off-balanced system.

"Our records indicate her name is Halah Shirota," Braden answered. "A Class 1 Xylon Warrior before she turned. The Egesa captured her sister, Josella, then captured *her* when she went in alone, against Council orders, to get her sibling back. Daegal apparently promised to free them both, if she completed the Earth mission and brought back information. He didn't fulfill the bargain, and Josella mysteriously disappeared. But Halah has obtained certain freedoms within the Egesa society."

"In exchange for Lair secrets, no doubt," Erik said.

"No doubt. She contacted me, via Laszlo's private communication board not long ago, wanting to return to The Lair."

"You can't trust her, Braden," Kam interrupted. "I found that out firsthand."

"We have some assurance. From the electromagnetic waves transmitted by her implanted Xylon brain chip, I've managed to locate Josella in one of the banishment zones."

"I thought the tracking chips were only short range," Alexa responded.

"They are with our hand detectors. But a booster tracking computer, available here on Xylon, was recently repaired. The chip codes are still loading as we speak. The long-range device allows tracking as long as the person remains in this system."

"Has Laszlo been tracked?" Kam asked.

"His chip code cannot be found," Braden replied.

Erik snorted. "Big surprise."

Next to her, Leila felt Kam stiffen.

Braden flipped off the monitor. "Tomorrow I'm sending Pitch and my sisters out to the Sand Moon to find and hold the girl captive. We'll keep that information and Josella's safety as leverage until we successfully complete this mission. That will ensure Halah's cooperation."

"Sounds risky to me, Braden," Torque replied. "Anytime you depend on the emotions of a female, you're apt to get screwed."

Leila and Alexa turned their heads to stare at him.

"What?"

"It's settled," Braden answered. "Study the plan in the notes. Kam and Erik, wait out in the Council antechamber. I want to talk to you two again, in a few minutes. Torque, you and Leila stay in here, please." His gaze settled on his mate, and his eyes filled with compassion. "You can go, Alexa. Get some rest. Then maybe later you could help out with the new arrivals. Two Earth females are being brought down."

Leila saw Alexa frown. Xylon routinely recruited DNA-compatible women from other planets to breed with, since so many of their own females were sterile. Alexa, though one of those recruited women herself, never had agreed with the process. But she'd proven invaluable in calming Earth women and helping them adjust.

"Yes, I can do that," she replied.

It looked to Leila like she wanted to say more, but she held her tongue. Alexa wasn't one to fear speaking her mind, so she was certain Braden would get an earful later. Alexa understood her mate's position and knew when to keep silent on a matter while in front of other Warriors. Leila often marveled at how quickly the woman had adjusted to Xylon society.

Braden aided Alexa to her feet and caressed her slightly rounded stomach. "I'll join you later."

She nodded, her eyes softening. She lightly kissed his lips, then looked around the table. "Good luck, everyone. Be careful. My thoughts will be with you." She dematerialized out.

Chapter Two

An ominous silence settled over the interior of the Council Chamber. The dim lighting added to the oppressive feel in the air. Strange, how Leila had never before noticed the dreariness of the room.

She watched Kam and Erik step out the door. Erik glanced back at her once before the portal closed. A worried look briefly crossed his face, an emotion she normally didn't see him display.

As such, she fidgeted and began to worry, too, about why Braden wanted her and Torque to stay behind. A bad case of nerves hit as possibilities flickered through her mind. She suspected major trouble lurked in the planning of this Marid mission.

When she looked over at Torque, and he winked at her, she didn't feel any better.

The door closed and auto-locked, leaving the three of them in the room alone. Neither she nor Torque spoke. They simply waited for Braden to resume control. Leila studied his face, trying to figure out if good news or bad was forthcoming.

When he looked at her, his eyes narrowed slightly. "Leila," he began. "Torque has informed me that you're unable to self-heal."

"What!" Her head snapped toward the man relaxing on the other side of the table. "How could you tell him?" He'd found out purely by accident on their mission to Earth, after three Marid Assassins injured and captured them. She'd received a wound to her thigh, and he'd noticed she wasn't healing at an accelerated rate.

"It's the truth. He needed to know. How did you keep the fact out of your records? We couldn't find the notation."

"It's in there. You just have to know where to look. Laszlo said it wasn't anyone's business, but his and mine." She thought her secret would remain undiscovered. How stupid! Of course Torque would tell. He held no loyalty to her. They weren't even friends.

"Why didn't you tell me, Leila?" Braden asked. "You know the importance of healing information, especially on a Warrior."

Reluctantly, she returned her attention to the head of the table. She expected to see anger or frustration from Braden, not the look of tender understanding now directed at her. Alexa was a lucky woman to have such a man to love, and who loved her in return. Braden's strength, intelligence and, most importantly, compassion made him the perfect leader to revive Xylon's floundering society.

As far as her inability to self-heal, she hadn't completed the third step of her Initiation Rite, which sexually transferred the ability. No way was she sucking the needed elements from the cock of the devil who had participated in her ceremony. The first two steps of the Initiation had proceeded typically, but as the third step had approached, and her sexual appetite had grown, the trio initiating her had turned to abusive, sexual behavior.

She'd always craved a darker, more carnal sexual experience, but they had pushed her too far. By the time she had realized what she'd gotten herself into, the power of the sexual stimulant chemicals had prevented her from defending herself.

Even so, while in her state of heightened sexual need, she'd refused to take Dare's ugly, deformed cock into her mouth. And now the choice was coming back to haunt her. Ironically, the Warriors who'd initiated her, now Marid Assassins, were the same ones who had captured her and the Xylon team on the Earth mission, where she'd been injured. All of her troubles traced back to those three, who had betrayed The Lair in every way possible, before ending up banished for life. *Damn them.* At the memory, her entire body trembled, and she gripped her hands together to stop their shaking.

"Leila?" Braden prompted.

"I didn't think it mattered that much," she lied. When Braden had never confronted her about the issue, she'd figured he hadn't watched the full video of her Initiation Rite, otherwise he'd have known. She'd respected him for allowing her that privacy. Most men wouldn't have done so, if they'd known of the video's existence and had access. Still, she wasn't about to mention the fact, nor the permanent injury she'd received. No good would come from it, in her opinion.

"Leila…" He stared into her eyes for a long moment, not speaking. Then, "A few of our women still refuse to perform the third step. Punishment isn't given for that. However, I can't send you on missions involving anything more than research on Type F planets if you can't heal yourself when injured."

No! He couldn't decommission her for everything but "friendly" mission assignments. She'd never earn a promotion to a Class 2 rank that way. "I'll be careful, Braden. I'm the only one who can find what we need on this mission. You know that."

"Yes." He rubbed his chin. "Actually, I do. So, I came up with a solution." His gaze flicked to his brother, then back to her. "If you're willing."

She didn't like the look in their eyes. Braden seemed overly cautious with his words, which wasn't normal for him. And Torque appeared strangely expectant, almost eager. Her heart thudded dully in her chest. "What?"

"You'll need re-initiating."

Her heart slammed against her ribs. "Forget it!" In an Initiation Rite, she'd have no control over what happened to her body. Or very little. "I won't chance a repeat performance of last time. I wouldn't survive it."

"That won't happen," Torque interjected, greater compassion in his voice than she would have expected from him. Even so, the look in his eyes told a lustful story.

She studied his intensity and wondered if he'd already been chosen to lead or participate in the ceremony. Rumor had it that his cock was enormous, and he liked aggressive sex, and using restraints and special sexual devices on his partners. When moisture filled her vagina at the erotic thoughts, she silently cursed herself. Her body often craved more than her mind would permit. Even as a Healer, with all her training, she never fully understood the inconsistency between body and mind, or perhaps consciousness and sub-consciousness, represented the more accurate contradiction. "Can a re-initiation even be done? I've never heard of one."

"It's rare, but I found a few cases on record. It's either a re-initiation, Leila, or you don't go on any more potentially dangerous missions," Braden told her. "This one included. I'll send someone else."

"No one else qualifies." They needed her knowledge. She had to be the one to go.

"Then I suggest you agree, for the future of all Xylons. If you refuse, I will delay the mission until another Healer becomes trained in what to look for."

Damn. She'd hoped his words were a bluff, and he would back down, knowing the importance of obtaining the substance as soon as possible. But hardheaded men rarely changed their position. Still, she hadn't expected this of Braden. "It will take too long to train another Healer, who also holds a Warrior rank, in the testing procedures to ensure no mistakes are made. We need the correct formula, Braden. You're well aware of that. You're just trying to blackmail me into doing this." She forced her voice to remain calm and steady. He wouldn't deal with her if she lost her temper or broke down.

"I'd rather you didn't look at it that way, Leila. This ceremony is necessary. I understand why you didn't complete the third step originally. Rave, Shear, and Dare abused their power over you. I'll make certain you're taken care of this time around. I'll personally choose the Alliance."

So he hadn't chosen yet.

"You won't have to go through the entire rite. Just the third step. A minor sexual appetite afterwards. Much shorter and easier than the full ceremony."

"Unless you've never sucked cock," Torque said. "And you're opposed to it with any man."

"I've sucked..." She shook her head and stemmed her words. "I'm not opposed to it. I'm opposed to the loss of control."

"Even with men you know and otherwise trust?" Braden asked.

"I-I don't really know. When I need relief, I always choose partners for the one time only. Since my original Initiation, that is."

"And people talk about me," Torque mumbled.

"Hey, I'm not some whore!" Leila picked up a laser pen and threw it at him. "Don't you dare imply that I am."

Torque batted the pen out of the air, then chuckled. "That was not my intention."

"I've only been with a handful of men."

Torque shrugged. "If you say so."

Damn him. She felt like jumping across the table and throttling the man.

"Enough." Braden looked thoughtful for a moment. "Maybe, with this re-initiation, we can help conquer your fear and trust issues with sex, as well as get you protected."

Leila didn't say anything. Men always made the solutions sound so easy. If Braden, instead of the Council chose the Alliance, she wouldn't have to worry about abuse, she supposed. He'd see to it. He knew her past. No one would dare defy Braden.

But who would he choose? Warriors she trusted, but whom she faced and worked with daily, which might become awkward afterward, or Warriors he trusted, but she didn't know? If so, she wouldn't have to interact with them on a regular basis, but she might panic when they started touching her, because they'd be in control, not her, and she'd have no idea what to expect from strangers. Maybe that's why he'd asked her the question, to get an idea of how to choose.

"Go to your quarters, Leila," Braden told her. "Rest. And don't worry. You have my word that nothing will go wrong this time."

"Isn't there another way?" Although she asked, any hope of a reprieve had already faded from her mind.

Braden approached and took her small hand between his much larger ones. "Trust me, Leila. This is for the best all the way around."

Nodding, and sadly resigned to the situation, she stood. She held a Class 3 Warrior rank, and she would maintain her dignity by doing her duty, and doing what was best for Xylon. Regardless of her personal feelings. All she had to do was complete the ceremony, and then it would be done. She didn't have to enjoy it.

Too bad she couldn't take some sort of medication to get her through the ordeal. Medicine would counteract the preparation chemicals they needed to pump into her pussy, using a special dildo. Otherwise, the healing elements wouldn't absorb properly once transferred. Whichever way she looked at this, smooth and easy weren't part of the equation.

Unable to meet Braden and Torque's eyes for fear of revealing the extent of her inner turmoil about the situation, she pulled her hand from Braden's and dematerialized out.

* * * * *

"You want her," Erik said to Kam, while they waited for Braden to call them back inside. Just saying the words made his gut clench. Even though he voiced the concern as a statement, not a question, he still hoped for a denial from Kam.

"Leila?"

"You know that's who I'm talking about." He tried to convince himself that Kam's response didn't matter. He'd fight for the woman, if necessary. Still, he preferred that the man just step aside.

A half-grin appeared on Kam's face, and he clamped a hand on his shoulder. "Not as my breeder-mate."

That didn't make him feel better. "Have you fucked her?" He knew Leila's answer, but he wanted to hear it from Kam, too. Their gazes locked and held.

"No."

"Would you?" He swallowed hard, waiting for the answer.

Kam pulled his hand away and stepped back. "Could you blame me if I said yes? She's a beautiful, sexy woman."

He clenched his fist. "Maybe."

"I could ask you the same question about Braden's mate, my sister, but I won't, considering I already know the answer."

Raking his fingers through his hair, Erik sat on a tall stool near the room's control panel. Given their society, and his own past actions, he had no right to be overly territorial, he supposed. He'd helped Braden sexually initiate Alexa and had watched the two of them have sex more than once since her Initiation. She was one hot lady, and loved getting her ass spanked — the thought alone made his dick ache. Leila had a perfect ass for spanking, but would probably deck him if he tried.

Even today, if Braden and Alexa invited him into their bedchamber, he'd have a hard time refusing. But still, Alexa didn't consume his thoughts as Leila did. Leila touched him emotionally, challenged him intellectually, and his body craved hers physically, like no other. She belonged with him. She belonged *to* him.

"Leila is special, Erik."

"I know that." Kam was well aware of how he felt about her. The man didn't need to state the obvious. His frustration level increased. He clenched his fingers, then slowly released the fist, forcing his hand to relax, much as he remembered Kam do inside the Council Chamber. "What's your point?"

"She needs you. Don't give up on her."

His interest perked up, and a sense of hope filled him. "Did she say that?"

"No, but I know." Kam pulled the mood sensor from his belt. "I've registered her emotions enough times."

His gaze flickered over the palm-sized machine. His belief in its readings ranked low for the most part. Tracking emotions was far from an exact science, and the best that electronic device ever did, in his opinion, was come close. Kam would argue differently, he was sure. He relied on the device during missions and often swore the readings helped him out of scrapes.

"She has a lot to deal with emotionally, Erik."

"Yes, she does." So did he, and Kam knew it. If not for him… "What do you think is going on in there?" He nodded toward the Council Chamber.

"Nothing good. Otherwise, Braden wouldn't have separated us."

All the energy drained out of his body. Too many personal issues pulled at him. He needed an anchor in his life, a woman who truly cared, to help him through the days. A unique woman. He'd been alone too long. "I need Leila, Kam," he confessed in a low, strained voice. "I need her body. I need her softness to balance me. But she won't even give me a chance." His voice hardened and sounded tight even to his own ears. "We should have killed Rave, Shear, and Dare when the chance presented itself. Their deaths might have brought her a measure of peace."

Kam's eyes filled with understanding and compassion. "We didn't even know what had happened to her at the time."

"We did with Rave. I was standing over her unconscious body after we saw the partial video of the way they hurt Leila while they fucked her." Rage rushed through him, and his hand once again clenched. This time he didn't relax the fist. He couldn't. "It would have been easy to take Rave out of commission."

"Erik, don't think about it. I doubt that would have changed things, even if you had terminated Rave. The only peace Leila will ever find lies within herself."

* * * * *

Daegal stood face-to-face with his Top Commander. The man in the full facemask wasn't delivering good news. "What do you mean the compound is temporary?"

"The sterilization only lasts ten months. We're now getting reports of supposedly sterilized breeders in the slave quarters being with child."

Daegal's gaze shifted from monitor to monitor, watching The Dome's activities, as he let the Commander's words sink in. He couldn't face the man. Looking at him brought back the memory of their failure to capture, or at least sterilize, Alexa Sandor Koll, the new Xylon Leader's bitch, and the last super breeder known to them. Her special-combination DNA could have helped provide the answers they needed to defeat the Xylon Warriors for good.

Now with this news, he realized they had made virtually no progress in the campaign to reign supreme in this system, other than entrapping a number of Warriors who had fled The Lair to join their side. After The Lair hadn't fallen, many had tried to return. Unsuccessful, their heads now decorated the walls of his trophy room. "Increase the potency."

"Our Healers say it's not possible. We can't inject the formula directly into the women. The active elements neutralize. The fluid only works when transferred through our cocks, and a stronger dose causes impotence in our males."

Daegal hung his head at the information. Sexual transmission was required for many of their medicines. Formulas could often be injected into one gender, but proved ineffective to the other unless passed on through bodily fluids. "Can we multiple inject using the same strength?"

"No. One time only. Additional doses don't activate."

As his anger took hold, he felt his blood pressure and body temperature rise. "Keep this top secret." Frustration clearly laced his voice, and he fought to control the tone. "I don't want our failure known."

"Word will get out. Secrets are hard to keep these days."

Damn. Everyone on Xylon had to die, and he needed to defeat them quickly. His power weakened more and more with each passing day. Laszlo might be able to make him strong again. The man's research and development abilities rivaled those of any Healer. And Laszlo had to be suffering the same weakness. He needed to destroy Laszlo's Warriors first, then flush the man out of hiding, and force him to test and use whatever methods necessary to return them to full strength. If the only way existed through primitive methods, he'd gladly comply.

The Egesa often fought to the near-death for him, his Commanders, and Assassins. Success brought them great sexual and monetary rewards. As long as they believed he still possessed the special mental powers he used to control their minds—the minds of all lesser-developed creatures on Marid— they'd never betray him. They'd be too fearful of the consequences.

For his amusement, he'd let the creatures sexually play with Xylon's people, both the males and the females. Then he'd instruct them to tear off the Xylons' limbs and leave them to bleed to death in their own forests.

Finally, he'd reign supreme in this system, with all the riches and followers needed to expand his army of Assassins. "Dispose of all breeders currently in the slave quarters or owned privately. Just keep the necessary number for research purposes. Then call a meeting of all Commanders and set up new invasion plans to be implemented as soon as possible."

"As you desire."

Daegal clicked a button, bringing a blue and green planet into view on his screens. After defeating Xylon, he'd pursue his next target. Earth…

* * * * *

"No!" Erik slammed his fist down on the table. "She's mine, and I don't want anyone else touching her." Even as he said the words, he knew the response he'd get.

"That's unreasonable," Braden replied. "You know the law, and the necessity of it. One man will not be able to sexually fill her needs, once her increased appetite hits after the chemical transfer. I know you don't want any damage done to her. She's already been through enough. If her sexual appetite remains unsated during the ceremony, the imbalance in her brain waves will cause permanent injury to her mind. She could even die, Erik."

Erik couldn't believe what he was hearing. He knew the risks as well as Braden. Of course, he didn't want Leila harmed, but her rite was a special situation. "It's a partial re-initiation. Three people aren't necessary. Two will do." The fewer, the better. One would be best—him. But Braden would agree to two. Alexa had only had two, and she had gone through the full ceremony. Her mind hadn't snapped, and Leila was just as strong, if not stronger. In fact, Braden himself had originally insisted that he alone initiate Alexa. *She's the one who wanted me to stay. So, you should understand my feelings, friend.* He would never protest if he really thought a danger to Leila existed. "You know two will do, Braden."

As the seconds ticked by, Braden stared at him in silence, until finally he nodded. "Two. Fine. If a problem arises, you can call in a third. I don't want to argue about this. We need the Initiation finished quickly, no matter what I said to Leila earlier, so we can get on with this mission. Who do you want with you? Torque or Kam?"

"Neither," he answered without hesitation. "I don't want them touching her." He'd initiated with Kam in the past, but he didn't trust Kam like he used to. He glanced briefly at the two men, then his gaze returned to his best friend and leader. "I want you in the Alliance, Braden." He and Braden had initiated lots of women together before Braden had mated Alexa. Partnering with him was the best solution, and the safest for his own peace of mind.

"Braden?" Torque snorted.

"Me!" Braden's eyes widened. "Alexa would rip off my balls."

Ouch. Erik cringed, wondering about the truth of that statement. Braden might be right. Not raised in their society, Alexa's sexual upbringing differed. But he'd try to convince Braden otherwise. Perhaps a selfish move on his part, but Leila meant too much to him not to at least try. "If she knows it's Leila you're helping, she won't protest."

"Well," Braden scratched his chin, "perhaps."

Kam cleared his throat. "I think Leila would be fine with me as part of the Alliance. That way, Alexa wouldn't need to make a decision."

"I'm not fine with it," Erik replied, shifting his gaze to the man.

Kam's eyes narrowed.

"No offense." He again turned to Braden. "Ask Alexa. It's our way. No other mate would object."

"Alexa is an Earthling. It's not the same for her."

"She's half Xylon. She's accepted other sexual situations." He didn't want to say too much in front of the others, out of respect for her and Braden's privacy, but the memory of pumping a dildo into Alexa's pussy, fucking her hard, immediately came to mind. They'd even gratified themselves while watching each other, until they both came. And he'd licked her asshole, while Braden watched. She really liked that. Granted, all of those things occurred during her Initiation Rite, but still, she wasn't some sexual neophyte.

"Maybe Alexa could be the second," Torque tossed in with a huge grin on his face. "I'd pay big to see her tongue Leila's pussy and lap up her cum. Wouldn't you, little brother?"

Braden looked less than happy about the sexual conversation concerning his mate. "What's the problem with Kam doing this?"

"He's part of the Marid mission. We'll all be working closely together. I think it's best that—"

"Bullshit. Erik is jealous," Torque interjected with a laugh. "The thought of another cock challenging his doesn't sit well, so he wants you in there instead, Braden."

Braden looked at Torque as if he'd lost his mind. "What do you think I have between my legs?"

"You're mated. It's not the same. This argument is ludicrous. I'll do Leila, and with great pleasure. I have more experience than any of you with Initiations. Let's just get on with it. We have a mission pending. And I'm horny as hell."

"Back off, Torque. This doesn't concern you." Erik feared Torque's sexual tastes were too close to what Leila really needed deep down. The competition made him uncomfortable, because Torque wouldn't hesitate to take advantage of her need, if he discovered the truth. He wasn't the type of man to do what was right, over what served him best. And Leila would be the one who ended up hurt in the long run. He couldn't allow that to happen.

He pulled Braden aside. When he spoke, he lowered his voice. "You know that Kam is unstable. With Laszlo disappearing, and the two of them working so closely together, I'm not as comfortable with him as I used to be. And Torque, well, there's no way. He's huge. Leila is too delicate. He'd rip her in two."

"Kam is fine, for now. Leila confirmed that in her reports to me. Kam would never hurt her. You know that. I understand about Torque, even if the 'delicate' and 'ripping her in two' parts are a bit overblown. His size does intimidate most women. But

Kam shouldn't be a problem. I think you're simply less threatened by me because I'm mated, like Torque said."

"I'm not threatened by Kam. Leila will belong to me, officially, as soon as I arrange a Branding Ceremony." Their joining would be permanent and for life. She'd bear his mark and everyone would know she belonged to him.

"Branding? You haven't even fucked her yet, Erik. Have you? She'll never agree to Branding. Besides, you need Council approval to bind her."

"I've had the visions, Braden." He hadn't told anyone else. But he knew Braden would understand. He'd experienced visions of Alexa before they joined.

Braden's eyes narrowed. "Predestined visions? Are you sure? Has she experienced the same?"

"I don't know. But they're real breeder visions, not fantasies. I know it."

With an impatient look, Braden ran a hand down his face. "You're aware, as well as I, that those visions most likely aren't genuine at all, but implants by Laszlo. A manipulation of our minds."

"Laszlo's not around. He might even be dead, for all we know. And even if he's still alive, how could he project such images in his supposedly weakened state? If Kam told us the truth about Laszlo's powers waning. I'm still not so sure about that, or about either of their loyalties. But the visions have to be real. We found other cases in the records and Xylon legends. And we've all heard the stories. You and Alexa experienced the visions, too."

"Visions, yes. Whether real or —"

"Another case of Laszlo using whatever he deemed necessary to get us to do his bidding." When Braden nodded, he acquiesced partially. "All right. Maybe some of these visions truly are fantasies, and some might be created by Laszlo, but others could very well be real. No one actually knows for certain. Regardless, I'd bind Leila tonight, if she'd allow it. I feel that strongly about her."

"You love her."

He shifted uncomfortably. His feelings weren't open for discussion. Not even with Braden. "I owe her." And that's all he intended to admit. He'd already said too much to Kam, and he now regretted voicing his feelings aloud. It put him in a vulnerable position that made him uneasy.

Braden frowned. "Erik, if your actions in regard to Leila come from some false sense of responsibility —"

"I *am* responsible. Now let's leave it at that. If Alexa agrees, will you help initiate? It'll be easier for everyone, all the way around."

Braden shook his head. "You're overreacting. Kam is chosen. Leila trusts him. This joining with the three of you will bring all of you closer and help make the upcoming mission a success. It's our way. It's best. You two work it out."

Erik growled deep in his throat and slammed his fist into his palm. So much for his best friend. He didn't understand why Braden remained so hardheaded about participating. Must be his love for Alexa. *That* he understood, he supposed, though he didn't like the position it put him in. "Fine. But Kam's not touching her unless there's a real need, and I approve it."

"Understood."

* * * * *

The water streamed over Leila's naked body. She sighed. The warmth relaxed her muscles and soothed her emotions.

Long ago, she had turned the open shower into her special retreat. Filled with greenery and stone on the floor and walls, the area felt like a private grotto, complete with waterfall. The bath reminded her of Xylon's deepest, secluded forests in all their peace and beauty. When off balance, she oftentimes spent hours here regenerating her mind and soul.

Her hands glided over her body, washing the vanilla-scented cleanser from her skin. She imagined several men's hands doing the same, and her entire body became sensitized. She'd decided to face her re-initiation with a braver attitude. She'd hidden too long from a problem she held no responsibility in, and allowed it to take over her life.

Not that she expected her entire mentality to change like a snap of a switch, but getting through this ceremony would be a first step. A major step. She trusted Braden to make the best choice for her in the Alliance. Maybe she'd even ask if he would attend. His presence, whether participating or not, would ensure her safety. Then she could allow whatever to happen, without anxiety. She'd vid-cell him later and see about arranging it.

A noise drew her attention.

She shut off the water and glanced toward the bath's entry. Her gaze followed the stone pathway, leading out to her bedchamber.

A shadow appeared at the corner.

Her heart skipped a beat. Before she could move, a man stepped into partial view. A very naked man. She hadn't expected anyone so soon! Certainly, she'd receive advance notification before the ceremony began.

The man's face, and one shoulder, remained covered by shadows, so she couldn't identify him. He didn't speak. He just stood in the entry, tall and muscular.

Maybe he wasn't here for the Initiation. Maybe he'd illegally materialized into her quarters. Momentary panic hit. Her disruptor, a banned weapon for a Class 3 to carry, but she owned one anyway, was hidden in the other room.

Her eyes zeroed in on the man's cock, which grew hard and impressive under her scrutiny. He stepped further into the light, and her gaze snapped up to his face. "Kam." She relaxed, but only slightly.

She crossed her arms over her breasts as he approached. His gaze slid down her body, stopping briefly at her pussy, which she attempted to hide by turning to the side. She wasn't ready yet. She hadn't concealed her scars. And she needed to contact Braden.

She'd thought he might send... She shook her head. No. It did no good to think about *him*. Kam would be gentle. That's what she needed now, not what she secretly craved in the safety of her fantasies, but what she could handle in reality.

Warily, she scrutinized the foreign look on his face. Gone was his half-grin and easygoing stride. Right now, he looked completely serious, and headed toward her with a definite, sexual purpose.

Her gaze lowered to one of his hands. He carried a dildo with him. An Initiation Dildo. It contained the chemicals needed to prepare her internally.

Kam stopped in front of her. "You're beautiful, Leila," he whispered. He touched her cheek. "I need to fuck you."

She felt a blush creep up her neck, and wondered if his need was personal or bound by duty.

After a moment, his signature half-grin appeared. "Disappointed?"

The safest answer was another question. "Did you request this assignment?"

He didn't respond immediately. Instead, his thumb grazed her bottom lip. "What answer would make you feel more at ease?" he finally asked her.

"I don't know." And that was the truth. Her feelings were one big jumble right now.

"You smell good." He brushed her cheek with his. Looking down, with a slight smile on his face, he tugged her arms away from her breasts. "Let me see these beauties. I've indulged in many a fantasy about them."

"About my breasts?" His confession surprised her, and her pussy contracted. She gradually lowered her arms.

He visibly gulped, and his free hand rose to cup one mound. "Oh, yes. So soft. So absolutely perfect. Just like I imagined."

Leila chewed at her bottom lip. His hand felt warm and exciting against her skin. How long had he sexually fantasized about her? she wondered.

His thumb grazed her nipple, which had already hardened. At her sharp intake of air, he smiled. "You like that."

She didn't respond, nor meet his gaze. She did enjoy the touch very much, but feared admitting it aloud. She rarely admitted her pleasures aloud.

Peeking up at him from behind lowered lashes, she saw Kam's eyes glow with desire. She'd always believed him to be a gentle lover, but now their previous conversation came back to haunt her. *Don't for a moment underestimate what I might demand from a woman.*

He rubbed the dildo along the front of her thigh. "Spread your legs for me, Leila. Let me ease inside you."

She wasn't sure if he was speaking about the dildo or his own hard cock. Kam was one of the sexiest men she knew—a combination of heart, mind, and body that made most women melt. His cock looked so long, smooth, and almost elegant that she had a difficult time not reaching out to touch it. Still, she'd hoped Erik would be the one…

"Um, can you wait in the other room for me? I'll be out in a minute, then we can continue." She needed to cover her scars first. She hoped changing their relationship to a physical one wouldn't ruin their friendship. They'd been close for a long time now, and she enjoyed their camaraderie.

"I like it in here. The shower adds to the erotic mix. You've turned your bathing room into a paradise. Let's lick every wet drop from each other's bodies."

Her stomach fluttered. "You're not wet," she whispered.

"A part of me is." He released her breast and tangled his hand in her hair, directing her head south. "Look."

She glanced down and saw beads of moisture on the tip of his cock. "Oh."

"Go down on your knees and lick the head, Leila. I want to watch you taste my cum. I want to see just how much you love the taste of cock." He lowered his voice to a deep, sexy timbre. "Suck my dick all the way down your luscious throat. I'll fill your mouth with the best cum you've ever had."

Her eyes met his. "Not too modest, are you?"

He smiled and leaned forward, whispering against her lips. "Find out for yourself whether it's true."

Her heart pounded in her chest. Should she? Before doing anything, she glanced around him. Certainly he wasn't the only one who would come tonight. Maybe—

"Relax." His hand eased under her wet hair and down her back. "We'll go slowly." When his fingers contacted rough skin, she jumped away as if his touch had burned her. He frowned. "What the hell?"

"Sorry. You took me by surprise. I guess I'm a little more nervous than I expected. Even with you, a friend. Go ahead and wait for me in the bedchamber. I'll be out in a bit."

"I felt something. Turn around," he ordered in a stern voice that she rarely heard from him.

"I'll join you when I'm ready."

He grabbed her arm and forced her around.

"Stop it!" Leila protested. Her hands caught against the stone wall to keep herself from stumbling face-first into the rock.

With the dildo still in hand, he swept aside her long curtain of hair. "Damn it. I didn't know about this."

Leila jerked free and spun around. "It's nothing!"

"Nothing?" Kam's voice rose. "Someone whipped the skin right off you!" His eyes revealed his sudden realization. "The ones who initiated you did this. They left the scars." He spoke the words in the form of a statement, not a question.

He knew. He lowered his voice, and compassion shone in his eyes again, like the Kam she knew and loved as her friend.

"Our healing cream won't remove the marks?"

"No," she answered, trying not to sound defeated. "They run too deep. It helped, but only to a degree since…"

"Since you couldn't self-heal." Kam turned and left the bath.

Leila's anger, frustration, and overwhelming sadness broke free. She kicked over a pot with a Purple Starleaf in it. Ironic, considering Starleaf plants gave off a calming agent.

A tear slid down her cheek, and she swiped it away. "I can't blame him for leaving. I'm hideous. I'm—" *No!* She raised her chin, not about to put herself through more emotional turmoil. *This is not my fault!*

"I look the way I look, Kam. Get over it," she said to no one in particular. She grabbed a drying cloth and dried her body, and as much of her hair as she could, then she donned her favorite white, fuzzy cover-up.

She entered the bedchamber and stopped short. Erik materialized beside Kam, fully clothed, which looked odd since Kam still stood naked. They spoke a moment, then quietly argued about something, most likely her condition. She couldn't make out most of their words.

So, Erik actually was part of the Alliance, too. She felt disappointed that he hadn't entered the shower instead of Kam. Maybe he thought Kam a calming presence given her wariness and allowed him to approach her first. Well, neither of them would want her now. And that was fine. She didn't care.

Liar.

She swiped away another tear, before anyone noticed.

Erik pushed Kam.

"Hey!" She rushed forward. "What's going on?"

Neither man said anything. They just stared at each other with fire in their eyes.

Without warning, Erik turned and dragged her into his arms. He kissed her soundly, for just a moment, then released her. When she teetered backward, and her hands sought purchase, both men reached out to steady her.

"Point made, Erik," Kam said. "Even if done a bit barbarically."

"Next time, I'll rip off your head. And I'm not necessarily speaking about the one on top of your shoulders."

Confusion filled her. They stared at each other like mortal enemies. Whatever was going on had to be a male thing. She touched her mouth, still tingling from Erik's kiss. His spicy taste lingered. She drew her tongue along her lips, trying to capture the unique flavor.

Erik's head turned, and his eyes met hers. She quickly slid her tongue back into her mouth. A look she couldn't discern, almost like possession, crossed his face. No man had ever looked at her like she belonged to him. Her independent nature bristled at the thought, but deep down something about the idea warmed her and made her feel complete.

Kam had certainly told him of her damaged back, given the intensity of their conversation. She wondered about his thoughts. She normally applied skin patches to the scars, which made them virtually undetectable, even on naked flesh. But she hadn't had time, not expecting the re-initiation to take place without notice.

The air by the door shimmered. Braden materialized in. A moment later, Torque followed. Kam must have called them. *Shit.*

"What's the problem?" Braden asked.

"Limp already, boys? You had to call for backup a little soon, didn't you? Can't get 'em up?" Torque laughed.

"Shut up, Torque," Kam ground out.

Erik stood uncharacteristically quiet. His eyes held a hard look. This could not be good.

Kam turned toward her. "Drop your cover-up for them, Leila."

She glanced around the room at the four men staring at her. She didn't want to be gawked at. They couldn't change her appearance anyway. So, what did it matter? "No. I want a few minutes of privacy." Even though Kam would certainly tell Braden and Torque what had happened, she still wanted to cover the scars, so they wouldn't look at her with pity, if they did continue with the re-initiation.

"Drop the cover," Kam repeated. "Or I'll rip it from you myself."

Her eyes widened in shock. His voice had come out deceptively calm. But she saw the seriousness in his eyes and suspected the medicine contributed to his harsh words and maybe his actions too, which might have caused the problem with Erik.

"Back off, Kam," Erik warned.

She retreated a step. If he dared touch her in anger, she'd never give him another shot. That formula adversely affected his personality, too adversely. He could end up hurting someone, and she didn't want that someone to be *her*. Even as she thought the condemning words, she knew they weren't true. She'd never let him suffer, no matter what.

"She has the right to choose what to do." Erik pushed Kam aside and wrapped his fingers around her arm. "Come over here with me." He pulled her toward the far side of the room.

Kam hesitated a moment, looking at Erik like he wanted to punch him out. As she and Erik passed, Kam went to speak with Braden and Torque.

"Someone want to tell me what's going on?"

With her back turned, she heard Braden ask Kam the question. After that, all she heard were whispers. She was surprised that Kam had let Erik shove him twice, with virtually no response. True, Erik outranked him, stood taller and more muscular, but Kam wasn't a pushover. "You shouldn't treat him like that."

"Kam needs to learn his place." Erik stared into her eyes. "Did he hurt you in the shower?"

"No, of course not. He'd never hurt me. You know that." A strange question for him to ask.

Erik raked a hand through his hair and grumbled. "Yeah, I suppose. Did he touch you?"

"Just my breast." Clarity struck. Erik hadn't known about Kam coming into her bath until after it happened. She glanced at Kam, then laid a hand on Erik's arm. "I'm all right. Really."

His jaw tightened, and he nodded. His eyes held a combination of anger mixed with what looked like sorrow. "I knew they abused you and made you suffer. I didn't know they beat you and left you scarred, Leila. You should have told me." A muscle in his jaw ticced.

She didn't want to talk about this, didn't want to think about what had happened to her. "It's done, Erik. Over. There's nothing you can do to change what happened."

His voice rose and sounded strained. "But it matters to m-" he stopped, lowering his volume. "What happened matters to the Council. Even though I don't agree with how Kam approached you tonight, we're going to need to see, and record the scars, for The Lair records."

"Everyone doesn't need to see." She hated the way the scars marred her body and certainly felt uncomfortable showing them off. She'd never even sought medical treatment for them, not wanting anyone to know about her abuse. She'd treated the wounds herself. She'd known at the time, if she said anything, Dare would kill her...or worse. The three had threatened her with unspeakable things, guaranteeing her silence.

If older, with more experience, she'd have gone straight to Laszlo, but her fear had held her back. After Laszlo found out and banished the three, no reason had remained to fear, but by then nothing could be done. Laszlo didn't offer to re-initiate her.

Even if he had, at that time, she never would have agreed. Maybe he'd known that.

"It'll help us to know the scope of what happened to you. It's time to stop hiding. Get everything out into the open. Finally. Deal with it. We can help you. We want to help you." His gaze darted around the room, before finally returning to meet hers. "I want to help you."

"I know." She saw the compassion in his eyes. "We're friends, of sorts, right?"

"I'd like to think so." The look in his eyes softened even more. "I'd like to think we're more."

Her breath hitched in her throat. Instead of responding to his statement, she took the coward's way out and continued with what she'd originally planned to say. "Even so, you were disgusted when you saw the video of my Initiation, those few moments of it anyhow. We never talked about it, but I remember your face. You wouldn't even look at me right after."

He looked at her now, directly, and honesty shone in his eyes. "Yes, I was disgusted and angry as hell. At them. At myself, for not being able to change what happened. Never at you. I intend to kill all three of them, Leila, if we ever cross paths." His hand rose toward her cheek, but then he curled his fingers inward.

"Leila," Braden said, drawing her attention.

Erik dropped his hand to his side, and she turned away from him. Despite his caring words, he couldn't even bring himself to touch her now that he realized how terrible she must look naked. A dull thud started in her chest. Since he could probably possess any woman on Xylon he desired, she couldn't blame him.

"We need you to take off the cover." Braden walked toward her.

She fidgeted at his words, not quite knowing what to do. Nakedness wasn't normally a problem within their society, but she felt vulnerable and didn't want to see her imperfection reflected in their eyes. Besides, she'd never been as free with her body as most others. Somehow revealing herself to a stranger had always been easier than the thought of being intimate with a friend or Warrior who served on the same team as she. She'd worked hard becoming a Warrior, even harder to become accepted and respected among their exclusive ranks. She didn't want them looking down on her. "Braden—"

"Come on," he interrupted and reached for the belt on her cover-up.

Once he made up his mind, no one changed it. She could absolutely refuse, and she doubted he'd push. But what was the point? They already knew, so the damage had been done. And now that her injury was known, she realized just how tired she'd become of running from her past. "All right." She nodded and allowed him to open the cover-up.

From behind, Erik slipped the garment off her shoulders.

Kam pushed aside her still damp hair.

Not wanting to see their reaction to her scars, Leila kept her eyes closed. She heard a muffled curse from Erik. When she felt them moving around her, but nobody said anything further, her curiosity got the better of her, and her eyelids fluttered open. They stood surrounding her, staring at her, no longer moving. They barely seemed to be breathing. And she didn't see pity in their gazes, but…lust.

Braden's eyes locked onto her breasts, and her nipples grew long and hard. His nostrils flared, making her feel more desired than in ages. He'd seen the rough and damaged skin on her back and apparently didn't care. Torque stared at her pussy. His tongue grazed his lower lip, and her vagina throbbed in response. An image of him licking her until she came entered her mind. She almost groaned. She heard Erik's heavy breathing behind her and felt his fingers trace the scars on her back and ass. Nobody had ever touched her scars. His tender caress made her lose her breath. She couldn't see or hear Kam, though she felt his hand tighten in her hair.

She reached for her cover-up.

Braden pulled it out of range and dropped the garment to the floor.

Her heart pounded wildly as the men continued to stare at her body. "Um, somebody say something. Please," she whispered, afraid to speak any louder.

"Sorry," Braden said, clearing his throat. "You're just so gorgeous."

Gorgeous? She gulped.

"I wasn't expecting—" He shook his head. "Kam, record her injuries. We're going to do things differently tonight, Leila." He looked over at Erik and made a few hand signals.

Though a Warrior herself, only Class 1 and Class 2 ranks trained to communicate this way, so the significance of the signals were unknown to her. Braden's words and reaction had taken her completely by surprise. And Torque looked at her with such fire in his eyes that she almost went up in flames. Instead of fear, an unexpected sense of excitement filled her, a feeling she hadn't experienced in years.

Erik said nothing as Braden continued signing. Finally, Erik growled and puffed out a large breath. "For observation only, until I otherwise direct."

"Agreed," Braden replied.

"What's happening?" she asked, worry starting to replace her excitement.

"We're going to put you through an immersion, of sorts," Braden explained. "And the full Initiation."

"Full? Why?" He couldn't be serious.

He reached toward her breast, then glanced up at Erik, and let his hand drop before touching her. "After everything that happened to you, I can't be confident the original three performed the first two steps of your ceremony correctly."

"The first step isn't effective anymore, Braden." She felt an urge to cover her breasts and pussy, but refrained. Standing there naked while the rest of them watched, unsettled her now that they were in conversation and her sexual arousal had waned. "And we're not even so sure about the second step, given what we know."

"The protection may not be completely effective, but some protection is better than none. You'll be protected from the Egesa, just not Marid Assassins and Commanders. The preparation of your entire body needs redoing to make sure that you're ready for breeding when the time comes to choose a mate."

Though she hated to admit the truth, what he said made sense. "And the immersion?" He couldn't mean what she thought he meant with immersion. As a Healer, she understood the process. As a woman... "Wh-what did you mean by that, exactly?"

His gaze again dipped to her bare breasts, before he answered. "We're all staying, Leila, and we will put you through a full sexual experience to help you overcome what they did to you. Get in bed."

Staying? All of them? Her heart slammed against her ribs, and her gaze flickered over the four men. "Fucking me, over and over, isn't going to make me forget, if that's your plan."

"What we do to you will break through your sexual barrier and start the healing process."

She automatically turned to Erik, realizing right at that moment she trusted him more than any other to protect her. They'd always had a volatile relationship, but he'd never let her down when she needed him. "Erik?"

He leaned close. "I'll take care of you."

"Erik, let's talk a moment," Braden said, pulling him away. "Then I'll get the rest of the needed equipment so we can Initiate her properly."

Torque smiled from ear to ear. Erik punched him in the shoulder as he passed. "Ow." Torque cringed, but didn't retaliate. He just chuckled.

Leila's mouth went dry. She hadn't time to question what Erik meant by his words. Maybe he simply meant he'd take care of her sexually, but her soul felt his words emotionally. The blood rushed through her body so swiftly that she broke out in a sweat. She looked to Kam, her friend, for additional support. She'd never heard of an Alliance of four. Though Braden would probably only watch.

"It'll be all right," Kam told her. "Get into bed."

Unable to control herself, her body began to tremble, in excitement or fear, she wasn't quite certain. She stumbled over to the bed.

Normally, Initiations took place in the Ceremony Room. The fact that they wanted to perform the rite in her quarters did make her less jittery. No video of the event would exist, and in her own surroundings, she felt more in control. Though she suspected, with these four, the control would really be all theirs.

Chapter Three

Leila leaned back against the headboard of her large, iron-framed bed. An orchid-colored sheet covered her body. Her private quarters. She never engaged in sex here, always preferring a neutral location with whoever ended up as her partner of choice. Not that she'd slept with a parade of men these past few years, barely any since her original Initiation. She could count the number on one hand. Still, her bedchamber had always remained solely hers, up to now.

Tonight would mark a change for many things in her life.

A while ago, Braden had dematerialized out. He hadn't yet returned. He needed to get a special anal dildo for the second step of the Initiation. And Erik had requested some other specific items, but she wasn't near enough to him when he'd asked to hear exactly what.

Her only Initiation experience was with her original ceremony. She'd never participated as part of an Alliance, so other than the sexual transfer of protective elements, she wasn't certain what to expect from this group of men.

Across the room, Torque sat in a purple, overstuffed chair. His gaze roamed up and down her form, making her feel naked. She held the sheet tighter, as if that provided her with greater protection from him. He looked at her in a way that sent sexual thrills, and at the same time, a good amount of sexual trepidation deep into her very core.

Earlier, Erik had left for the bath or living area. She hadn't seen which door he went through. He'd looked troubled before he left, but hadn't said anything. That worried her.

Kam, still here and hovering close, sat beside her. He'd temporarily put his pants back on, for which she was grateful, simply because she felt less vulnerable, given the situation. Xylon's men, especially the Warriors, felt so comfortable with their bodies, they'd probably walk around unclothed all the time if allowed. Not that she would necessarily object, since most of them were quite handsome and solidly built.

She shifted under the sheet, trying to get more comfortable. Her nerves, still a bit on edge, prevented her from relaxing completely. But she'd be all right. She trusted these men, even Torque, regardless of his arrogance and intimidating presence, more than any others in The Lair. If she decided to give over control, these were the men to do it with.

"Everything's transmitted to the records, including the images of your scars. Are you going to be all right with this, Leila?"

"Ask me after the Initiation is over." She attempted a smile, but didn't quite succeed. "Where's Erik?"

"In the bathing room. I don't think he's handling your scars well. He feels responsible."

"Responsible?" That made no sense. What could Erik be thinking? The man was a total enigma to her these days. Sometimes, he acted so cold. Other times, he burned hotter than a lava pit. And so often, he said things that made no sense to her. Now this. She never knew what to expect from him.

Somehow though, the unpredictability fueled her attraction to him—to this one Warrior she admired more than any other. He'd fought unselfishly for Xylon on many dangerous missions over the years, all without complaint or desire for reward. He was a true planetary hero to their people. To this day she wondered about the source of the internal struggle of emotions she often saw in his eyes, and it tugged at her heart. "It's not like he was present when the abuse happened."

"Well, actually, there's news about that period of time that you're not aware of. Braden and Erik might bust me for telling you, but we found out something after returning to Xylon with

Alexa, and Braden took over control. The information appeared in Laszlo's records."

"What?" From the look on Kam's face, she knew whatever they'd found wasn't good.

"The Council chose Erik to lead your Alliance back when it originally took place."

The blood rushed through her body like a tidal wave. She felt unsteady and unsure that she had even heard him correctly. If she were standing, she probably would have toppled over. "Erik?" Her voice broke. When Kam nodded, she turned nauseous. She forced herself to swallow several times just to keep her stomach from heaving.

Oh, how things could have differed if he'd participated in her Initiation. All the years of pain would never have occurred. One thing she did know about Erik, he'd never have beaten her, like those other three. Nor would he have allowed her to be beaten by anyone in his presence. The news, like a stab to the heart, crushed her, and she fought hard to hold back tears. "What happened? Why didn't he do it?" she whispered, wondering what had lured him away that dreadful night.

Recently, Erik had made it quite clear that he wanted her sexually. She wasn't so sure about emotionally. Back then his feelings must have been ambivalent, or even uninterested, on both points. Their entire history consisted of a love-hate relationship she'd always found strangely stimulating. Up until now.

"Leila, he didn't know you were the initiate. I swear."

She closed her eyes. So, at the time, he didn't know. And now he did. Were his thoughts and feelings as troubled as hers? Most likely, if he now felt responsible, as Kam said. Her eyes opened, and she glanced toward the bathing room. Seemed she might not be the only one who needed some heartfelt healing from this painful ordeal.

* * * * *

Erik smashed his fist against the bathing wall, cracking one of the stones. *My fault. All my fucking, damn fault.*

He already felt guilty about Leila's Initiation, and now she was scarred, probably for life, because of him. She deserved better.

The marks on her back and ass, obviously caused by some strap applied excessively hard, made him sick. The horror she must have endured, he couldn't imagine. He opened his fist and shook out his throbbing hand.

Nobody had realized that Rave, Shear, and Dare were going too far during Initiations. Video existed, but the new initiates had apparently been too intimidated by the trio to say anything. So the disks had never been reviewed. Until Laszlo, for reasons unknown to him, had watched Leila's ceremony. Maybe the man was simply looking for a cheap thrill one night. Who knew? But afterward, he'd informed the Council, and those three monsters had been immediately banished.

Erik had tried to stay calm in the bedchamber for Leila's sake, but the knowledge about what had happened to her tore him up inside. She was so beautiful, inside and out, despite her ravaged flesh. All the pain she'd gone through, and was still going through, could have been avoided. He felt like the biggest bastard ever. Maybe all the times she'd called him that in the past, she'd been correct. What he'd condemned her to hadn't been on purpose, but it didn't matter. The result ended the same.

He should have insisted on completing the Initiation, instead of going on that mission to Tamara. He'd been itching for an off-planet assignment and jumped when the opportunity had arisen.

The Council hadn't informed him who the female initiate was, so he hadn't thought twice about passing on the lead position in the rite to another Warrior. Even if he had known, he wasn't sure what decision he'd have made.

Back then, he was more than a bit wild. Young and stupid, too, if he admitted the truth. And he'd thought any woman he wanted would fall at his feet, whenever he wanted. Even today, he rarely met with a refusal when he went on the prowl. Except with Leila—she was one special lady and didn't fall for his lines. He was determined to capture her heart. He'd have to resort to the truth with her, and lay his emotions on the table. She wouldn't accept anything less, and she deserved so much more.

When Laszlo had found out that the Initiation hadn't gone as planned, he'd been angrier than Erik had ever seen him, even before he'd found out about the abuse, according to the date and notation in the file.

Maybe Braden was right, after all. Maybe Laszlo really was manipulating them, and even back then the man had wanted him and Leila involved for some reason. Whatever the truth, everything had turned into one big, fucking mess.

Braden had come across all the information in Laszlo's records shortly after he'd taken control of The Lair. He, Braden, and Kam had always shared data whenever possible, and Braden had thought it important for him to know what he'd found.

None of them had known about her scars though. Braden wouldn't permit viewing of the video and never watched it himself. Leila deserved that privacy, he'd said. Laszlo hadn't noted her specific injuries in the files, only that he'd watched the rite, had seen physical abuse, and reported it.

Laszlo kept many secrets, it seemed.

Hearing a familiar voice from the bedchamber, his thoughts switched to another who kept secrets—Kam. No wonder Laszlo and Kam worked so well together. They were two of a kind.

Kam had always been a good friend, but each year he changed more and more, withdrawing into himself so much that Erik barely felt like he knew the man any longer. Kam's actions tonight proved that once again.

He was the one who was supposed to initiate Leila with the dildo. Kam purposely arrived early to do it himself. His excuse of her needing a more tender touch didn't fly with him. He knew how to show and give tenderness when needed. The man simply wanted a chance to fuck her. The discovery of Leila's scars was the only thing that had stopped Kam. He should have ripped the guy's head off, like he'd threatened, for overstepping the bounds already set down on how they were going to deal with her.

These last few years, so many changes and tragedies had plagued Xylon and its people. Sometimes he felt like taking off and never returning. Then he wouldn't have to deal with the shit anymore. Though he looked at Braden like a brother, he had no real family here, no personal ties. Except his feelings for Leila. He needed to decide one way or the other what he wanted to do with his life, and not look back.

Continuing to argue with himself in his head, he paced and grumbled. *Who are you kidding, Rhodes?* He had responsibilities. And he could never leave Leila, no matter what. He knew that above everything else. No further decision or thought was necessary.

He vowed right then to do anything and everything to protect her, to give her all the pleasure she'd missed out on, and see to it she felt secure and cared for. The idea of other men touching her didn't sit well, but he'd be in control, directing the action, and if their combined efforts brought her more pleasure, all the better.

Braden's argument about the necessity of the lot of them staying tonight seemed valid, he supposed. Time would tell. Braden had signaled his wishes, and he'd finally, though reluctantly, agreed. She did need to be put through the entire ceremony again. He understood that. More so, she needed to break through this fear and mistrust during sex that she still harbored, or her life would be overshadowed by that fear from now on. For Xylons, sex was a major part of life. He wanted her to feel free to enjoy that sexuality. But he would be the one to decide how the others participated tonight. He'd do this for Leila. *Only for you.* He'd do anything.

* * * * *

Leila watched Kam walk past Torque on his way to the bathing room. She hoped he and Erik didn't end up in another confrontation. She hated when they argued.

Noticing that Torque seemed suddenly distracted, her gaze settled on the man. He was up to something. She felt it, and that made her nervous.

Torque glanced over his shoulder and scooted toward the end of the chair. When Kam disappeared into the bathing room, he stood up and swung his gaze over to her. Their eyes locked, and a smile tugged at the corner of his mouth.

As he approached, she shrank back a little. *I knew it.* He wanted something all right, and she feared asking him aloud what, like she didn't already know. The hungry look in his eyes gave him away.

"You're frightened of me."

His low, deep voice rumbled through her. "I'm wary." With reason. As a trained Warrior, she could normally protect herself if necessary. But Torque was a Class 1, and a renegade, which made him more dangerous than simply any Xylon inhabitant. At least she knew Kam and Erik remained near, as long as they hadn't dematerialized out. She wished they were still in view, so she could be certain.

"Why wary?"

"I've heard rumors." To say the least. Some female Warriors gossiped endlessly after Joining Parties. Or maybe bragged was a better word. Torque almost always made it into the conversation. She couldn't help but overhear the talk, from time to time.

"Sexual rumors?"

She nodded.

A huge smile crossed his face. "All true."

Her pulse jumped. She'd expected a don't-believe-everything-you-hear response. But Torque never responded as expected, from what little she did know about the man. "That doesn't make me feel better."

"It wasn't meant to." His eyes darkened and grew more intense, turning almost black as he looked at her. "What you heard about me makes you hot. I see it in your eyes."

She averted her gaze, settling it somewhere in the vicinity of his massive chest. "Torque, you've got a mouth on you. And a huge ego."

"And an even bigger cock. I know. But I excite you sexually. As does Erik. Yes?"

She couldn't help lowering her gaze to the front of his pants. The large bulge caused more panic than intrigue. He looked huge. She quickly glanced away. He wanted her sexually stimulated. That was why he'd said what he had, instead of putting her mind at ease. She knew that, but she wasn't about to admit to anything. Not with him.

He sat down next to her. "You just don't want to acknowledge that danger makes your pussy wet."

She shook her head in disbelief. The man was incorrigible. He never stopped until he got what he wanted. Well, she wasn't playing.

He gripped her chin, turning her head toward him and commanding her complete attention. "What women fear sexually is often what they secretly crave the most."

"That makes no sense." She pulled her head back, out of his hold.

He cocked an eyebrow. "Are you certain? Think about it, my dear." He reached out and tugged at the sheet, but she wouldn't release it. "I just want another look at your gorgeous breasts, and maybe a small taste before the others return."

"Are you serious?" He had more nerve than any man she'd come across in a long time. Even more than Erik. She ought to slap him, but no telling what his reaction might be.

"Yeah, I'm serious." His hungry gaze raked her body.

Still clutching the sheet with one hand, she waved her other hand toward the far side of the room. "Go back and sit in the chair." His words about her fear and cravings disturbed her. Could he be right? Her vagina was indeed soaked right now. She'd never been fully satisfied with her lovers. Maybe they'd been too tame and too submissive to excite her sufficiently. Even so, Torque was overly dangerous, in her opinion. She wouldn't want to be completely alone with him in a sexual situation. Erik possessed the right amount of untamed sexuality and heartfelt caring. Her body throbbed just thinking about the man. All she needed to do was trust him enough to let go with him. Maybe, in the future, she'd even feel comfortable enough to let him know how she truly felt about him.

"I'm going to see your breasts eventually." Torque leaned closer and whispered, "I'll be touching them, licking and biting your nipples, sucking them deep into my mouth until you scream over and over for me to fuck you like an animal." His lips grazed her ear. "Once that happens, the things I plan to do with your pussy—"

"Torque."

They both jumped and looked over to see Braden standing by the door. She hadn't seen him materialize back in. Instantly, she felt more at ease.

Torque frowned and stood up. "Just setting the mood."

"Try dimming the lights." He glanced around. "Where are Kam and Erik?"

"In the bath," Torque answered. "Taking a group piss or something, I guess."

Braden set a small black case on the floor. He walked over to the bed, a concerned look in his eyes. "Are you ready to start, Leila?"

"You're staying, right?" She needed to double-check, just to be certain. Now that some time had passed, and he'd had a chance to think over his decision, he might have changed his mind.

Reaching out, he allowed the tips of his fingers to stroke her cheek. "Yes, I'm staying. It's going to be all right, Leila."

She tried very hard to believe that. "Are *you* going to…touch me, tonight?" Just because he intended to stay, didn't mean he intended to participate.

His eyes never left hers. He didn't immediately answer, only looked at her with sympathy and compassion. Finally, he asked, "Do you want me to?"

She turned her head and lightly kissed his fingers. She felt his surprise, even before the look crossed his face. He always treated her so gently, and as Erik's best friend, and a friend of hers too, she didn't fear him. Sexually, she wasn't completely sure about any man. But she knew Braden only wanted the best for her. Her learning to trust in all aspects of life, including sex, needed to start somewhere. "I will trust you, Braden, and the others."

A small smile appeared on his face, and he pulled away his hand. "Well, our participation, specifically mine—if any—will be up to Erik."

She nodded, understanding. She felt good that Erik would be in charge. Still, anything could go wrong as far as her emotions went. Once the rite began, she hoped to relax enough not to go into a panic attack. "Alexa?"

"I talked to her. That's why it took me so long. We came to an understanding, and she's accommodating us only because it's you."

"I see." She didn't ask for details. And he didn't offer any.

Worry worked its way into her mind. Sometime after this was over, she wanted to speak with Alexa to make certain everything was indeed all right. She didn't want to be the cause of any problems in her and Braden's relationship. They were an ideal couple, with one of the strongest commitments she'd seen on Xylon.

Xylon's born-and-bred women understood Alliances, but Alexa's perspective as an Earth woman would differ. Though if she were Branded to Erik, she might not be so understanding if he wanted to continue participating in Alliances. Her thoughts weren't politically correct for Xylon's society. But then, she'd never actively tried to conform to society standards.

Her thoughts registered. *Branded to Erik.* Not Branded period, but she specifically chose Erik in her mind. A big difference existed between attraction and Branding. Her visions definitely had made an impression on her psyche. She needed to speak with Erik, and see if the same visions plagued him. She watched Braden glance over at Torque, who was leaning against the wall and looking sullen.

"Don't worry about him," Braden told her. "He has a soft spot. He just doesn't like to show it."

Staring at Torque's expression, she wasn't convinced of the truth of those words. She'd never noticed anything soft about the man. She didn't believe he'd purposely hurt her, not with the others around to make sure he didn't get too wild, but that didn't mean she felt comfortable enough to allow him total access to do anything he might want to her, sexually.

Braden pulled a small tube out of his pocket, flipped open the top, and dispensed a tiny, brown pill into his palm. "I want you to take this."

Leila looked at the square pill. She didn't recognize it. "What is that? Medication? Medication counteracts the Initiation chemicals."

"Not these. They belong to Laszlo. We found them in his quarters, along with the research on them. They are only used in extreme cases of Initiation fear, and only on special high-level breeders."

"Am I high-level?" Alexa, as a super breeder, would be considered high-level. But her?

"You are in my opinion, and that's all that matters right now. They'll make you more accepting, let's say, of what we're going to do to you."

"A relaxant?" From his words, she gathered the Council wouldn't agree with his assessment of her status. Not a big surprise. If she wasn't close with Braden, Erik, and Kam, she wouldn't be privy to many perks, including special medical equipment received over the last couple of years, for use in her research studies, which she knew they'd arranged.

"A relaxant of sorts. And a sexual stimulant of sorts. The chemicals affect the mind more so than the body." He handed her the pill. "Take it."

A mind-altering drug. Dangerous, especially since the Initiation itself already altered one's brain waves. "Why wasn't I informed of these and allowed to run tests on them?"

"You don't have high-enough clearance."

Irritation grated along her spine. "I'm in charge of the medical facility. How high up do I need to be?"

"Sorry. Council regulations. Only research specialists with a crypto clearance qualify, in addition to certain Xylon Council members. Since we already possessed the research results on them, I didn't fight the decision. I'm making an exception by showing you these now and telling you what they are for, because I think you need the help tonight. If you mention you know about the pills or have taken one, all of us will end up banished."

Somehow, she doubted that. The Council would never banish Braden or Erik. No other Warrior qualified to lead and control The Lair.

She didn't normally like to take medication she wasn't familiar with. She trusted Braden though. And Laszlo had apparently tested them. If the medication helped her get through the ceremony without incident, she'd be grateful. "All right. I'll take it."

"Do you need some water?"

"No, the pill's small enough." She placed the square on her tongue and swallowed. She wondered how long before the effects kicked in and whether she'd realize what was happening.

"Remember, Erik's going to be in charge tonight. You'll enjoy everything we're going to do to you." He leaned forward, and his voice lowered. "You'll come all night long."

Leila laughed, but her humor was halfhearted at best. "You sound confident."

"I am." Braden kissed her cheek. "Trust us. Trust Erik." He straightened and turned around. "Erik, Kam. We're ready to start."

Leila's heart rate kicked up a notch. *Here we go.* She squirmed beneath the sheet.

The two men strolled out of the bath.

She studied their faces. They didn't look angry. Maybe they'd formed a truce. The two of them had been friends for a long time. She'd hate herself if their friendship ended over something involving her.

Erik sat down on the bed. Just looking at Leila made his heart ache even more so than his dick, which said a lot, given how much he wanted her. Finally, tonight, he'd know what it felt like to be inside her.

An Initiation wasn't how he'd pictured their first time together. He hoped to find some private time with her later. Kam had agreed to follow his instructions tonight. At least that was one less worry.

He took Leila's hand in his and laced their fingers. Her skin felt cool to his touch. "You know there are certain things we have to do to your body with the dildos to inject the protective elements inside you."

Her fingers squeezed his. "Yes."

She was trying to be so brave, his beautiful and sexy Warrior. She'd been through this before, and she had enough sexual experience. And she was a strong woman. Still, he worried about how she'd handle the ceremony. "Don't fight us. Just let it happen."

Braden leaned down and whispered in his ear. "I gave her the pill."

Erik nodded. "Good." He felt better. The medication would help keep her mind open sexually. He didn't want her to fear sex, or even be uncomfortable with the act, but crave all that a man, that *he*, could give her. He released her hand and tugged on the sheet. "Let me pull this off you. You have no reason to hide, Leila. Your body is incredible."

Slowly, her fingers loosened, and she let go of the sheet. He slid the cover off her, exposing her naked flesh to all of them. Erik had never seen a woman more beautiful. Her long, silky hair and sultry eyes alone made him ache with need. Along with a perfect face, her breasts were full and round, her stomach flat, nicely flared hips for cradling a man, a gorgeous pussy, covered with satiny-looking curls, and long, shapely legs.

The men surrounded the bed, looking down at her like a group of sex-starved youths. When she tried to cover her breasts, he stayed her hands. Erik glanced at each of his friends. "Give us some room." He didn't intend to let them just jump on her.

Torque frowned and returned to the chair. Kam leaned against the wall. Braden perched on a padded bench under a grouping of three scenic pictures.

Without their intimidating presence, Leila seemed more at ease to Erik. As his appreciative gaze roamed over her flesh, a blush covered her body. Xylon women rarely blushed. He found the reaction endearing.

She smiled slightly, looking more nervous than happy. "I guess this is it. Do what you need to do to me."

His emotions turned to mush. Her eyes held such trust. Trust in him. He leaned over and brushed his lips against hers. "Give me your tongue, baby," he whispered.

She opened her mouth and gradually eased her tongue forward until it touched his. He groaned at her sweetness and wondered whether the flavor was natural, or if she'd artificially enhanced her taste.

She sighed and sank into him.

His hands cupped her breasts. Full and soft. Her tender skin aroused every nerve ending in his body. His cock stirred in his pants and grew semi-hard. When his thumbs grazed her nipples, she gasped, and he captured that gasp in his mouth, slanting his lips across hers.

Erik felt the heat building on her skin. If they gave her what she really needed, instead of what she normally allowed, her emotional healing might move along faster, whether she agreed with the process or not. He'd already spoken to one of the other Healers about the situation, presented in the hypothetical, of course. And the Healer had agreed. He'd never force, if she absolutely refused, but he planned to push her to her limits tonight.

Deepening their kiss, his tongue explored her mouth. She responded, kissing him back with desire and building passion. One hand stroked down her silky body, and his fingers grazed her pussy — the curls covering her felt softer than he'd imagined, and her folds, moist and open, beckoned for a deeper exploration.

"Mmm." She arched slightly against his hand.

Breaking the kiss, he raised his head and stared into her eyes, hoping she knew he'd never do anything to harm her, only to help and protect and arouse. "She's wet, but not wet enough," he told the others. He wanted to make love to her, regardless of who remained in the room watching. But his desire would have to wait until later. Tonight was about pure sex, protecting her body, and preparing her for later breeding.

"That's easily fixed," Torque said. "Lick her pussy. We'll each take a turn. She'll drip cum by the time we're through."

Leila gasped, and her gaze darted around the room to each of the men.

He had to know… Her response would set the tone for the night. Gently turning her chin back toward him, Erik locked his gaze with hers. "Would you like that? All of us eating your pussy." He watched her chest rise and fall. Nerves? Excitement? The skin around her nipples puckered. He leaned over and sucked a bud into his mouth. He couldn't resist. No matter her answer to his question, he intended to be the one eating her. First taste. He needed the first taste.

"Yes," she whispered, her fingers tangling in his hair.

"Yes to what?" Torque asked, his tone antsy. "Erik sucking your tit or all of us tonguing that tasty-looking, pink cunt of yours."

Erik felt her squirm, and he sucked harder. *Say it, baby.* He would direct the action, but he wanted to know her needs, and how far she'd be willing to let them go.

"Yes. Lick my pussy," she finally said, her voice more than a little shaky. "I want to know how your tongues feel inside me."

"All of us?" Kam asked.

"Yes, yes. All."

Kam groaned. Torque and Braden remained silent, but Erik felt the sexual energy in the room skyrocket. He lapped at Leila's rosy nipple, admiring the shape and length. A Xylon woman's nipples were a little longer than an Earth or Tamarian woman's. He found that asset incredibly sexy. And they possessed their own special flavor. He could suck those buds forever and never tire of the taste. He looked into her eyes. "Will you accept Braden's tongue on your nipples, while I lick you, Leila?"

She swallowed visibly and glanced briefly at Braden, before her gaze returned to him. She cupped his cheek. "Is that all right with you?"

Damn. The very last thing he expected was for her to ask his permission. He leaned into her hand, his heart tumbling in his chest. He looked over at Braden. "Do you want a taste of her?"

Braden stared at her breasts. "Definitely." He approached, and Erik stood up, moving aside.

"She tastes like dewberry," Erik whispered to his friend. The flavor still lingered in his mouth.

Smiling, Braden sat on the mattress and reached for one mound. He palmed her lightly. "Perfect, Leila. Beautifully shaped and full, with nipples just made for sucking. A man's dream."

Leila's hand touched his. "Taste me, Braden. I want you to."

Erik bristled slightly. He knew the pill affected actions and words, and made her open to more sexual experimentation. Still, he wanted to find out just how much the medication was talking and how much were her true emotions. *How do you really feel about me, Leila, any different than you feel about the others?* His heart squeezed in his chest.

"Go on, brother," Torque urged. "Eat that ripe tit while you can. You won't get another chance after tonight."

Without warning, Erik grabbed her ankles. He pulled her flat on the bed, so they could service her better. He planned to make tonight an experience she'd never forget.

"Oh!" Her eyes widened in surprise.

Braden leaned over, and the tip of his tongue touched her hard nipple. She made a little sound of pleasure at the moist contact. He circled the bud as the others watched, sucked on the nipple, then took as much of her breast in his mouth as he could. A look of delicious delight crossed his face, and joyous bliss crossed hers.

Watching Braden suck Leila's tit didn't make Erik as crazy as he'd expected, especially after Leila said she wanted him to taste her. He knew Braden was committed to Alexa, and the pleasure on Leila's face made the sacrifice of allowing another man to touch her worthwhile.

Erik pushed apart her legs, spreading her thighs, and readying her for his attention. He settled comfortably on the bed and stared down at her pussy. His. No matter what happened tonight. Leila's body, mind, and soul would always be his.

Torque slid forward in the chair. "Lick her, Erik. Make her pussy quiver. I get next taste. Afterwards, Kam can fuck her with the dildo, while we all watch."

"I want a taste, too." Kam licked his lips, moving closer.

"I'm in charge here," Erik responded with a growl, not about to let Torque or anyone else direct things tonight, or any night, where Leila was concerned. Not that there would be another night. After this ceremony ended, he'd provide her with all she needed to stay sexually satisfied, from now on.

"I know what'll get her off." With a hard look on his face, Torque stood up and approached the bed. "Let me in there. I'll make her squirt cum all over the bed. You're too soft with her and taking too damn long."

Leila tensed. Erik felt it. He also saw Braden react, who'd obviously felt Leila's discomfort, as well.

Braden raised his head. "Torque, Erik is in charge."

"You guys have no damn balls. I'd show her how real men fuck. She'd love it and beg for more."

Leila's fingers tangled in the sheet.

"Back off," Erik warned in a low voice, trying to maintain his control and not erupt into a rage. Leila felt unsettled enough without them breaking into a fight and making her stress worse.

"Relax." Braden kissed her cheek, letting his tongue graze her skin. "You're all right."

Erik caressed her thighs, working also to relax her. "Braden and I will take care of you," he told her, hoping she trusted him enough to believe his words. When he felt her tension slowly ease, he leaned down and spread her pussy with his thumbs. Lightly, he licked her fleshy clit. Just once.

Leila gasped at the touch of his tongue.

Perfect. He really wanted to bury his face, his tongue, deeply within her pussy and eat her fast and furiously until she came, but this first time he needed to go slowly. For her. "Stimulate her tits again, Braden. She liked that."

Leaning over her body, Braden circled one nipple with his lips. He brushed his tongue across the top of the bud. Alternately sucking and brushing, he kept up the gentle touch.

Erik watched Braden work his magic. The man loved breasts. He was a pussy man, himself. The scent of a woman's sex always drove him wild. And he craved the taste of Leila's. He waited for her reaction, grateful that Braden understood this first taking of her body by them needed to be special.

As if afraid to make a sound, she chewed at her bottom lip.

Erik felt her arousal. She needed to come badly. "Moan, cry out. Don't be afraid to let go with us." He lowered his head and inhaled her special, sexy scent—his pulse kicked up a notch, and his heart pounded in his chest. His tongue eased out, and he licked her pussy, slowly and thoroughly, not leaving an inch untouched. Delicious. Her cum probably tasted even better.

Little mewls of pleasure escaped Leila's lips.

Not enough. He wanted to hear more, to *make* her cry out her pleasure. His tongue swirled around her clit. Her pussy tasted slightly sweet, unique, a flavor he couldn't exactly describe. He could eat her all night long, except he wanted inside her too. He slowly pushed one finger up her pussy, while he continued tonguing her. The thought of his dick enveloped in her heat almost made him come in his pants. He worked a second finger within her moist folds, barely able to get his thick digits in. It must have been a while since she'd been fucked.

She groaned and spread her legs a little wider, bending her knees.

Yes, she wanted it. He glanced up at Braden who was licking her nipples, first one, and then the other. Her hands, buried in his hair, guided him to what she wanted. She obviously enjoyed the multiple stimulation. And they hadn't even injected the chemicals into her yet, which increased sexual need exponentially, once the elements took effect. The pill was doing its job.

After tonight, she'd crave more of what they were going to give her during the session here in her bedchamber. She wouldn't fear submission any longer — with the right man.

While his tongue circled her clit, he slowly finger-fucked her. Each time he pushed in deep, he felt her shudder. Good. He wanted her to come for him. He needed to make her climax first. He hungered for her to know that he gave her that ultimate pleasure before any of the others.

He pumped his fingers a little faster, demanding a reaction. *Come on, baby.* His tongue swirled around her clit. He sucked it into his mouth and drew on the bud, scraping his teeth against the sensitive flesh.

"Yes, Erik!"

The more intense the stimulation, the better she responded. That worked well. He'd see to it she got plenty of intensity tonight.

From the side, Kam approached. Erik didn't know what the man planned, but he'd better keep his dick in his pants. At least for now.

Kam sat on the floor and leaned over the mattress. He grasped Leila's ankle and licked the bottom of her foot and between her toes. Much as Erik had thought about doing earlier tonight. How could a man not? She had the sexiest feet Erik had ever seen.

Leila moaned, and her leg jerked. But Kam held her firmly.

"What the hell." Torque took the cue and moved to give her other foot a tongue-bath as well.

He made small grunting sounds of enjoyment, which Erik found almost funny. Apparently, every part of Leila tasted good.

"Oh!" She gasped and wiggled on the mattress. "Too much stimulation."

Never too much. They were just getting started. Erik lifted his head. "More, gentlemen," he directed. "Overload her senses." At his instructions to the others, Leila let out a little squeak. He almost chuckled. Soon she'd be shouting. Her ecstasy would prove too much to contain, he had no doubts about that. "More intense, Braden."

Nodding, Braden lightly bit one nipple and pinched the other one, which caused her to squeal and squirm. He sucked on her tit again, drawing deep, while his fingers massaged her mounds.

"Spread her out for me," he said to the other two. Kam and Torque both pulled Leila's legs wider, and the erotic sight of her so open and vulnerable was incredible. Erik lapped at her clit. He thrust his fingers as deeply as he could, curling his digits inside her and stroking her internally.

"Erik!" She cried out and arched her back. "I'm coming! Yes! Oh! Ah! Keep licking me. I'm coming. I'm coming. What— Ohh! I...can't...stop!"

Yes! All for her pleasure. He felt great giving that gift to her, especially tonight when she must feel completely out of her element.

"Don't try to stop, Leila," Kam told her. "Let your body go. Let us show you the wonderful possibilities of total, sexual fulfillment."

"To hell with the flowery words," Torque responded. "We're gonna show you how great it feels to fuck like crazy and come hard."

"Uh, uh!" She twisted and moaned through another massive orgasm.

Braden lapped rapidly at her nipples. His hand caressed her stomach and hips.

Trying to draw out her climax, Erik varied his licks, touching her clit on all sides. With his fingertips, he brushed along a specific, tender spot he'd found up inside her. Her cum covered his fingers and dripped onto the sheet.

"Ohhh!"

Torque pushed her leg up and licked the entire length of the back of her thigh, getting as close to her pussy as he could, without interfering with Erik.

Her body jerked, and she gave out another squeak. She mewled and finally collapsed on the mattress.

After a few more licks to lap up some of her cum, Erik lifted his head and pulled out his fingers. "You can stop, gentlemen. She's done."

They all released her.

Erik stared down at her flushed body. So beautiful. He held his fingers to her lips. "Suck them clean, Leila. Taste yourself."

While the others watched, she opened up and sucked her essence off his fingers.

"Get it all," he told her, rotating his fingers slightly. Such a sexy sight. She looked like she enjoyed the taste. When he pulled back his hand, her eyes fluttered closed.

"Oh, yeah. That showed her we mean business," Torque said, staring down at her pussy. He rubbed his dick through his pants. "Fuck her with the dildo now, Kam. I want to see how she takes a cock up her cunt."

"No," Erik responded. "I'm doing this. Let me have the dildo." This involved more than sex. The chemicals needed to be properly injected. Otherwise, her state of protection wouldn't change. He didn't trust anyone else to do this part.

Kam handed it over. "Do we get a taste of her? Her pussy looks like there's still plenty of cream left."

"No." Erik hefted the dildo in his hand, unconcerned about Kam and Torque's frowns. Their pleasure meant nothing to him, only hers. "She needs to orgasm again in order for her body to pull the dildo's special chemicals deep inside her. I hope she isn't too exhausted to respond." He'd wanted to give her an orgasm simply for her pleasure first, which he had. Now, they needed to get down to business.

"She's still got plenty of life in her," Torque said, his eyes locked on the curls between her legs. "Believe me. Go on. Fuck that wet cunt." He licked his lips.

Erik growled. Punching Torque in the nose right now held a lot of appeal. Though Torque meant no harm, his abrasive nature turned irritating at times. Especially tonight. He wanted Leila treated with respect, not as some off-world cantina babe, out for a hard and fast fuck. But he didn't want to cause a problem that might erupt into violence. Not now. He'd deal with Torque later. They'd fought more than once in the past. Torque never changed.

Taking a cleansing breath to keep himself calm and centered, Erik held the tip of the dildo against Leila's pussy. "Tell me you want it, Leila." He didn't intend to simply shove the thing into her.

Even though she lay breathing hard, with her eyes closed, she didn't hesitate. "I want it."

"Tell him to fuck you," Torque urged. "Beg him to give it to you hard."

"Torque," Braden said, pushing the man back a step. "Give it a rest."

Leila didn't say anything, but her eyes opened and locked with Erik's.

Staring into those beautiful cinnamon eyes, he saw her need and pushed the dildo inside her, one slow inch at a time. After about six and a half inches, she tensed and looked unsure. The Council had ordered an increase in the size of the Initiation Dildos a couple of years ago to accommodate more vaccine. She knew about that, but hadn't experienced it personally until now.

"Relax. You can take it." After another gentle push, the entire eight inches slipped inside her, everything but the base. He curled his fingers around the flat, electronically controlled end and pulled the thing halfway out of her. The long instrument glistened with her juices.

"That's so fucking hot," Torque said, moving closer.

"Ah... Nice," she said, with a slight smile. "Feels good." Her eyes clouded with desire.

All eyes turned to her pussy. Even Leila rose up on her elbows to watch.

His cock hard as steel, Erik shifted uncomfortably. He rested his other hand on her thigh, holding it down, and slid one knee onto the mattress. He planted his other foot firmly on the floor. Hoping to give her a memorable fuck, his hand tightened around the dildo. He moved its length back and forth slowly for several strokes, then increased the rhythm a little at a time. "Still good?"

"Good. Yes." She nodded. Her eyes never left her pussy.

Erik heard the others breathing heavily as they watched. His determination set, now that he had her approval, he moved faster and faster, until he was finally pumping the dildo hard.

"Oh, oh, oh!" Leila moaned, still watching, her gaze locked on the dildo moving rapidly in and out of her pussy.

"Keep going, Erik," Torque encouraged. "Harder. Damn, that's nasty. Look at her cream coat that cock. You ever watch yourself getting fucked like this, Leila?"

"N-no." Her fists clenched in the sheet, and she groaned, spreading her legs wide.

Torque signaled Kam, who nodded in return. They each hooked a hand under one of her knees and spread her to her limits. Braden sat behind her and supported her back with his chest, so she could watch more comfortably. He caressed her breasts, while his eyes remained locked on the dildo.

"I need more access, guys. I want this cock deeper," Erik said.

"Deeper?" Leila squeaked out.

Torque and Kam lifted her up a little. Braden stopped his caressing long enough to slip a pillow beneath her, to raise her pelvis for better penetration.

"Good." Erik thrust the dildo into her with driving force, as deeply as he could get it in.

Leila gasped.

"You like that?"

"Yes." She moaned. "Fuck me. Fuck me. Fuck me."

"Oh, man," Torque groaned.

"Do it, Erik," Kam encouraged. "She wants it. Give it to her."

Without the pill, Erik doubted she'd have spoken so graphically. His body broke out in a sweat, as he pumped the dildo wildly. Until she came, nothing short of a planet-wide, land quake was stopping him. "Kam, rub her clit," he directed, his voice full of sexual excitement. He heard the tone, but couldn't control it, nor did he want to. Let her hear his anticipation of her climax.

Kam sucked his finger. He reached down and circled her clit. "Let go, Leila."

"Relax your cunt muscles," Torque said. "You'll spasm harder."

"Come for us," Braden commanded. "Right now."

As if following Braden's order, she screamed and came. Her body shook violently, and for a moment her eyes rolled back in her head.

"Yeah!" Torque shouted.

"Chemicals are injecting," Erik told them. As she orgasmed, her internal muscles drew the elements deeply into her body, protecting her from sexually transmitted diseases and poisons.

He continued fucking her, slower now, until Braden moved aside and lowered her back flat onto the mattress. "Her pussy is protected, and she's ready for breeding."

All breeders remained essentially sterile until approved for impregnation by the Council. But she was now capable. With his arm and hand exhausted from pumping her so fast, he barely eased the dildo out of her, without shaking. Even so, he knew they needed to continue. "Turn her over for the second step."

Leila mumbled something, but he didn't understand her words. He didn't ask her to repeat them. Nor did the others. If she'd issued a protest, she needed to say it louder, so they could hear.

Braden and Kam gently turned her onto her stomach. When she didn't voice any objections, he figured she must be all right. Though she probably felt too weak right now to protest much of anything they might do to her.

"Damn, I'd love to shove my dick up her ass," Torque said. "I'm hard enough to fuck that hole all night long."

"Me, too," Kam agreed, his eyes locked on her full cheeks. "I bet she's as tight as a vise."

"You're too big, Torque," Braden said. "You know that. So don't even suggest it."

He grunted. "Yeah, I know. One of these days I'm gonna find a woman I can fuck as hard as I want and go up her ass whenever the mood hits, without worrying about hurting her."

Once Leila's sexual appetite hit, she'd probably welcome a multiple ass fuck. Not that he intended to allow the others at her. Erik stared down at her, submissively lying on the bed. The sight of her scars ripped at his emotions. Once they completed the ceremony, her flesh would begin to heal. He hoped. If not, he didn't know what he'd do. Leila lay strangely quiet, and he wondered about her thoughts. He leaned down and whispered in her ear. "Are you all right?"

She turned her head toward him and smiled. A lazy, satisfied look graced her face.

Feeling a sense of relief, he smiled back. She'd enjoyed herself. He'd make sure she enjoyed everything. He lightly kissed her lips before pulling away.

Kam touched his arm. "Let me prepare her, Erik. I want to lick her asshole."

Uncertain, Erik stared down at Leila's nicely rounded ass. His gaze shifted to his friend's eager expression. He knew Kam loved doing a woman's ass. And he was good at it. Leila would most likely enjoy his tongue penetrating her. As long as it wasn't his cock… "All right, lick her. Get her really wet."

A frown marred Kam's face. "I know how to go up a woman's ass, Erik."

"Yes, I'm aware." He caressed Leila's ass cheeks, tracing the scars there. She lay passively, which surprised him. He wondering how much anal experience she'd had, beyond her original Initiation—probably not much, given her propensity for control. Though, she hadn't opposed their words and actions, so far, and she knew her ass was next. "I just want to make sure she's completely slick. Braden, hand me the anal dildo. Even though she doesn't need to come for the anal elements to work, I want her coming anyway. Let's make this come blow her mind." If they could do that, he doubted she'd be wary of much of anything sexual afterwards.

She sighed. "I can't come any harder than I just did." She hugged the pillow, and her lips quirked up into a slight smile.

"Really?" Braden cocked an eyebrow. "That sounds like a challenge to me."

They all chuckled.

Erik shook his head. Wonderful. Now they'd try extra hard to make her scream, or even pass out from pleasure. Warriors never liked the idea of *not* being able to do something. And Leila knew that quite well. She'd issued the challenge on purpose. He almost made a quip about it, but didn't want her to know he realized what she'd done.

"Relax, my sweet," Erik said. "We're going to send you soaring. Raise her up a little, guys, and push another pillow under her. Get her ass up."

Braden and Torque lifted her hips and positioned her properly.

Kam spread her cheeks and lapped at the small, puckered hole, circling the tender skin. He speared his tongue inside.

"Mmm." She squirmed.

"Lick it thoroughly," Erik said, then chuckled when Kam slanted him a look.

Leila wiggled on the bed and began to pump her ass.

"Look at her beg for it." Torque chuckled. "Shove that tongue deep, Kam. She loves it."

Over and over, Kam reamed her.

With only mild emotional discomfort, Erik watched Kam tongue-fuck her ass. He'd done the same to Alexa, during her Initiation. It didn't mean anything more than what it was. Later, he'd be pumping something much bigger than a tongue or an anal dildo up that tight hole. She'd enjoy that, too. Kam wasn't the only one talented at ass fucking.

"Oh, yes, more! I'm going to… I'm going to…"

Before she came, Erik pulled Kam back. He was in charge of her orgasms, not Kam or anyone else. And he wanted them all to understand that. Leila and Kam both moaned their disappointment. "Don't worry. We're just getting started here. Hold her ass open, Kam, while I insert the dildo."

"Don't tease her next time, Erik. Let her come, even if it's one of us she's coming for." Kam spread her cheeks and pulled gently at the skin around her opening.

Erik adjusted the settings on the dildo. "Don't forget this is a one-time event for the rest of you. And I decide what happens tonight."

Leila glanced up at him. Their eyes locked for a long, heated moment. She smiled just barely before putting her head back on the pillow.

While Braden, Kam, and Torque watched intently, Erik slowly pushed the much thinner anal dildo into her ass. He flipped the vibrator on low.

"Ahh!" Leila's hands fisted.

"Easy." Braden stroked her hair and back.

Erik fucked her slowly, letting the dildo do most of the work. She mewled, but then relaxed and wasn't responding as much as she had to Kam's tongue. She needed more tactile sensations, he surmised, from her earlier responses. She needed all of them working her body to his direction. He wanted to focus on the big picture, and he knew that he couldn't do everything himself, so he'd employ their help, regardless of his wariness to do so. "Torque, take care of her clit."

"Finally."

Before Torque touched her, Erik grabbed the back of the man's neck and leaned close. "You *will* treat her the same as you'd want your sisters treated."

"I don't fuck with my sisters, in or out of bed. They can take care of themselves. As can Leila. She's not helpless." His eyes darkened with his anger. "You know damn well I'm not going to hurt the woman. But I *will* lay you out if you put your hands on me again. Now let go of me."

"We'll settle this later."

"I look forward to it, Erik."

The tension in the air increased as Erik stared intently into Torque's eyes. Finally, he released the man's neck. If Torque made one wrong move with Leila, he would knock him out. He'd done so before on Earth, when Torque showed up unexpectedly and wanted to fuck Alexa, and he'd flatten Torque again, if he needed to.

Torque licked his finger and reached under her. "What do you want, boss? A gentle glide, or something more demanding?"

From the look on Torque's face, Erik knew the man only asked as a dig and to see if he'd compromise Leila's pleasure. Torque never asked permission to do anything. Erik caressed Leila's ass. He intended to order what he knew she needed, in her heightened state of arousal, no matter who executed the touching. "Tug on her clit. Torture her. Make her crazy."

His eyes sparkling with mischief, Torque chuckled and nodded. "One of my favorite things to do to a woman."

"Kam, come down here. We're both going to put a finger up her pussy," Erik said. She'd get all the stimulation any woman could need. "Braden gets to watch."

A frown crossed Braden's face. "Thanks."

"That's what you get for being mated, and for refusing my initial request." On principle. As his friend, Braden should have backed him up. All right, so he was being petty, maybe. But he needed to know how the Initiation turned out first, before resting easy about Braden's judgment call tonight.

"Payback is beneath you, Erik. And I have permission to participate, in part."

Torque laughed. "Permission. I love that. The mighty Xylon Warrior—Commander of The Lair—obtained permission. Alexa's leading you around by the short hairs."

"I make my own decisions."

"Apparently not."

"Shut up, Torque." Braden grumbled something else under his breath, but not loud enough to be heard. His frustrated expression spoke volumes though.

Erik did hope Alexa understood about Braden's participation. After all she'd been through, he admired that lady tremendously. He pushed a finger into Leila's soaked pussy. Then he slowly pulled out almost all the way. "All right, Kam. Get yours in here."

"Flatten your hand and move up a little, so I can get in." A little awkwardly, due to their positions, Kam pushed a finger deep, along with Erik's.

"Mmm." Leila shifted on the mattress, and the dildo wiggled precariously in her ass.

To keep it firmly inside, Erik pushed the instrument in a little deeper and kept his fingers wrapped around the shaft. "All right. Now, fuck her hard."

Instead of building slowly, the men showed her no mercy, fucking her hard immediately, as directed.

"That's...oh! Good." Leila thrashed and moaned. The mattress bounced and shifted beneath her. She grabbed onto the iron headboard and held on tight.

Reaching down, Braden squeezed one of her ass cheeks. "I'm doing more than just watching."

"Fine. Slap her ass." Erik wanted to know how she'd respond to that type of dominance over her body, given her history. And Braden was the most skilled with spanking.

"No... No!" she protested, reaching back with one hand. "That's what *they* did to me. That's how it started."

"He won't hurt you, baby. He'll use his hand only. And it won't go any further than that." Erik nodded toward the case. "Bind her first."

"Bind? Erik, you can't," she pleaded, trying to get up.

"You're not going anywhere," Torque told her, his hand pressing against her back, keeping her in position.

"Let me up!" This time her voice sounded more angry than scared.

"Listen to me, Leila. You're all right," Erik said, trying to soothe her with his voice. "We're going to make you feel things you've never experienced before."

"I can't do this."

"Too bad," Torque said.

"Shut the fuck up!" Erik ordered. Torque wasn't making this easier on any of them. "Relax, Leila. Nothing bad will happen. Trust us."

Braden took a long tie out of the case he'd brought earlier. He returned and tugged Leila's arms behind her back, despite her protests.

"Braden..."

"Stay calm. It's all right." He bound her wrists together. "She's secured."

She whimpered, and a tear slid down her cheek.

Damn it. Apparently, the effects of the pill and main Initiation Dildo chemicals weren't enough to get her past this last block. Erik removed his finger from her pussy. "Keep pumping yours lightly," he instructed Kam.

Erik sat down beside her. He leaned close, stroking her hair. He couldn't continue like this. He wouldn't, without her trust and permission. He didn't want her traumatized. The other Healer had said this would work. He knew that wasn't the case, now that he saw her distress. The Healer had said she'd issue a mild protest, then acquiesce. The idiot. *He* should have known better. He still intended to push her to the edge, but it would be her decision to allow it to happen or not.

"I'm right here. We're not going to hurt you, baby. I promise. Just a mild sting, for stimulation only. Like in your visions and fantasies." He whispered the words in her ear, so only she heard, hoping she'd indeed experienced the same visions as he. "I want to fulfill everything you've always craved to enjoy sexually, without fear."

She gasped, then hiccupped and nodded.

He'd hit a nerve. "Let go of your apprehension. Let us sexually dominate you tonight...completely. You can trust us. Trust me." He caressed her back. "But this *is* your decision, Leila. I'll stop right now and remove the tie, if you say so." He heard Torque grunt. "I promise." He repeated the vow slowly, needing her to know his seriousness. "But if you do give us complete access and control, you'll come harder than you ever have. I guarantee it." After a moment of quiet, for her to contemplate what he'd said, he asked, "What do you think, Leila? What do you really want, deep down?"

She bit her bottom lip, releasing it a moment later. "I trust you, Erik. If you say it'll be good, I believe you. My memories of last time clouded my judgment, that's all. I know you're not like them. None of you are. But, still... If I change my mind once it starts —"

"Say *stop* at any time that you really need us to, and we will. But give it a chance."

"All right."

The trust she was putting in him made him determined to give her the best experience ever. If he let her down, he knew she'd never trust him, or probably anyone, ever again. Still, he needed to ask her once more. "Now, you're certain it's fine for us to continue? To spank you?"

She nodded. "I want to try."

"This could totally change your life, for the better. Believe me." It wasn't so much about the spanking. Some women liked the stimulation, some didn't. This was an issue of trust. He kissed her lips, then returned to the dildo and changed the angle. He pushed a button to allow the tiny feelers, coated with the necessary protective elements, to emerge inside her.

At their penetration, she jerked slightly. That reaction was normal, so Erik didn't worry, especially since she calmed immediately afterward.

"Go ahead, Braden. Spank her, but go easy."

Braden lightly slapped her ass, just to the right of the dildo.

The men groaned as her cheek jiggled and a slight pink mark appeared.

Leila tensed.

"Are you all right?" Braden asked. "I know that didn't hurt."

"I'm all right. It didn't hurt." Slowly, she relaxed. "I'm ready. Go ahead."

Erik re-inserted his finger up her pussy. He and Kam finger-fucked her, moving not quite in rhythm, which pulled along her sensitive nerve endings and stretched her even more. Torque concentrated on her clit. Braden slapped her ass again, just enough to cause a slight sting, nowhere near as hard as Erik had seen him do Alexa.

Leila took in a lungful of air, but didn't tell them to stop.

Think about your fantasies, baby. If she did that, Erik knew she'd be all right. In his visions, and hers too, if they were true visions, she craved to enjoy all types of sexual experiences. Those desires he'd try to fulfill for her.

Braden spanked her again, slapping his palm harder against her ass this time.

She began to shake.

Even though she didn't voice a protest, they all immediately stilled.

"Damn it, don't stop now!" she practically growled. "I think I'm going to come."

"Yes, ma'am," Braden replied with a grin.

They all laughed and resumed stimulating her body. Erik eased his finger deeper. Kam did the same, jostling a bit for better penetration.

Braden's palm contacted with her ass. A light pat, then a more forceful one.

She screeched and climaxed hard.

"Keep fucking her," Erik ordered, as she came. "Spank her just a little faster now, Braden. Maintain the stimulation."

He complied, slapping one ass cheek, then the other, over and over.

"Yeah, do her good, brother. Oh, this is hot!"

Leila practically wailed as her body continued to shake and thrash. "Don't stop," she begged. "Don't stop."

"We're not stopping," Erik told her. "We'll keep this up as long as you keep coming." Torque was right. Her body, bound and at their sexual mercy, caused something primitive and possessive to rise up inside him. He'd always gotten off on control, but with Leila, this proved so much more powerful because he knew she never submitted...until now.

Braden continued smacking her now very pink ass. Erik and Kam's fingers moved steadily back and forth within her pussy. Torque's fingers kept her clit stimulated. Erik began moving the dildo inside her ass, pumping it quickly to work the elements deep.

"Oh! That feels great!" She started to cry from the intensity of her orgasms, coming one after another, hard and fast.

While Braden switched to spanking one ass cheek only now, Torque slapped the other one, the fingers of his second hand still tugging on her clit. "We're gonna wear your body out, babe."

"Yes!" She jerked, coming again.

With each successive orgasm they gave her, Erik felt better. In the future, sex wasn't going to be something she did just to relieve the tension in her body. She now knew the pleasure and enjoyment possible with the right partner.

Finally, she collapsed, her body still twitching, but done coming.

While the others continued to slowly finger-fuck her, Braden unbound her and rubbed her arms to return the circulation. Torque finally stepped back. Erik and Kam pulled their fingers out of her pussy.

Erik flipped off the dildo and removed the thin vibrator from her ass. "She's protected from rear penetration poisons and illnesses now. Are you all right, Leila?"

Lying on her stomach and breathing hard, she wiped her eyes. "That was the best ever. I never thought so much pleasure possible, especially from giving over control."

"That's exactly why you came so incredibly hard," Erik spoke in a low voice, so as not to break the sensual mood. "But never agree to that kind of submission because someone intimidates you, only if you have complete trust in your partner should you allow something like that to happen."

Lightly, he caressed her pink ass. When Torque had begun spanking her, he'd almost pushed the man back. But he'd kept the slaps light, like Braden. Maybe Torque understood more than he let on.

Too bad that once the major sexual appetite hit Leila, she might not remember most of what happened here tonight. Some women did, some didn't. They'd know in the morning. He'd question her when he got the chance. Even if she forgot the actual events, her apprehension about sex should remain gone. After an emotional wall broke down, a Xylon's psyche remained stable, in most cases anyway.

Hopefully, he'd get more chances than just tonight to touch her intimately, to show her how he felt about her, and not in a group setting. He wanted one-on-one time. He wanted her to clearly remember everything he did to her body, and know he was the one giving her that pleasure.

She glanced up at him. "I trust you, Erik. All of you. And, um…"

"Yes?" he asked when she hesitated and blushed.

"I wouldn't even mind…doing it again."

At her admission, he gulped, but then his muscles tensed. When the others issued no comments, he relaxed and felt grateful. She'd exposed herself, and none of them said or did anything to lessen that. They were good men.

No more sexual barriers existed for her. She was now completely free. "Are you ready for the final step?"

He stroked her hair and leaned down to kiss her. Their lips touched. Their tongues touched. And, at that moment, a new connection of trust and understanding formed between them.

Chapter Four

In a military stance, Halah stood alertly before Rave, who leisurely stretched out on a long, green lounger in her quarters. No matter how relaxed Rave appeared, Halah had learned long ago never to let down her guard around this woman.

As expected, Rave didn't invite her to sit. Her superior attitude always grated on Halah's nerves, more so recently, as her own frustration with life in The Dome increased. The woman gave the word "bitch" new, intergalactic meaning.

Rave pulled open the black robe she wore, revealing her naked body. She smiled slightly at Halah, and her eyes held a challenge.

Yeah, so? was Halah's first thought. The woman's breasts sagged down to her waist. Was she supposed to be impressed by their heft? She held her tongue. Halah didn't want trouble. She needed something from Rave, although she hated to admit that fact.

Rave slid apart her thighs and bent one knee along the back of the lounger, intimately exposing herself. She snapped her fingers, and a female slave immediately rushed over and knelt between her legs. The girl lapped at her pussy, like an obedient pet. Rave stroked her head gently, almost lovingly. "What do you want, Halah?"

If she didn't have business that couldn't be ignored, she'd have turned and left. Halah couldn't wait to get off this rock and away from these people. She was no innocent herself, but even she couldn't stomach the former Warriors who now enslaved others and enabled the Egesa to do the same, especially since the majority of those enslaved ended up used for sexual pleasure, torture play, or horrific medical experiments.

Her thoughts briefly flickered to the male Warrior she wanted to tie up and fuck until he couldn't walk. Perhaps she wasn't so different from those she despised. Pushing aside the unappetizing thought, she concentrated on her reasons for coming to Rave's quarters. "Leila Abdera will be captured on Marid tomorrow."

Rave laughed. "What nonsense are you speaking?"

"Not nonsense. I made a deal with Braden Koll to capture Leila, plus whoever accompanies her to Marid, then help them find the sterilization formula, along with important information about Daegal and The Dome. Afterward, I'm to aid in their escape."

Rave's eyes narrowed. "In exchange for?"

"Information on my sister's whereabouts. Braden says he knows where she is."

"He's lying. That knowledge isn't even in The Dome databases. I've looked. Her tracking chip is not operational, according to the intelligence. There's no way he's located her."

"Maybe the intelligence is wrong."

Rave frowned. "The girl disappeared, and no one knows where she is, Halah. Don't become that man's fool."

The fact that Rave sought out the whereabouts of her sister made her shudder. No telling what Rave would do, if she got her hands on anyone who held Halah's heart. "Braden is a man of honor. I have to take the chance he's not lying."

"Honor." Rave snorted. Her fingers tightened in the girl's hair. "What's your angle with this, Halah? I assume you have one, and you're telling me everything because…"

"I know you, Dare, and Shear, as well as Daegal's Top Commander would like to possess Leila. Maybe even Daegal himself, for all I know. Why everyone is so obsessed with her, I'll never understand. But I can give her to you, to do with as you please."

"Our obsession, as you call it, is personal and, frankly, none of your business."

Like she really wanted to know. They could pass the woman around or have a team fuck for all she cared. "I will need clear transport off this moon, once I find out the information. You can arrange that for me. My other problem is that Leila's a breeder, as the ones with her will most likely be. Now that all breeders are being rounded up and killed, I won't be able to clear them through processing." Halah had learned of Leila's status from Rave herself. The woman bragged to her endlessly about how she, Dare, and Shear had initiated the Healer some years ago.

"The breeder sterilization formula isn't permanent." Rave twirled her fingers in the slave's hair. "Does Braden know that?"

"No, I don't think so. The rumors are true, then?"

"From what I hear."

"I don't intend to mention it. Let him find out for himself. I need my sister's information from him. However, the new directive will make getting it nearly impossible without help. The Warriors will be executed once we enter The Dome, and I'll never find my sister. Braden may even have her killed in retaliation."

"That I doubt, not his style." She held up a hand. "Hold on, while I come." She pushed her pelvis forward. "Get with it, girl. Cunt-lick me better, or I'll whip your pasty skin right off your back. Yes! There, that's the spot. Now, faster. Oh, oh, ahhhhh!" She sighed and relaxed against the lounger. With a grunt, she shoved the girl away. "Bring a wet cloth."

"Can we continue now?" Halah asked, disgusted with Rave's display.

Rave's attention switched back to her, and she chuckled. "You need a personal slave, Halah. I think it's been too long since you've received a good lick and a hard fuck."

"And I think you're a bitch-whore with a power complex. Can we focus this talk on the situation at hand?" Perhaps her words weren't wise, but she couldn't hold back.

"It takes a bitch-whore to recognize one, my dear. Besides, I take that as a compliment."

"You would."

Waving her hand in a dismissive gesture, Rave shook her head. "I don't have time to swap words with you tonight. I'm expected elsewhere. If I clear Leila and company as slaves into your keeping, they'll think you're helping them, and give you the information, then you'll betray them and give Leila to me, right?"

"That's the plan."

"Why should I agree? Now that I know, I can just take her. I don't care what happens to your sister." Rave looked up at the girl who'd returned with the cloth. "Clean me."

Halah tried hard not to lunge forward and punch Rave out...or worse. Her hands fisted at her sides.

Rave grinned up at her, and she spread her legs wider for the girl. Halah knew Rave had only had sex in front of her, and ordered the slave girl to wash her, to try and put her off balance. Rave always wanted the upper hand, and she didn't know how else to get it. Sad, because Halah wasn't impressed.

After everything she'd been through, not much rattled her anymore. She'd attended many Lair Joining Parties in her day. Public sex and voyeuristic sex didn't faze most Warriors. Rave's attitude was what grated on her nerves. "I know your secrets, Rave, and I might let something slip if I don't get the help I need—from the stress, you understand." She shrugged. "So, it's to your advantage to help me."

A look very close to a pout formed on Rave's face. Halah almost laughed.

"And if I still refuse or seek my own agenda?"

"I go straight to Daegal. Your association, business and personal, with Gabriella, will be revealed." Halah simply stated the obvious. Rave was only buying time by asking what she already knew the answer to. Halah glanced around the room.

She wouldn't be surprised if Gabriella, Daegal's mate, was watching this entire scene from some hidden surveillance.

"Nobody sees Daegal, except Gabriella and the Top Commander. Ever. Unless you have a death wish."

"I'm sure if I try hard enough, I can get safe passage and an audience. Or at least attract his attention, considering this whole complex is monitored on video."

With Rave's help, Gabriella was slowly poisoning Daegal. They'd found a way around many of the healing elements. Or maybe the chemicals just weren't as effective on Daegal for some reason. Halah wasn't sure which, nor did she care.

Whatever the case, the two women were causing havoc a little at a time, behind the scenes. The two were also having an affair, though she suspected Daegal wouldn't much care about the latter. He often shared Gabriella with others, even the Egesa. Halah's stomach churned at the thought of allowing the smelly, lizard-like creatures access to her body. They were nasty fuckers. Literally.

Totally by accident, she'd found out about Rave and Gabriella's alliance. One day, as she'd covertly looked for information on her sister, she had overheard the women plotting to take over The Dome. Halah had decided that it might be in her best interest to record their meetings.

With the help of a few loyal friends she'd made on Marid, she had placed some listening devices in strategic locations. A couple of the placements had paid off. The existence of those recordings now kept her alive, safe, and the recipient of certain perks. She didn't intend to lose the advantage she'd gained.

Rave's upper lip curled. "I should have you killed. Gabriella wants you dead. And Daegal doesn't care, according to her. Supposedly, he's said you're too trivial for him to deal with, and he's left your fate up to her. So at best, your time is limited, Halah."

Yes, she was certain of that truth. Still, she needed to remain strong and confident, and not allow Rave to think any of her threats hit home. "Don't try to intimidate me. You won't have me killed. Neither of you will. We've been through all this before. Whether you choose to believe me or not, Rave, I am more powerful than you and Gabriella know. I have many more followers here than you realize." A small lie, but effective, given the wary look that crossed Rave's face.

"You're dreaming if you think you can overpower us."

"Really? I'm never unprotected as you allow yourself to be, like now. I could easily electrocute you, right here." She almost always remained wired with power. Halah was smart enough to know that she needed to be ready to defend herself at all times.

Her training as a Class 1 Warrior in electrical warfare came in handy. In a one-on-one fight, Rave wouldn't stand a chance. Neither would Gabriella. If they combined forces or sent a team to destroy her, Halah didn't know her chances of survival. But she wouldn't go down or give up easily.

The slave girl scurried to her feet.

Halah caught her arm. "You stay quiet about this. Or you will die." If the girl ran to the Top Commander, Halah would lose her advantage.

"Leave us!" Rave ordered, then waited until the girl disappeared around the corner before continuing. "Do not threaten my servants. Blackmail is so unbecoming."

"But effective. Once I'm gone from Marid, you won't have to worry about your secrets or me any longer, Rave. This will work out best for everyone involved."

Rave whipped her robe closed and surged to her feet. "We will do this your way, for now. But if I don't get Leila out of this, I will watch you die. You are little more than a slave yourself, Halah. Don't fool yourself into thinking otherwise. This knowledge you have is powerful, but not complete."

At Rave's acquiescence, Halah relaxed slightly. If she thought Daegal would release her from The Dome, she'd have already bypassed Rave and told him of the women's deception. But she'd been double-crossed by Daegal in the past. She couldn't trust him. This time, she needed to play her advantage smarter.

The thought of actually locating her sister, alive and well, kept her determination strong. "All I want is to find Josella and leave this life far behind. After that, I don't care what happens to Xylon or Marid or any of the moons, for that matter. You can destroy them all, if that's what suits you."

* * * * *

Erik stared down at Leila, resting on the bed. Such an incredible woman. No other compared in his eyes. Sexually, she made him hot and hard. Emotionally, she kept him calm and centered. Around her, he became a better man.

Two of the three Initiation steps were now complete. The third and, in his opinion, most important step, remained. Leila had skipped the third step last time. Not that he blamed her. But she wouldn't have the option of refusal this time. She'd already agreed. And he'd make certain the thought of refusal never entered her mind. "Let's get her ready for the final step." He stripped off his shirt.

"Too tired," Leila said.

"Too bad. We *are* finishing you off," Torque answered. "Don't worry. We'll get you going again. Your sexual appetite will be kicking in, too. So, don't get too comfortable. You're going to be begging for it soon."

Kam tossed a pillow on the floor. "Whose dick will she be sucking?"

"Mine first." Erik dropped his shirt, then with Braden's help, carefully eased Leila off the bed. She looked worn out. "Are you sore?" Trying to assess her physical and mental state, he looked deeply into her eyes. "Tell me the truth."

"I'm all right, just a bit tired."

"We need to continue." He wished they could let her rest, but the timing tonight was essential for everything to work correctly in her system. He caressed her hair and back.

Meeting his gaze, she nodded. She touched his bare chest, and her fingers skimmed his flesh, trailing slowly down to his belt. "I know."

His stomach tightened. He loved the feel of her touch. He leaned down and brushed her lips with his. "Soon, you can sleep. Just a little while longer, and we'll be done." He helped her onto her knees atop the pillow. "Try to relax."

"You have plans for her to multiple suck?" Braden asked.

"With her scars as they are, while her body is in the correct state, if she sucks the healing elements from more than one of our cocks, maybe she'll be able to heal better. I don't think it's been scientifically tested before, as far as I know. But the theory seems valid."

Her ability to self-heal meant more to him than worrying about the sexual participation of the others. The elements only absorbed properly while the Initiation chemicals still coursed through one's system. Tonight was their last shot at transference. According to Braden, and Laszlo's once sealed records, re-initiation was the end of the line. The rite couldn't be performed a third time. So far, the Initiation had gone well as far as getting her protected and breaking down her sexual barriers. He hoped for that success to continue.

"I'll volunteer for number two," Torque said.

"I think Leila should choose," Kam offered. "She might prefer me."

"I will choose." Erik knew what needed doing, and Leila's judgment might not be the best while the chemicals controlled her system. Her safekeeping was his foremost responsibility, and he took that responsibility seriously.

"Leila, does that sound reasonable?" Braden asked. "About the multiple sucking."

"Yes." She nodded, her head hanging in exhaustion, her hair covering her face. "It's a plausible theory."

Erik stroked the back of her head. So silky soft. He wasn't certain about her sucking Kam yet, but he'd let her suck Torque.

Unless she objected. The man spewed cum like an erupting volcano. He'd watched Torque fuck at Joining Parties. The man was practically legendary. Between the two of them, she'd receive plenty of self-healing elements.

After tonight, though, she belonged only to *him*.

Leila felt the chemicals stimulating her system, slowly changing her exhaustion once more to sexual desire. She raised her head and tugged at Erik's belt. She needed his cock in her mouth, wanted to experience the taste of him on her tongue. The healing elements she required seemed secondary to her at this point. Right now, she simply wanted him.

She glanced up at his face. He was breathing deeply, his eyes heavy-lidded with passion. Because of her. Even on her knees, a sense of power filled her, more so than any dominant position she'd ever assumed during sex. She took her time unhooking his pants, tormenting him, making him wait.

When she finally reached inside, he sucked in a sharp breath.

Her fingers curled around him, not quite circling his thickness. His cock felt hot and incredibly hard in her hands. She pulled him out and caressed the long, purplish length. Velvet over steel. Perfect.

Erik groaned, long and deep.

She leaned forward and licked the head, swirling her tongue over the thick top and around the rim. She flicked the sensitive underside and dragged her tongue along the lightly ridged shaft, up and down.

"Oh, damn!" Erik's hands fisted at his sides, and his muscles visibly tightened.

Behind her, Braden sat on the bed. He slowly massaged her shoulders, then tugged her long hair behind her, wrapping the strands around his hand. "Suck his cock, Leila. Put the man out of his misery. He's waited for this longer than you know."

Smiling slightly, she leaned forward again, wondering if Braden held her hair simply to give the others a better view of the action. She slid her lips over the bulbous head of Erik's cock and sucked. "Mmm." Even after everything they'd done to her, she found this act the most erotic.

"Oh, yeah, Leila." Erik moaned. "Your mouth on my dick feels better than I ever imagined."

"Deeper," Kam said from the side.

"Yes, come on, Leila. You can swallow more of him than just the head." Braden pushed gently on her head.

Yes, she could. His cock was big, but not unmanageable. She slid her lips down further over his shaft. So good. Erik's musky taste invaded her senses and made her crave more. He'd waited for this, Braden had said. Well, so had she.

In her fantasies, she sucked him almost nightly. Now, he filled her mouth in reality, and her fantasies paled in comparison. Her body grew warmer as the flavor of his cock completely filled her mouth. Sucking him made her edgy, and her whole body ached. Needing relief from the sexual cravings building inside her, she began to caress her breasts.

Beside her, Torque knelt on the soft flooring and pushed aside her hands. "Let me take care of those tits for you, babe."

Her hands shifted to Erik's thighs, and her fingers curled into the fabric of his pants. She welcomed a stronger touch. And she knew Torque would give that to her. His hands, warm and assured, covered her breasts. He rubbed them softly. When she pushed her breasts firmly against his fingers, he increased to a harder and more demanding manipulation of her tender flesh.

"Easy, Torque," Braden said.

No. She didn't want easy. Torque knew, and he ignored Braden's words. Instead of letting up, he massaged her breasts even harder. Leila moaned around Erik's cock.

Normally, she smacked anyone who handled her so roughly. But Torque's touch felt good. When he pulled on her nipples, she moaned again, deeper this time, and bobbed up and down on Erik's thick shaft.

"Oh, yeah!" Erik responded. "Whatever you're doing to her, keep doing it."

"See, Braden. She loves it," Torque said. "Don't you, Leila?" he whispered against her ear. "You were made for pleasuring and receiving pleasure in return, and you know it." He traced the rim of her ear with his tongue.

At the erotic sensation, she shuddered. Torque's words surprised her. Not the fact that he'd just reduced her worth to one of some concubine. That was pure Torque. She'd work up being offended later. But she'd expected him to use more crass language. Maybe he did have a soft spot in him, although an archaic attitude concerning females.

Her pussy throbbed. She needed to come so badly. She needed Erik to come, too. Her body and mind ached with the need. Something…

Odd. For some reason, she suddenly didn't feel right. She felt— Oh! Her head started to pound, and she cringed.

"Kam," Braden said, a tone of concern in his voice. "Go up her pussy with your fingers. Erik, I think she's suffering some ill effects. We need to increase her stimulation. Approve it."

"Yes. Do it." He nodded, holding her shoulders steady. "Quickly."

Kam knelt on the other side of her. He pushed two fingers inside her pussy and pumped. "Relax, Leila. This will help."

"Mmm." She stopped sucking, but she couldn't move her body.

As soon as Kam penetrated her, her muscles relaxed. She squirmed, able to move again and instantly felt better. Not perfect, but the pounding in her head eased significantly. Kam kept moving his fingers, gently but effectively. For the first time, she understood the adverse affects the chemicals produced on the brain, if the sexual stimulation of the body waned too much.

"Harder, Kam," Torque said. "She needs it. She knows she can trust us, so she won't object." He continued to squeeze her tits and brushed her nipples with his thumbs.

"Do it, Kam," Erik ordered.

"No problem." Kam pumped his fingers harder.

She mewled at their insistent touch and resumed sucking Erik's cock.

He made a low, sexy sound from the back of his throat, and his fingers squeezed her shoulders.

To completely stop the pressure in her head, she did need the harder stimulation, while the chemicals exerted their sexual effects on her. A gentle taking didn't ease the discomfort enough. Gentle could come later, hopefully alone, with Erik. She looked forward to some private, intimate time with him, to lie in his arms and enjoy him fully, without the presence and watchful eyes of the others.

Erik tangled his fingers in her hair as best as he could with Braden still holding the silky strands. "Make sure she's all right with this, Braden, and that it's helping her."

Braden unwound her hair from his grasp and clutched her hand. "Squeeze my fingers if what they're doing to you is too rough, Leila, or if you need something different."

If her mouth wasn't full, she'd have told him that she felt better now. Braden had immediately picked up on her discomfort and handled the problem. She'd definitely protest if something happened she didn't like.

Kam and Torque's hands felt great on her body. But she didn't want to pull off Erik now and break the momentum simply to tell them so. Braden would figure it out.

"She's not squeezing," he said to the others.

Torque laughed. "I told you hard was what she needed."

"This makes you feel good, huh?" Kam poked a third finger against her pussy. "Spread your legs then. Take another finger."

The way she felt now, she wouldn't protest his entire hand. She widened her legs to allow him access, and her mouth sank further over Erik's cock. Her long hair fell forward and covered her face, brushing along her body and his.

"Oh, yeah," Erik replied. "Good."

Kam pushed all three fingers deep inside her.

Internally, she throbbed, her pussy stretched. Her breasts felt tender from Torque's caresses. Their touching demanded a response from her body. Even Erik pulled her closer, his fingers insistent on the back of her head.

The more aggressively Torque and Kam manipulated her flesh, the faster she bobbed her head, and the deeper she sucked Erik's cock. Fear didn't control her tonight, only need. Torque and Erik were right. Knowing she could trust them, along with the chemicals adding to her need, opened a whole new world for her sexually.

"Oh, Leila! Yes!" Erik shouted, when she tightly suctioned her mouth around him and sucked hard.

"Hold out," Braden encouraged. "Let more of the protective elements build up."

"I can't," he panted, pushing his cock further down her throat. "Her sucking feels too damn great."

The excitement in Erik's voice spurred Leila on. She needed him to climax, to taste his cum. She slid her mouth almost all the way over him, surprising herself at how much of him she could take.

She burrowed her fingers inside the back of his pants and scraped her nails across his ass. When she felt his body tremble in response, her heart raced, knowing he was close.

Suddenly, her pussy contracted around Kam's fingers, and she came. Oh! So good! Waves of pleasure washed through her, and her nails dug into Erik's cheeks. "Mmm. Mmm. Mmm."

"Yes!" Erik's body tightened, and he shot his cum down her throat.

Leila sucked him fast and deep.

"Swallow as much as you can." Torque circled her nipples with his thumbs, then tweaked each one.

Yes, yes. The pain-pleasure of Torque's touch had her following his direction, sucking and swallowing over and over, and wanting more. The chemicals, it had to be the chemicals, making her crave all these things. Or so she tried to convince herself.

Erik bent over her, holding her close, one hand buried in her hair, while he tried to keep every last drop in her mouth. "Get it all, baby."

The others slowly pulled back, as she continued to swallow everything she could.

Finally, when Erik had nothing left to give her, she let his cock slip out of her mouth. The absence, that lost connection with him, made her groan in disappointment. She'd wanted his cock hard in her mouth longer, wanted to give him endless pleasure, so he thought of her differently than just another fuck.

"I'm spent." He turned and collapsed on the bed. "She's good, guys. Really, really good."

At Erik's words, Leila warmed inside. Maybe she had given him something he wouldn't forget, after all. She wiped her mouth and leaned over to lick the bottom of his foot, which hung over the mattress.

He jerked, then chuckled. "Wench."

A smile crossed her face. She liked teasing him. She loved sucking him. And she hoped later to do so much more.

Unfortunately, or maybe fortunately—depending on one's perspective, even though she'd climaxed, her sexual appetite continued to grow. Strangely, she didn't feel the "fog" that had occurred during her first Initiation. The pill might have something to do with how she felt, or just the fact that this was a re-initiation.

Knowing she needed more tonight than just what Erik could give her, while still on her knees, she turned around and faced Torque. "I want you to fuck my mouth." The sudden urge to see what Torque had in his pants overwhelmed her. His was the only cock she'd never seen. She'd purposely never watched him fuck at Joining Parties, not wanting to appear awestruck like other women, especially since she'd wanted very little to do with controlling men. But tonight, her curiosity burned too strongly to deny.

In obvious surprise, Torque's eyes widened. He laughed, his eyes crinkling, and the color changed from near black to a liquid chocolate. "Oh, yeah, babe."

From the bed, Erik raised his head.

Everyone looked over at him.

He frowned. "She needs your protective elements. That's the only reason, Torque. She doesn't actually realize what she's doing and saying. Understand?"

"Yeah, and?"

With a sigh, Erik dropped his head back to the mattress. The tone of his voice dropped low and deep, "Fuck her mouth."

* * * * *

Halah sat in her quarters, looking over her plans. A male guard, not a slave, but a friend she'd teamed up with to help ensure their mutual safety, set a tray of food next to her.

From what she understood, Dak had never attained Warrior status on Xylon, but was a WAIT—Warrior In Training—when he'd decided to defect. He'd since regretted his decision, but once one pledged alliance to The Dome, death was usually the only way out. She'd never pledged her alliance, much to the Top Commander's chagrin.

"You need to eat, Halah, and keep up your strength. You're too thin already."

"I know. I just can't seem to keep anything down lately." All food tasted like sewage to her.

"Nerves."

"Me?" She puffed out a breath of air. "Hardly." She never showed her nerves to anyone, or her emotions. Not even to Dak.

"Yes, you. Pretend all you want. I know you."

Not really. He only knew what she allowed him to know. Even with friends, she kept her feelings closed up inside. She'd been betrayed too many times in her life. "You should get some rest, Dak. Tomorrow may be a long day."

He nodded. "Let's hope all goes as planned. I'll meet you at the transport center in the morning."

"Very well."

He swiped a piece of fruit from her tray, then left her to her own devices.

After he'd gone, she returned to studying her plans. If she pulled this off, everything she wanted would soon be hers.

Her orbiter was supplied and ready to go. She'd exchanged her smaller model for a larger though still manageable ship, capable of longer travel, to ensure they wouldn't end up stranded somewhere too close to their current danger zone. After she found Josella, they needed to leave this system to stay safe.

Rave had set up false information for the Warriors to access on the computer about Daegal and The Dome. Guilt struck, as it often did about betraying her people, but she forced it aside. "I owe allegiance to no one but myself."

The Council had refused to rescue her sister after the Egesa captured her, not deeming the girl important enough to risk sending in a team. That decision had showed Halah just how alone she was in the galaxy. With no other family to turn to, she'd taken on the task herself. So far she'd been unsuccessful, but she refused to stop trying.

Halah popped a piece of red-ice melon into her mouth. "Blah. Sour." She pushed the food tray aside.

Once the Warriors landed, Leila would be allowed to get her hands on the sterilization formula. Since she wouldn't be leaving the moon, no harm would come of it. Even if she did somehow manage to escape, the formula, in its present state, only worked for a limited amount of time. They'd end up spending a lot of time and effort combating something that didn't actually work.

Halah needed to make certain she got the information about her sister before Rave got her hands on Leila. She figured Rave would double-cross her. The Warriors might, too.

At the knowledge that she had no one to really trust, a sense of loneliness filled her. "No, I'm not going to indulge such foolishness." Weak emotions. They served no purpose. She took a cleansing breath.

What if they gave her false information about her sister's whereabouts? She shook her head. She couldn't think about that. Besides, it went against their code of ethics. Braden had made a deal. He would hold up his end of the bargain.

Though a Class 1 Warrior herself, she no longer felt bound by the same Warrior code. As such, she intended to seek her own agenda, as Rave was fond of saying.

Since she couldn't afford to trust anyone completely, she'd put her own plans in motion. "No matter what any of you do this time around, I'm the one who will come out victorious. I have to. This might be my last chance."

Chapter Five

Torque stripped his chest bare and tossed his black shirt into the corner. He unlatched his belt and slid down his uniform pants.

Leila gasped, as his shaft grew even longer and harder before her eyes. She'd never seen a man so big. He must be at least ten inches. And thick. She doubted she'd be able to wrap her fingers halfway around him.

His cock was much thicker than the Initiation Dildos, and he was twice as thick as Kam. Or Braden, from what she remembered of his and Alexa's official Branding Ceremony, when they'd been mated for life. She'd been a witness, along with Erik. Like most of Xylon's ceremonies, the Branding was sexual in nature. To her, Erik's cock seemed longer and thicker than the other two, but Torque even outdid Erik in proportion. And the head of his penis looked huge.

"You're gonna have to lean over, with your ass in the air, and let Braden spank your gorgeous butt again, if you want some of this." He gripped his cock and sat on the floor. "It makes me hard as steel to watch a woman get her ass smacked. And the harder I get, the more I spew."

Leila sighed. She needed to draw the line, while she still had the ability. Though his comment about her *gorgeous butt* did make her feel good. "No more spanking, Torque. You do know the need to always dominate, engage in dominant acts, or watch someone else being dominated exhibits the inability to trust," she told him.

"You should know."

All right, she'd set herself up for that one, she supposed. Still, she couldn't let him get away without some response.

Sometimes, an innocent reply worked best with men like Torque. "Because I'm a Healer?"

He grinned and lightly stroked his cock. "You know that's not what I meant, Leila. Don't play naïve with me. Your theory is a load of psychological crap, and you know it."

Well, that didn't go as she'd planned. He wasn't going to let her off easily, it seemed. "I know a lot of things, Torque. Probably more than you think."

"That's very possible, my dear." Looking at her intently, his eyes narrowed. "I don't think we're doing our job properly tonight. You're too clearheaded, if you're capable of such a debate. We need to change that. How about you *dominate* my dick? Just to show that I trust you."

"Like trust is what's motivating you here." She knew better. His eyes shone with a bit of humor, but mostly lust, and he continually raked her naked body, especially her breasts. She pulled her hair forward to cover herself, a discreet move on her part. Or, so she thought, until Torque grinned.

"Kind of late for that, don't you think? And just so you know, giving someone dick-control requires ultimate trust."

"Does it?"

"I know you want my cock, and Braden's palm slapping your butt. I heard you admit to Erik that you liked what we did to you in bed. Admit it to the rest of us."

"Torque, stop badgering her," Erik said from the bed.

Leila's heart warmed when Erik gave her a small smile and a wink. His presence made her feel confident and free. She knew he'd keep her safe.

"Come on, Leila," Torque continued. "Stop denying what gives you pleasure. That's part of what tonight is about, not just providing you with the ability to self-heal."

"I'm not denying anything." Surprisingly, she had enjoyed Braden's spanks. And Torque's hand, too. Considering her past, she wouldn't have thought that possible. But she knew they'd never hurt her, so she was able to enjoy the act, like she did in her fantasies. Just as Erik somehow knew. Even though she had said she wouldn't mind doing it again, that didn't mean she wanted to engage in the activity over and over, during the same session. Her butt couldn't take it.

And as far as Torque's cock was concerned… "I did enjoy the spanking you and Braden gave me, but I've had enough for tonight. And I can't suck that enormous cock of yours." There was such a thing as too big, even though few men or women admitted it aloud.

"Enormous? I like that." Torque laughed. "But…" He shook his head, and made a tsking sound. "You wanted a mouth fuck, babe. So, you're gonna get a good one. Now start sucking."

Not so fast. She wasn't about to be ordered around. Confident in her control with these men, she smiled slightly. "You said *if* I wanted it. I don't now."

"Really?" He cocked an eyebrow. "Well, irrelevant actually, since you need my healing elements." He wrapped his large hand fully around his cock, moving his fist along the shaft's thick length, stimulating himself, until beads of liquid appeared on the tip. "Lick those off. Then decide. You'll change your mind."

"Torque, you're impossible." He had an ego the size of, well, his cock.

"But lovable."

"Now, that's debatable." Leila hesitated a moment. She supposed she could at least lick the tip of that monster. From the side of him, she leaned over, her ass high in the air. An undignified position for certain, but considering what they'd done to her on her bed, she had no cause for embarrassment now. She glanced back at Braden. "No spanks or I'll floor you."

"Yes, ma'am." He chuckled, giving her a small salute.

Her tongue dipped down and swirled around the top of Torque's extra-thick head, gathering the clear drops. When his hips surged forward, she felt a sense of triumph, knowing he'd be a prisoner to her lips and tongue if she decided to suck him.

"Mmm. Nice tongue action. Now put my dick in your mouth. We'll see how good you really are."

The challenge in Torque's eyes reflected a typical male dare. She looked over at Erik, who lay on the bed, watching intently. For several moments, they simply stared at each other. She saw tenderness and understanding in his gaze.

At his slight nod, she switched her attention back down to Torque's huge shaft. She needed more protective elements in her system. She'd see how much of him she could take. Maybe she'd even find out if those rumors she heard about his never-ending cum were true. She changed positions for a better angle and slid her lips around the top of his cock head, which was as much as she could take. She sucked lightly.

"Harder, babe."

A little at a time, she increased the suction. His taste was different than Erik's. Muskier. She reached down and fingered her clit.

"I think I'm getting her hot, guys. I know she's heating me up good. She's got the softest lips I've ever felt. What a rush!" Torque slowly pumped his hips. "Relax your jaw, Leila. That's right. Yeah. Take just a little more of me."

The compliment from Torque took her by surprise. She sucked him deeper, but not by much. She was certain he'd had better. Even so, he seemed to be enjoying himself.

"Yes, that's good," he groaned. "Oh, yeah!"

Leila's skin tingled, and she felt hands caressing her ass. Erik. She jerked in surprise. She hadn't even seen him move off the bed, but she recognized his warm and tender touch on her skin.

He shifted beside her. Her whole system reacted to his nearness, his smell, his touch. She needed him. His fingers trailed up her back and into her hair.

She started to pull off Torque. Erik was the one she wanted. She craved the feeling of his arms around her, his cock inside her, his mouth on hers.

His sexy voice stopped her, and his lips brushed her ear. "Keep sucking him. You need what he can give you. Tonight, we're going to give you everything you need. And fulfill every fantasy you've ever had. But after tonight, *I'm* going to be your fantasy. Me alone."

His hand reached down and covered the fingers stimulating her clit, so that they moved together. Slowly. Gently. She mewled. Erik was already her fantasy. He just didn't know it yet. With him helping her masturbate, she couldn't hold back her feelings and moaned deeply around Torque's cock.

"Oh, damn. That sound vibrated right up my dick. I'm gonna shoot."

Leila curled the fingers of her free hand around Torque's cock, as best she could, and prepared herself to take his cum.

"Keep your throat relaxed," Erik told her. "And take down as much as you can."

Torque's fingers tangled in her hair. "Here it comes!" He roared, and his cum shot down her throat—a massive amount. "Ahh!"

Sucking hard, she lustily drank all he shot into her mouth.

So that only she heard, Erik whispered in her ear, "We will heal your body and spirit, Leila. That's what this is tonight. But for all our tomorrows, I will fulfill your emotional and sexual needs, and you will fulfill mine."

She practically melted at his tender words. As she swallowed, she experienced a small orgasm from her fingers. Though not a toe-curling climax, the pleasure fluttered through her body and warmed every inch of her from the inside out.

After the mild climax faded, her attention re-focused on Torque's cum. When she couldn't take the rest of what he spewed into her, she let some flow from her mouth, down her chin. The slightly sticky warmth rolled along the skin of her throat and between her breasts. And still, he continued to pump his seed into her mouth, groaning low and deeply the entire time. She'd never known a man who emitted so much.

Finally, Torque finished, and she pulled her lips off his cock. She swallowed the remainder of the cum in her mouth and tried to sit back, but wasn't able to. "Torque…"

Torque had collapsed flat on the floor, and he held her head in his lap, keeping her in the same ridiculously vulnerable position. "Oh, man. You can really suck, Leila. Get her off, Erik."

Oh, yes! Please. After hearing that, she didn't try to struggle free. Though nicely satisfying, she needed to come more than the climax she'd experienced at her own hand.

"Spread your knees, baby. Give me more room."

She immediately complied, scooting her knees further apart for Erik. His finger circled her clit. She felt so exposed in this position, she almost came right then, imagining what she must look like to them. "More, more." Her voice came out muffled against Torque's stomach. "Give me your cock, Erik. Please."

"You heard her. Give her your dick, already," Torque told him. "She needs fucking."

From nearby, Kam said, "Use your tongue first, Erik. Lick her. Make her drip."

"Yes, yes, yes," she begged. *Anything.*

After a moment, she felt his tongue slide along her wet pussy. "Oh, yes!" He varied his licks in the most interesting way, driving her insane, but he concentrated on her clit. "Push inside, Erik. Fill me up." She needed something, anything, inside her. And it didn't matter what, at this point.

He teased her entry, circling and prodding her. She grabbed onto Torque's cock, just to have something to hold onto. She tried pushing back against Erik to get him to plunge his tongue deep, but he wouldn't enter her. She let out a little whimper.

"Give her what she craves, Erik," Braden encouraged. "Stop torturing the woman."

Erik lifted his head. He massaged her hips and ass. "You want a tongue-fuck, Leila?"

"Yes. Tongue-fuck me. Now." Her voice wavered from a commanding tone to a pleading one.

"My pleasure, baby." Following several more light licks, Erik finally pushed his tongue inside her pussy.

"Ah!" Incredible.

He curled and flicked his tongue, moving deep then shallow. She squirmed, unable to keep still. His licking felt so good. She needed everything sexual she could get. As she'd done earlier, she reached under herself to stimulate her clit. This time though, someone grabbed her wrist, stopping her.

"I have something better," Kam said. Then she felt a second tongue. On her clit. Kam! He licked her fleshy bud of nerves in short, rapid-fire flicks.

"Oh!" Never had she felt anything so intense.

With Erik's tongue inside her pussy, and Kam licking her clitoris, while Torque held her in position, the stimulation pushed her right over the edge. She screamed against Torque's stomach and came hard, her body shaking. "Oh, fuck!"

"Exactly." Torque chuckled.

After she finished climaxing, and her body relaxed, she tried to lower her ass, but they wouldn't release her. Their tongues continued to lick her. "I-I'm done." She wanted to collapse now and sleep until morning.

Kam slid out from under her. "No, you're not. Hold her, Torque."

"I've got her. She's not going anywhere," Torque answered, holding her securely.

"Let me back there, Erik."

Her pulse pounded, and despite her growing fatigue, her body responded to his words, weeping in renewed need. Damn, these chemicals. Or bless them. She didn't know which. She held her breath, wondering about Erik's reaction to Kam's words. Would they come to blows? Time seemed to stand still, while nothing happened.

Then, she felt the two men switch positions, and both resumed their licking. At the feel of their tongues in her pussy, the breath rushed out of her. "Oh!"

This time Kam's tongue went inside her, and Erik brushed the tip of his tongue back and forth along her clit. The only thing she could do was hold onto Torque and let it happen. She wasn't quite sure how many times she came, or how many times the two of them switched positions, but the delightfully orgasmic session seemed to go on forever. She felt some of her cum trickle down the inside of her thigh, before being licked up by one of the men. At some point she must have started stroking Torque's cock, because all of a sudden he came all over her breasts and stomach.

"Oh, yeah," he groaned. "You are so fucking good, Leila." He stroked her hair.

"Tired now." She barely got the words out.

"You done, guys?"

"For the moment," Erik replied.

"All right. Let's get her comfortable."

They pushed her down onto the floor, onto her back. She thought they planned on allowing her some rest, until Torque shoved his pants aside. He rolled toward her, and his tongue was everywhere—her throat, her breasts and nipples, her stomach—licking his cum off her skin. "Oh, Torque!" His tongue was raspier than Erik's or Kam's, and his licks stimulated every area of bare flesh he touched. Too tired to do much else, she simply laid there and allowed him to have his way with her.

He slid down her body and burrowed between her thighs, pushing her knees to her chest. His tongue lightly circled her tender clit, then he consumed her pussy, like some wild animal.

"Ahh! Oh!" Her eyes locked with Erik's, as Torque licked and sucked her, his tongue and mouth tormenting her pussy. "I'm going to...oh!" She climaxed again. The orgasm was stronger than she thought possible, after just peaking so often. The entire time, her eyes never left Erik's intense stare. In her head, *he* was the one making her come. And the vision, while looking into his penetrating green eyes, took her to the heights of pleasure. "Again! I'm coming again!"

He caressed her hair. "Enjoy it, baby. Come hard. You're so beautiful when you come."

His approval meant everything. She let go and allowed the pleasure to rush through her. "Ohh! Erik."

"Hey," Torque complained. "I'm the one licking you down here."

"I didn't think she had any more in her," Kam said. "Keep at her, Torque."

"Damn right." He lowered his head and lapped up every drop of her cream.

Erik leaned over her. "I'm the one who wants your heart. Remember that." He kissed her deeply.

Yes. She wrapped her arms around him. Their tongues brushed, and his lips caressed hers. Erik's touch was so gentle she felt like crying. Finally, her body stopped trembling from her climaxes.

Torque sat back and licked his lips. "That was fun, up until you called out Erik's name. But I won't hold it against you, babe, considering the circumstances. What's next?"

Next? As she lowered her legs to the floor, Leila stared up at him in disbelief. She lay limp and exhausted, and he didn't even look winded. His cock, once more, stood hard and proud. Impossible.

What would it feel like to have such a huge shaft inside her pussy, fucking her? Painful probably. She imagined he had exceptional staying power, given his urgency to continue after he'd just come twice like she'd never seen. But that's all he'd have, physical prowess. No real emotional connection existed between them. Not even as friends, at this point. He was more stranger than anything. Sex with a stranger was a common fantasy. Not one of her favorites, but she had indulged herself in the privacy of her own imagination a time or two.

She wondered if he used something medically to be able to get hard so quickly. The healing power they possessed helped their men attain and maintain erections, but Torque seemed extra talented in that respect.

She glanced over at Erik, who was now gathering up pillows from the bed. What would happen between them after tonight? Would he resent the others touching her, and her allowing it to happen, even begging for it? He couldn't possibly, given this was an Initiation and Xylon's way of life. Not to mention the fact that he controlled the entire rite's progress tonight. And he seemed all right with everything so far. Still, she worried. And she knew she worried only because she cared, probably more than she should. He'd said he wanted her heart. She couldn't get that out of her head. If that were true…

After locking eyes briefly with Braden, and knowing he saw her jumbled emotions, she averted her gaze. Tomorrow was soon enough to face reality. Tonight, she needed to finish what was required for her to attain the ability to self-heal.

Torque looked down at her. "You've got the cunt of a woman a man dreams of turning into his own, personal sex slave."

"Hmph." Knowing Torque, she supposed that was a compliment. A woman would need to be quite strong and independent to handle life as his mate. She looked forward to seeing him fall hard for someone.

She saw Erik frown, and she knew. This did bother him. At least partially. She wanted to soothe his brow and tell him not to pay attention to Torque's words, or anyone else's. *He* was the man she wanted inside her above all others. The rest of this was just sex, for tonight only. Her body needed any and all the sex she could get right now to douse the burning within.

* * * * *

Alexa paced in her and Braden's bedchamber. Once they had discovered she was expecting, they'd moved from Braden's smaller quarters to a much larger place. She felt more comfortable here because the new place was their space, instead of just his. He also had a home on the planet's surface, but they'd never dwelled there. The Lair provided extra security that Braden thought necessary for her safety as a super breeder.

Once the situation with Marid stabilized, he'd promised her they could spend more time atop. She was glad. She missed the feeling of sun and wind and real air, instead of an artificially processed atmosphere. And she wanted their children to be able to play outdoors, under the clouds and sky.

Only one light illuminated a portion of the room, keeping the rest of the area in darkness. She lightly rubbed her stomach. Twins. All super breeders bore multiples. She'd probably end up as big as a horse before she delivered.

She couldn't help but worry how their two different gene pools would affect the children. Braden had told her not to worry. She was DNA-compatible. She already knew that, but the knowledge didn't make her feel much better. She wouldn't relax completely until she saw the results herself and held her babies' healthy little bodies in her arms.

Normally, she was fast asleep by now. Something didn't feel right though. Not physically, she felt fine in that respect. Something else tugged at her from the inside. At first, she thought her discomfort came from Braden not being there. But he often worked late nights, and she'd never had problems sleeping without him before.

Her pregnancy was going well. She hadn't even experienced morning sickness or cravings of any sort, which was just as well. She couldn't get pickles and ice cream here, or whatever odd thing she might want.

She sighed. She knew the real truth. She might as well admit it. The truth was, even though she'd agreed to Braden participating in part in Leila's re-initiation, she felt uncomfortable with the decision.

Braden had explained that this type of "immersion" would break through Leila's wall of sexual mistrust. She'd tried to understand, knowing this was part of Xylon and the rites of its people. But, often, she still found their ultra-sexual way of life hard to adjust to.

Kam had been a great help to her, while she attempted to cope with all the newness. Her brother was half-Tamarian, had studied Earth culture and many others for years, and knew how it felt to live between two worlds. But she hadn't completely embraced this new world yet.

Stopping in front of Braden's private computer, she fingered the monitor. Maybe if she knew what was happening, she'd feel better. The surveillance system had been disconnected in all of The Lair's private quarters long ago though. Or so Braden had told her.

"A secondary, hidden surveillance system exists," a male voice said from across the room. "No one knows about it, and the system can't be picked up by sensors."

She spun around. "Laszlo." Her heart began to pound. The man's piercing blue eyes seemed to look right through her. Where had he come from? And how had he known her thoughts? He must be aware of the re-initiation. "Are you really here?"

"No. I'm projecting."

"Where are you?" The mystery surrounding the former leader of Xylon deepened each time he appeared to her.

"Execute file S114P for private monitoring."

"What—"

His image faded. "Wait! Geez." Laszlo often appeared to her. She never understood why. And Braden no longer really believed her when she told him about her experiences, she didn't think, so she'd stopped mentioning them.

One time, Laszlo had alluded to something about her children being the future leaders of Xylon and needing extra protection. Maybe that's why he stayed close. Who knew?

Maybe she was just going nuts and imagining all this. But if the visions were real...

"Hidden systems." She glanced around the bedchamber, wondering if any were located in their quarters. She shuddered at the intrusive thought. "Why would Laszlo tell me how to private monitor?" She fingered the computer screen again. Could she really see what was going on in Leila's bedchamber?

If she saw something she didn't want to see, the knowledge might damage her and Braden's relationship forever. Or what she saw could strengthen their bond. She did trust him, but...

Laszlo must have given her the information for a reason. He never did anything without a reason, she'd learned, soon after her life here began. She sat down at the desk, staring at the blank screen in front of her.

"So, what do you think, babies?" She rubbed her stomach. "Do we check up on your Daddy, or not?"

From the late hour, she knew they'd finish with the re-initiation soon. She also knew how to execute files on Braden's system. She'd never done it herself, but had watched him do it often enough. Now, she just needed to decide whether or not to try.

Chapter Six

Pitch Pantera grabbed the girl around the waist. "Keep still." Even though only in her early twenties, she fought like a seasoned she-cat. Lucky for him she didn't have Warrior training. Otherwise, she'd be even more formidable. He noticed the bandage on her arm. From her computer records he knew she was Sunevian, not Xylon, so she didn't possess the ability to self-heal. He couldn't imagine going through life so vulnerable to infection and disease.

His hand-tracker had picked her up shortly after the team had split to locate her. The main tracker on Xylon led them to her general location. But nothing had registered on their handheld tracking system upon landing, so each of them had taken a different path to speed up the search.

His nose twitched from the lingering odor of smoke. She must have built a fire earlier to heat the broken-down abode where he'd found her hiding. Her clothing — a long shirt only — dirty and torn, hung on her as if not her own, and didn't provide much coverage or protection. Her bare legs showed numerous scratches and wounds.

The air on the Sand Moon during the day often became sweltering, but at night the temperature dropped severely. No telling how long she'd suffered the effects.

She kicked his shin.

"Ow, damn it!" He should have refused this mission, and he'd known it right from the beginning. Females on the run for too long always caused trouble when found.

She flailed her fists and screamed, her long black hair flying. "Let me go!"

"Calm down, Josella. I'm here to help you." The Sand Moon was not a vacation spot, but the toughest Banishment Zone of the four to survive. He needed to get her to safety before she ended up enslaved or worse. She was a skinny little thing and wouldn't last long if one of the gangs got hold of her. From the feel of her ribs, she hadn't eaten properly in a long while. And she needed a bath.

She stilled in his arms. "How do you know who I am? Who are you?"

"My name's Pitch Pantera. I'm a Class 2 Xylon Warrior. Braden Koll sent me and two other Warriors to find and secure you."

She turned to face him. "Who sent you?"

"Braden Koll, the new Warrior Leader."

"Koll? What happened to Laszlo?"

Her wide green eyes took him by surprise. Beautiful. "Disappeared. Braden has made a deal with your sister."

"Halah?" the girl's voice broke, and a look of sadness formed on her features.

She raised her chin, feigning an outer strength he suspected would shatter if pushed much further. "Yeah. Now stop fighting me, and let's get out of here. This place is not safe."

Life in the Banishment Zones consisted of gang warfare, survival of the fittest. The worst of the worst ended up sent to the Banishment Zones. The occasional innocent got dropped on the moons too, which was unfortunate. They normally didn't live long. He glanced around, a shiver running down his spine. He could almost feel the evil in the air.

"Are we going to Xylon?"

The hope in her voice touched him, but he pushed the feeling aside. Personal involvement affected judgment. He needed to stay sharp. "Quiet. You've attracted enough attention with your screams. We'll have company soon if we don't get out of here now." He pulled out his disruptor and tugged her behind him. "Come on. I'll explain everything once we reach a secure area."

* * * * *

Leila caressed her breasts. She needed stimulation again, and more than she could give herself. She felt her discomfort growing. Her head didn't hurt this time, instead she felt itchy inside, which wasn't as painful, at least.

Probably, the chemicals were wearing off. She really would like to be fucked properly, by a real cock—Erik's cock—before the night ended. "Help me out, guys."

They turned toward her, then simply stood there watching her touch herself.

As an incentive to them, like they needed one, she squeezed her tits and spread her legs wider. From the lust in their eyes, she felt like some party girl, entertaining a pack of horny Warriors just back from a dangerous mission. Still, they hesitated. She sighed.

So no misunderstandings occurred about what she needed, she told them straight out, "I need someone to fuck me. Now." She didn't specifically name Erik, because she wasn't ready to deal with that admission in front of everyone.

Torque smiled. "I do so like a woman who knows what she wants. Get in there, Kam. Give her some dick, and let her suck down your cum. She needs it. Then we'll fuck her good."

"Torque…" Erik said, a frustrated tone in his voice.

"Oh, relax, Rhodes."

Leila looked over at Kam. His healing elements would help her. If any chance existed of her scars disappearing, having the maximum protection inside her tonight would do it. In theory, anyhow.

Some female breeders healed faster than others. She wondered if those who did sucked more than one cock during their Initiation. From a medical standpoint, she would love to research the theory, if she could acquire the necessary details.

She and Erik looked at each other. While waiting for his reaction, she chewed at her bottom lip. She wished she knew his thoughts. He cocked an eyebrow at her. She shrugged. Her needs were such that the idea of sucking Kam appealed to her, but the decision was Erik's.

Stroking his cock through his pants, Kam stepped in front of her. "Let me add to her healing ability, Erik. Or try."

Erik shifted his eyes to stare at Kam. He didn't look particularly happy, but finally Erik did nod. "Only to help her, and only tonight, Kam. I'm serious. You know the boundaries."

"I know. Tonight only," he agreed. "To help her."

Kam and Erik exchanged some sort of hand signal she suspected was a form of a promise. She knew Erik worried about Kam, because of their close friendship. But he had nothing to worry about. Sure, Kam's motives probably weren't completely altruistic. She wasn't naïve. But he'd never challenge Erik. And even if he did, the choice ultimately rested with her, unless otherwise ordered by the Council. Her choice was Erik.

With a slight smile on his face, Kam looked down at her. "My dick is yours."

Leila tried not to laugh. These Warriors... They talked as if each of them gave her some great gift by letting her suck them. Well, during an Initiation, she supposed, they actually were giving her the gift of self-healing. She ripped open his pants and gently massaged him from base to tip. Warm, long, and mostly smooth to her touch. She slipped his semi-hard member into her mouth. "Mmm." Within seconds, he became fully hard, and his unique scent filled her nostrils and mouth.

"Yeah. Lick and suck it, Leila." He caressed the back of her head.

She glided her tongue over him several times, then once more sucked him deep. She felt their eyes on her. She liked them watching, because she knew she was making them hard, which gave her a heady sense of power in the situation. She took Kam's full length into her mouth and lightly caressed his balls with her fingers.

"Ah, yeah." Kam widened his stance, planting his feet firmly. He held the back of her head. "Here we go."

Yes! Come for me, Kam, her mind shouted. She needed all the healing elements he could give her.

With a groan, he came, and his semen filled her mouth. "Suck it down, Leila."

She swallowed his cum, taking all he had and sucking for more. He did taste good, as he'd said in the shower. Not so musky. Even slightly sweet. Must be the Tamarian part of him. She'd never tasted Tamarian cock, so she had no real point of reference as to whether her theory was correct. Perhaps, he'd simply guzzled something sweet earlier.

She pulled off him and licked her lips, which got a groan from the rest of the men.

As Kam collapsed on the bed, looking spent, she smiled up at the others. When they didn't speak or move, she asked, "Are you all just going to stand there staring at me?"

"Erik?" Braden prodded.

"Get her down flat on the floor," he directed, a look of sexual intensity in his eyes. "She's earned that good, hard fucking we promised her."

Leila gulped, and her heart pounded. She couldn't pull her gaze from Erik's. The promise of sexual satisfaction in his eyes shone clearly. *Yes, Erik. Fuck me.*

* * * * *

Laszlo hunched over in pain. "Damn." He fell into a cushioned chair in front of his panel of monitors. With everything he was capable of, he still hadn't found a cure for this weakness and pain. He feared the solution didn't exist.

His gut clenched. "Ohh…" He didn't think he was long for this life. Though not harboring a death wish, once he did pass on, a lot of problems, for a lot of people, would be solved.

So maudlin. He sighed. Not a normal emotion for him. As his pain increased, his strength of character and emotional stability diminished in equal proportion.

Daegal and "the other" were probably suffering the same effects. They must be desperate to find him. They wouldn't succeed. Nobody knew of this place deep in the forest. Nor could the location be tracked. He'd made sure of the security. He had many of these hidden locations to ensure his safety, and moved often. Kam was aware of one of the areas, but only one, and not this particular one.

He'd been able to maintain his projection powers from this secret location with the help of his computers and other electronic sources as boosters. From here, he monitored Xylon, Marid, and maintained partial surveillance of the four Banishment Zone Moons.

His vision had been going lately, and he'd had to adjust the monitor settings to make out the images. What else would break down in his body? He stared at the monitor displaying Leila's re-initiation.

He should have monitored her first one. He could have saved her a lot of grief over the years. He'd never brought up the possibility of a re-initiation to her, believing she wouldn't agree. He admired Braden and his ability to set things right.

The way Braden now ran The Lair made him proud. If the man were his own son, he couldn't be more pleased.

His mate, Alexa, though half-Earthling, had grown into a special woman. Just as he'd hoped. Her children would become leaders one day, if they survived to adulthood.

Torque gave him pause. The man had turned unpredictable after his and Braden's mother had taken her life quite a number of years ago. Such a tragedy. He still blamed himself for not somehow preventing her death. If the Council hadn't pushed for her to multi-mate with different Warriors because of her super breeder status…

He shook his head. He couldn't change what had happened, so he concentrated on what he could change.

Finally, Leila and Erik would be together. Only a small matter of time remained now, until they joined. Their bond should have occurred years ago, in his opinion, but maybe they both needed time to mature. Leila possessed a brilliant medical and research mind. And Erik provided a great second to Braden, with his high military skills. Through the years, Erik had maintained his iron will and carried out his duties as a Warrior and a man of principle, whether he acknowledged it or not.

Kam. Also a man of principle. Perhaps too much for his own good. Inflexibility often got a man into trouble. They'd been out of contact for a long time now. He didn't even know if Kam still trusted him. Or if he would help him, should the need arise. He needed to find a cure for Kam's pain, before he passed from this life. Leila was working on it, but she hadn't cracked the problem yet. And Kam needed a mate, too. Still so much to do.

So far, he'd sabotaged Daegal's breeder sterilization formula without The Dome's knowledge. Also, he'd contaminated their food sources—the poison would only affect the Egesa. He couldn't take the chance of a Warrior slave succumbing to the formula, so the active ingredients specifically targeted Egesa physiology. They'd discover the problem soon and implement a counteragent. But by that time, a great deal of damage would be done.

He knew Braden was sending a team to Marid. Regardless of his sabotage, that mission needed to take place for reasons other than those Braden knew. Everything was slowly falling into place.

* * * * *

Erik watched Torque pull Leila's arms over her head and trap them against the floor. Torque enjoyed restraining women during sex as did most male Warriors on Xylon. Dominating women, expecting sexual submission, was normal in their society. Their females, especially the Warriors, developed as strong, independent women. To submit was the greatest gift they gave to the males.

"Clip her nipples, Braden," he ordered.

"Clip?" Leila's voice revealed her surprise and wariness. "You know I'm not into pain, Erik."

He heard the tremble in her words. She had nothing to worry about. "I know," he said. "You'll like it." Tonight was about discovery for her. He wanted to expose her to a large variety of sexual experiences, before he officially claimed her for his own. He never wanted her to resent not having enjoyed what most Xylon females took for granted.

"I'll like it? Hmm. That's what all men say. We'll see."

Erik smiled. "If you don't like it, you can clip *my* nipples."

"I'll hold you to that," she answered with a laugh.

And he had no doubt she spoke the truth. So, he'd better make this good for her, or he'd never live it down.

"No further protests?" Torque asked her when she said nothing more. "I think we've created a nympho here, who's willing to try anything. Isn't that the Earth term, Kam?"

"Yeah, that's it."

This time, Erik had to laugh. Hell, half of Xylon's inhabitants fell into the nympho category, if one wanted to place a descriptive tag on their society's people.

Braden retrieved the items from the Initiation case and knelt beside her. His tongue slowly trailed up Leila's stomach, over her ribs, to her breasts. He lapped at one nipple, then attached a clip.

Leila groaned and arched her back. "Mmm, decadent."

A sense of relief swept through Erik. He knew she'd experience some pressure, and maybe slight pain, but mostly intense stimulation. He thought she'd enjoy the feeling. Though, with sexual pleasure, nothing was assured. Each woman reacted differently.

Braden sucked her other nipple into his mouth, then clipped that one, too. He attached a chain, running from one clip to the other. Erik nodded at him, and Braden lightly tugged on the connector.

Leila gasped. "Oh! I can feel the pull from my nipples all the way down to my pussy. That's…fucking nasty. I love it."

"Man, and I love it when you talk dirty, babe," Torque said with a chuckle. "Makes me hot."

"Everything makes you hot, Torque," she replied a little breathlessly.

Erik barely heard her words. He remained focused on her body, and the pleasure he wanted to give her. "Keep the clamps tight on her nipples until I'm through with her." Going down on his knees, he slid his hands under her knees and lifted her legs over his shoulders. He supported her ass with his palms and buried his mouth between her legs. A delicious sexual meal, like no woman he'd ever tasted. His tongue licked every inch of her pussy, savoring her, like she was his last. He drew her clit into his mouth.

"Oh, yes! Eat me, Erik!" Leila moaned. "Eat me."

Her words spurred him on. Slowly and steadily, he sucked her clit.

"Ah!"

"Spread her, Erik," Braden said. "I want to push a lubed finger up her ass. Maybe two."

A small whimpering sound escaped her lips.

Erik pulled her cheeks apart. He knew she'd love having her ass filled. She jerked slightly, and he figured Braden was entering her at that moment.

"Oh! Yes, Braden. Push all the way in. Yes. Yes. Like that."

"Kam, get down here and hold her," Torque directed.

Erik looked up briefly to watch Kam take Torque's place and clasp Leila's wrists in his hands. He stretched her arms flat on the floor above her head.

Torque tightened the nipple clamps slightly, then began jerking the chain over and over, which jiggled her tits and pulled on her hard buds.

"Ah!"

What a sight! Completely at their mercy, with him in control. Erik's dick hardened painfully, and he lowered his mouth to her pussy once more.

With Torque tugging the chain, Kam restraining her, Erik licking and sucking her clit, and Braden's fingers up her ass, Leila felt just like their sex slave, as Torque had said before, and as she'd felt in the bed earlier when they'd worked her over sexually. *Yes.* She let go and allowed it all to happen, complete sexual surrender.

Torque leaned down and whispered against her lips. "You're gorgeous. And you enjoy being held down, don't you? I know you do, babe."

"I wouldn't—"

"Shh." He licked her lips. "You love getting gang-fucked by men you can trust. Don't deny it." He jerked the nipple chain harder.

"Oh!" He was right. She couldn't deny it. She did feel hot, and needy, and safe, and oh-so wet.

Erik's lips and tongue consumed her in a way that made her feel like he believed her pussy belonged to him. And Braden pumped his fingers inside her ass with wild abandon, back and forth, pushing deep.

So good.

Tugging only gently on the chain, now, to stretch her nipples, Torque whispered against her mouth, "Erik is going to ride you hard, babe. I can't wait to watch him drill that sexy, wet cunt of yours. That's what you've always secretly wanted, right, for him to fuck you, while others watched? That's why you really still go to the Joining Parties, hoping he'll push the issue and make you submit in front of everyone. Admit it." He pulled harder on the chain. "Admit it!"

Her answer was a scream as she came. Vaguely, she heard Kam and Braden praising and encouraging her. Her pleasure rose and peaked, then slowly ebbed to a mild tremor.

Torque released the nipple clamps. She groaned at the flood of hot sensation. His mouth covered one nipple then the next, sucking gently.

Erik sat back, watching her reactions. Just knowing his eyes were on her made her feel sexy and desired. Her eyes remained locked with his until Braden moved and blocked her view. He licked at her lips as Torque had done earlier, but he didn't kiss her. He tugged open his pants.

Oh, my!

Torque and Braden held their cocks in their hands and fisted themselves like crazy. Torque was completely naked, looking like some fierce, barbaric Warrior from Xylon's history. Braden simply knelt over her with his pants undone and pushed down to his knees.

"We're going to come on you," Torque panted.

Come on her? The idea had never appealed to her before, nor had she ever allowed a man to shoot his semen on her, but...

"Touch me," Torque said. "Anywhere. I need to feel your fingers on me."

Anywhere? Unable to resist the once in a lifetime opportunity, and needing to do something totally unexpected, she reached up and slapped Torque's tight ass. He'd feel that.

"Hey!" he protested, but with a deep, pleasure-filled groan. After a moment, he said, "Do Braden."

Braden's eyes widened.

She complied and smacked Braden's sexy ass, which got an equally deep moan from him. One at a time, she slapped them hard. Over and over. Now they'd both know how a spanking felt, in case they'd never been on the receiving end.

"Oh, damn!" Braden shouted. "That's good. Ah!" He came over her breasts.

Torque shouted and came too, his semen shooting over her stomach. "Ahhh!"

They squeezed and shook their dicks, spilling everything they had onto her body.

Somehow an action she'd once found unappealing seemed strangely erotic to her. The sheer ecstasy and satisfaction on their faces made the act worthwhile. They stayed on their knees beside her, breathing heavily, their heads down.

When Braden finally did raise his head, his look of ecstasy changed to one of guilt. He jerked up his pants.

Leila felt bad for him. She understood his thoughts and feelings without asking. "I know you love Alexa, Braden."

"Yes, I do. More than anything." His eyes reflected his inner turmoil. "I just got this strange feeling, like I was betraying her."

"Hey," Torque said, getting Braden's attention. "This is our way," he continued, his voice low and soft. "It takes nothing away from what you have with Alexa, brother."

"I know." He nodded. "I just hope she feels the same."

A lump caught in Leila's throat. Braden was a good man. She believed that with all her heart. If he truly thought Alexa wouldn't understand, she doubted he'd have even shown up tonight. The other three could have done this without him, most likely. Though, Braden *had* been a stabilizing force tonight. He'd known when she was suffering, before the others noticed. She was truly grateful he was here.

Torque leaned down and whispered against her mouth, "Loved the spanking. I've never been given one before. Not even when I deserved one." He chuckled. "You are one hot fuck, babe. Erik's a lucky man."

She didn't say anything, but she did reach up and stroke his cheek. His eyes widened briefly, and he cleared his throat. She'd obviously surprised him. Probably, he hadn't been shown a lot of tenderness from women. That saddened her. He might have turned into a less abrasive man, if he had. But apparently he did understand that something special bound her and Erik together.

After Braden and Torque got to their feet, Erik knelt beside her. "Now, you're all mine." He leaned over and kissed her deeply, briefly tangling his tongue with hers before pulling back. "Let's get you cleaned up."

That's the last thing she remembered, until some time later. She lay on the soft floor, amid a pile of pillows, with her eyes closed. Her body felt worn out, and her mind foggy. Someone had finally cleaned the cum off her. She wasn't sure who, but from his extra gentle touch, she suspected Erik was the one. She didn't have the energy to open her eyes to look.

The chemicals had almost worn off. She felt it. Her body was no longer on fire. She could probably make it through the rest of the night now just fine.

"One more wave, gentlemen," Erik said. "This is the last, then we'll call it a night."

She whimpered. "Again?" Her voice came out so low she doubted anyone even heard her. She remembered Torque's words about Erik fucking her and wondered if they were true. How could Torque know Erik's intentions unless they pre-planned this entire event? Or maybe Erik had simply stated his desire to the rest of them earlier.

Someone turned her onto her stomach. She seemed to drift in and out of awareness. Pillows were shoved under her hips. She felt her ass spread open and something warm and gooey was pushed up inside her. She raised her ass slightly and got spanked in return. "Ouch."

"Stay still," Erik ordered her.

Someone's hand, she thought probably Erik's, spanked her a second time. Harder. She squealed, and someone chuckled. Torque? When another sharp blow landed on her butt, she squirmed. Her ass was still sensitive from the last spanking.

"Enough!" The next person who spanked her tender ass was going to get kicked in the groin.

She felt her cheeks spread again and pressure against her hole. The head of a cock pushed into her ass and slid deep. The sensation was incredible. She rubbed her nipples against the floor's soft fibers, not sure who was inside her, but she loved the tight fit, and the way all her nerve endings screamed out for more.

"Oh, yes. Fuck my ass." Almost ashamed to admit, even to herself, she didn't care who was fucking her right now. She just knew that she loved the feeling.

The in-and-out motion increased, faster and faster.

"Yeah, Erik!" Torque practically cheered. "Give her all you've got."

Erik was up her ass! Yes! His cock felt more intense than the anal dildo, or Braden's fingers, or even Kam's tongue. He filled her completely, stretching her asshole. She moved her bottom in rhythm with his thrusts. Knowing he was the one inside her increased her pleasure so much more.

"Look at her," Torque said. "She loves getting her ass fucked. Pump that butthole good, Erik. Make her scream the roof off."

"Shut up, Torque," Braden said.

"You're breaking the mood," Kam complained.

Nothing could break the mood for her. She loved this. Erik knew what she needed, and exactly how she needed it.

Erik grunted, fucking her hard. As his hips pumped against her, he pushed aside her hair and licked the back of her neck in one long stroke.

Leila shuddered. She couldn't help but wonder if he wanted to Brand her. The mark was placed on the back of the neck of a female by a male, through a special implant in the man's mouth, at the moment they both orgasmed. Such a Brand meant they were bound together for eternity.

"Someday," he whispered in her ear.

She sucked in a sharp breath and almost came right then. He knew her thoughts! Or maybe he'd licked her neck on purpose, knowing the direction her mind would take. Did he mean what his actions implied? Or was this just another Erik tease? Certainly, he wouldn't play around with such an important subject, simply to get the reaction and cooperation out of her that he wanted.

"Clip her clit, Braden," Erik ordered.

"Oh, shit, yeah," Torque said. "She'll go nuts."

Her clit? She groaned. If the clip felt anything like the ones used on her nipples, she didn't know if she could take the intensity.

Erik rolled onto his side, taking her with him. "Get ready for the sensation of your life, baby." He drew one of her legs over his hip, while Braden retrieved the proper clip from the case.

Braden knelt in front of them. He held her pussy open wide with the fingers of one hand and stimulated her clit with his finger.

"Ah, oh. That's so good, Braden." She wanted Erik more than anyone, but if she had to choose a threesome, she'd pick Braden. He knew just how to excite a woman, or at least her. He and Erik made a good team.

A grin tugged at his lips, but he didn't say anything.

Erik lightly pumped his hips. "Make sure she's extended, so it doesn't slip off."

After a few more flicks, Braden tugged gently on her clit, then clipped the fleshy bud. "Done."

When the clamp closed around her, she tensed. The object contained little wave tips on the inside which moved back and forth, stimulating her on all sides at the same time. "Ah, ah, ah." She'd known of the clamp's existence, but had never used one.

Erik rolled her onto her stomach. She gasped as his cock pushed deep. In Braden's hand, she spotted a remote control.

"Turn it on medium," Erik ordered.

With the added power, the normal waving of the tips increased. The stimulators attacked her clit, the feeling ten times stronger than when her nipples were clamped. Pleasure vibrated to every pore of her body. "Oh!"

Erik moved his hips slowly, pumping his cock deeply, then more shallowly. "Keep increasing the stimulation, Braden. A little at a time."

"Doing it now."

"Wait!" Leila jerked. "Too much! I can't take any more." Her body began to shake, and she couldn't catch her breath.

"Yes, you can," Erik told her, moving faster and harder now against her ass. "Relax. Take my cock and don't fight the clip."

"The feeling of both is too intense." She bucked beneath him. "Ahh!"

"Scream! Let it out," Erik ordered, holding her down and fucking her ass like crazy. "Show me how much you love this."

"Yeah!" Torque said. "Fuck her, Erik."

"Yes. Yes! Yes!" Her body climaxed, and her asshole tightened around his cock.

"Oh, yeah, Leila!" Erik shouted, his voice full of excitement. "Again, come again!"

"Come on, Leila," Kam said.

"Yes!" She came hard, the feeling incredible.

"That's right, baby. Keep coming."

After two more orgasms of intense, mind-blowing pleasure, she collapsed. Breathing heavily, she felt perspiration trickling down her body. Erik pulled out of her ass and turned her onto her back.

What an experience! She watched him tear off a protective covering from his still-hard cock, as Braden gently removed the clip from her clit.

"You did good," Braden said, his voice low and tender.

"Thank you," she said, the words popping out of her mouth unexpectedly. She wasn't sure if she was actually thanking Braden, Erik, or both of them.

Erik's eyes darkened, and his facial expression turned intense. "That's how a great ass-fucking feels, Leila. Now, it's time for your cunt to get the same treatment."

She gasped at his language and the way his body visibly tensed.

"You're getting fucked the way I've wanted to do you, and you've needed doing, for way too long." With a primitive look—one she didn't recognize from him—he pushed Braden aside and shoved her thighs wide. He positioned himself between her legs and, with a deep growl, thrust his naked cock fiercely up her pussy.

"Oh!" She arched into him.

Without giving her time to adjust to his length and width, he pumped her pussy with solid, deep, forceful strokes. "Yeah! How's that feel, baby?"

Her whole body vibrated from the anal orgasms she still hadn't recovered from, and now Erik was fucking her pussy as if he'd never get another chance. So good. So right. So perfect. Her body shook and trembled. "Erik! Oh, yes! Harder! Harder! Do it!" Inside her was right where he belonged. She wrapped her legs around him and dug her nails into his shoulders, holding on for dear life. She never wanted this to end.

The others stood back and watched, just as Torque had said they would. She briefly made eye contact with each of them. Seeing their excitement in watching Erik wildly ram his cock into her pussy increased her own pleasure.

Her hips pumped up against him, fucking him back with more need and enthusiasm than she'd ever felt for a man. "Erik, take what you need from me. Show me what you want, what your most erotic desire is. I'll give it to you. Anything."

The other men groaned.

He whispered in her ear, flicking his tongue lightly against her skin. "Later, when we're alone, I'll tell you my most secret, carnal need." His hips moved more rapidly now, drilling her fast and hard, like a machine.

"Yes!" She undulated beneath him, moving her body like a woman starved for a man, because she was starved. For this man. And she wanted to know all his secrets, sexual and otherwise.

"Man, she's like a sex-crazed animal," Torque said.

"That's what happens when a woman doesn't get enough cock," Braden responded.

"Or when she's fallen in lo—" Kam stopped mid-sentence and cleared his throat, not finishing his observation.

Their conversation was lost on her. She fully focused on Erik now, not caring what anyone else said or did. As far as she was concerned, the two of them were alone in the room.

Erik slowed down, panting heavily from his exertion. He moved almost gently inside her now. "Come, Leila. Come for me." He stroked her cheek. "Let me see you explode. Just for me. One more time."

"I want you to explode, too," she said. She squeezed her internal muscles around his cock. "Come inside me."

"Oh, Leila. Ah!" His hips jerked forward, moving faster again. "Yeah, baby! I'm coming!"

Erik climaxed, and his semen filled her pussy. Nothing had ever felt so good to her. Now, he was a part of her forever. She screamed his name over and over as her muscles tightened, and her body climaxed in response, milking his cock.

After he finished coming, he collapsed on top of her. She bore his weight, too tired to move. A few moments later, when their breathing returned to somewhat normal, he shifted his body weight and kissed her deeply, brushing her tongue with his.

She accepted his tongue — would accept anything he wanted from her. She'd never felt so completely satisfied by sex, or anything else, in her life. Not only was her body sated, but her mind as well. Now, she felt like no boundaries held her back from the life she wanted and needed to live as a female Xylon Warrior.

* * * * *

Josella sat in the back of the orbiter, looking at Pitch and the two female Warriors. She didn't recognize the women, but presumably they were the sisters of the new Warrior Leader, according to Pitch. She knew they ranked as Class 1 Warriors from the markings on their jackets. They hadn't said much to her, other than to bark a few orders. Obviously, they didn't want to be here.

She heard the wind swirling outside from the approaching storm. Rain and sand. She felt relieved to be inside. She'd been unsheltered and mud-soaked before. Not a pleasant experience.

The women tromped out of the orbiter, looking surly.

"What's going on?" she asked Pitch.

"The orbiter sustained some damage while we were out looking for you. One of the gangs must have come across it and tried to gain entry. I can't blame them. I'd do most anything to get off this moon, too."

"Are we going to be able to take off?"

"We're working on it."

"I assume I'm being blamed for this." From the look on the women's faces, she did not feel safe with her situation.

He smiled. "Not by me. We'll have to wait out the storm. The sand is already clogging our external systems. We'll need to do a full flush. Our timing wasn't so good. I checked the weather before we orbited. Nothing notable showed up on tracking. This freak storm came out of nowhere."

"A lot of freak storms happen here."

"So I understand. The atmosphere isn't stable." He turned to a control panel and flipped some switches. "Don't worry about it."

How could she not worry, especially when she wasn't sure about these three who basically held her captive? She didn't recognize any of them. Nor did the name Braden Koll sound familiar, but then she couldn't really judge anything by that. When she'd left Sunevia, she'd lived atop on Xylon and never much followed the military or political goings on, even though her sister held a Class 1 rank. She did know of Laszlo, of course. And a handful of others.

She studied Pitch. He was one hunk of a man. Black hair and the bluest eyes she'd ever seen. But that didn't mean he was sincere.

They might be defected Warriors and not really taking her to her sister. But if so, how would they know Halah's name, and why would they care about her?

Maybe they were Dispensers—The Lair's equivalent of The Dome's Assassins. She shuddered at the thought.

Whoever these Warriors really were, she didn't feel comfortable just sitting around and waiting for her fate...

* * * * *

Leila's eyes fluttered open. Darkness surrounded her. She must have fallen asleep.

Her eyes took a moment to adjust. The light above a scenic picture on the wall cast shadows around the bedchamber.

Strangely, everything looked neat, clean, and in its place. A pleasant scent even wafted through the air. Vanilla. They must have turned on her scenting system.

The Initiation was over.

She stretched under the covers, feeling delightfully sore and tender. Her mind seemed clear, or relatively so, considering what she'd been through. Her memory was a bit patchy though.

The men had showered her, along with themselves, and then put her to bed. She vaguely remembered their hands cleansing her body, but that's all. If they'd had sex with her in the shower, she didn't remember that.

Her foot made contact with something warm. She turned her head. Erik.

Surprised by his presence, she rose up on her elbows. Nobody else was around. He lay beside her, quiet and still.

At the realization that he had stayed with her after the ceremony, in case she needed anything, she presumed, her heart softened. She lightly pushed back a few strands of soft brown hair that toppled onto his forehead, and kissed him gently. In sleep, he looked so adorable that she couldn't help but smile.

She snuggled next to him, laying her head on his chest. Strong and firm. His arm came around her, but other than that, he didn't stir. He felt so warm, and he made her feel safe and secure.

Thinking about tonight…she never knew fucking could be so incredible. She hoped what had happened wouldn't harm her relationship with the others. Sex did that sometimes, even on Xylon.

She rubbed Erik's stomach. Peeking under the covers, she saw he was naked. So was she. His words came back to her — *my most secret, carnal need*. Her body trembled.

Although she'd enjoyed the re-initiation — what she remembered of it — she really wanted to know how it felt to be precious to one, special man. This man.

Earlier, he'd said, *now you're mine*. Maybe he'd just meant for the rest of the Initiation, and didn't mean it for his entire life. She needed to find out, before too much more time passed.

Tonight was an experience she'd needed to complete for personal and professional reasons, but multiple partners wasn't something she wanted to do again. Probably. She held back a giggle.

The pill and Initiation chemicals had enabled her to be sexually free and beg for more. She couldn't believe all the things she'd allowed them to do to her, to her body. But she felt complete now, like she'd gotten back something stolen from her long ago.

Tomorrow, an important mission began. She hadn't expected to leave so soon, but she knew now that she was protected, they'd leave at sunrise. She needed rest. With her memories of the night held close, she shut her eyes and drifted off to sleep.

Chapter Seven

Strapped to a command chair, Leila sat at the orbiter's navigation and communication controls. She stared out the front portals and let her mind drift.

Xylon's orb glowed pink and blue-green in the distance. Two of Xylon's five moons also shone in the darkness of space, the spectrum of vivid colors a sight to behold. She couldn't see the other three moons from her vantage point.

Marid loomed closest. She had always believed the Xylon system one of the most beautiful with its variety of hues and unique planetary formations. Too bad such violence and conflict between The Lair and The Dome spoiled that beauty.

She glanced to her left at Erik, who sat in the pilot's command seat, a look of deep concentration on his face as he went over the pre-orbit check list. Kam sat behind them and to the side, operating weapons and tracking controls.

Her body still tingled from the group fucking last night. She thought today would be awkward, but everyone treated her as always. The only difference she noticed appeared in Erik's eyes, when she sometimes caught him staring at her with a combination of passion, tenderness, and what looked to her like possessiveness.

Nobody had mentioned anything about the rite to her, so far. The morning had been too busy for anyone to think much about the Initiation, she supposed, though she certainly managed just fine.

She thought Erik had stayed in her bed last night, holding her close, but this morning she'd woken up alone. Maybe everything had been a dream. She held back a nervous laugh.

She remembered most of what had gone on during the rite, or thought she did. Strangely, she didn't feel embarrassed by any of it. The ceremony certainly hadn't been what she'd expected.

Though a society ruled by sex, Initiations weren't generally discussed openly, not the particulars of what happened in a specific rite, anyhow. So, her only real reference was her original Initiation, which she'd rather forget.

The re-initiation was something she would never forget. They had showed her things about her body and needs that she'd never even imagined in her fantasies.

She felt a little nervous about eventually facing Torque. If anyone was going to make lurid comments or references to what had happened last night, he would be the one.

After showering earlier, she finally worked up enough courage to look at her scars. Her heart had beaten faster than she'd ever remembered. She had feared seeing no change. Fortunately, the marks had looked significantly faded. She had almost collapsed in relief. The disfigurement would never totally disappear since the scars cut so deep, and the damage had occurred before she'd attained the ability to self-heal. But, she figured within another forty-eight hours, unless you knew what to look for, the once ugly wounds would hardly be noticeable. If she'd been able to suck Braden, too…

"Status?" Erik asked her.

Switching her thoughts back to the present, she turned her attention to the panel in front of her. She studied the readouts. "On course. Estimated time of arrival is…six point three minutes."

"Anything on tracking?"

"All is clear," Kam reported. "We're looking good."

Erik's hand brushed hers on the control panel and their eyes locked. Her nipples hardened and moisture gathered between her thighs. Amazing. She wanted him again.

She didn't think the dose of chemicals, along with the pill they gave her, had worn off completely. She still felt some residual effects. Or perhaps that was just a way of giving herself permission to feel horny again. As if she needed permission.

She'd spent so much time pushing Erik away that it now felt exhilarating to admit she wanted him and be able to act on the desire. She no longer feared his sexually controlling nature. In fact, she craved it.

Giving up control sexually resulted in such strong orgasms for her that she yearned to experience the explosive power of submission again. With Erik alone, this time. She wanted to strengthen their bond to each other and learn everything possible about him.

Multiple sex partners on Xylon were the norm. But, only *his* cock had penetrated her pussy and ass. The rest had used tongues and fingers and dildos. Still, she wondered if Erik resented the others touching her.

She had sucked everyone off except Braden, and that fact might make him uncomfortable. But her actions were necessary for her healing. And he'd approved everything that had happened.

Most breeders had three people in their Alliance doing the initiating. She'd had four. She wondered if that was a first.

A low beep drew her attention to the sensor screen. "We're coming up on their outer shields."

Erik took the controls. "Switching to manual. Tighten your straps, and hang on, everyone. It's going to be a bumpy ride."

As the craft hit Marid's first line of defense, the orbiter shook. The vibration rattled Leila's bones and made her see double.

Kam aimed a laser, blasting a hole through the energy net. "Go! We're clear of the outer shield."

Erik quickly maneuvered them past the temporary entry, before Marid reset the net.

"They've picked us up," Leila said. "I see two interceptors on my nav screen. Kam?"

"Nope. There are four. I've got them on tracking."

She adjusted her settings. "Yes, you're right. I see them now." Her heart picked up its pace. Four against one.

Erik grumbled. "So much for Halah's assurance that only one interceptor team patrols this sector. Damn woman. Braden said to be prepared for deception. Good thing he had us fitted with additional power."

"I hope it's enough." Leila switched on the extra weapons loaded for this mission. "Supplemental weapons active." Her nerves were frayed enough about infiltrating The Dome, and now it looked like Halah Shirota might have betrayed them already. "Should I send a distress message back to Xylon?"

"No," Erik said. "We're all right. The Egesa don't know we came from Xylon. We could be from Tamara or another neighboring planet. Let's keep it that way. No need to announce ourselves as loyal to Xylon, or worse in their eyes, The Lair, if they tap into a transmission and find out we're Warriors. Maybe they'll get sloppy if they think we're just galactic merchants or something equally unthreatening."

"Locking weapons," Kam said.

"Hold your fire, unless they shoot first. Let's see if we can get out of this the easy way. Go ahead and contact them, Leila. And lie, please. Maybe they'll be receptive to a female voice."

Leila chuckled, though felt little humor in the situation. "Right." She clicked on a generic, ship-to-ship channel, knowing they'd connect. "This is Orbiter 9-0. We are currently experiencing navigation problems and have drifted off course. Request permission to land for repairs."

A laser struck their side. The orbiter rocked once, but stabilized quickly.

"That worked well," Leila mumbled. "So much for the easy way."

"Minor hit only," Erik told them.

"Can I fire now?"

"Fire at will, Kam," Erik ordered.

"Firing." As the shot exploded, the orbiter's lights dimmed from the power drain. "A missile hit directly into the engine of the leader. He's useless."

They sustained a hit in return, and then another stronger shot jolted the ship severely.

"Shit!" Erik struggled to maintain control and keep them on course. A burning smell filled the orbiter, but no fire or smoke. "Hit to port side. What did that do to us, Kam?"

"Damn lucky bastards. They took out regular and supplemental weapons' control, except for minimal laser operations."

"Enough to blast through their net? We're coming up on Marid's internal shield," Leila warned, watching him struggle to find more power.

Kam pushed several buttons and turned a control knob. "We'll find out. Brace yourselves."

* * * * *

Torque slapped an electronic pad on Braden's desk. "We're getting in reports of massive executions on Marid."

Braden's heart squeezed tight. He grabbed the lighted pad. "Slaves?" Most of Marid's slaves were former Xylon residents or Warriors. His stomach churned at the thought of their deaths, and he felt sick.

"Just those who are Xylon breeders. The females. I can't get verification about the males. The numbers are significant though."

"Why only the breeders? They're sterile and no threat because of The Dome's new formula. Is Daegal trying to prove some sort of point or something?" Braden threw down a laser pointer he'd been attempting to fix.

"Unknown. But the data is all there, what we know of it. We're also picking up large movements of equipment, ships, and personnel. They're getting ready for something, Braden. I can feel it. Should we call the team back?"

"It's too late. They'll be through Marid's defensive net by now and out of communication until they get inside The Dome." Besides, they had to get their hands on that formula. Otherwise, within three generations the Warriors would be practically wiped out. And this system, as well as others, would be at the mercy of the Egesa Slave Masters. This mission might be their best opportunity to infiltrate The Dome. He had to see it through.

"They'll be picked up as breeders when Halah tries to get them processed. And now that all breeders are being executed…" Torque shook his head.

Braden dragged a hand down his face. "We'll have to trust in their ingenuity for survival. They knew the risks going in. This mission is too important to scrap."

"Damn. That sounds cold, coming from you, brother. They don't even know about the executions. They can't protect themselves from an unknown danger."

"I have a whole planet to worry about right now. I have to make the best decisions for everyone. Halah will know about this turn of events and figure something out. She has too much at stake personally to fail. They'll be all right."

"You're going to trust some female who betrayed her people? They're your best friends, Braden. Kam is Alexa's brother. What are you going to tell her about this?"

"Damn it, Torque! Support my choices or get away from me. I don't want to argue with you about every decision I make." He raked his fingers through his hair. Leaving the others at Daegal's mercy tore him up inside. But he had a duty to Xylon and its people. He couldn't start making decisions based on personal feelings. At this point, he had to trust Halah.

"Let me go in as backup."

"Forget it. I need you here. At least, for now. Gather all team leaders and issue a standby alert. Start shutting The Lair down, as a precaution." He stood up, slightly hunched over, and walked over to the monitor panel. He hadn't recovered yet from the pain Alexa had inflicted on him last night.

"What's wrong with you?"

Braden frowned. He wasn't keen on discussing private matters, but at least it gave him something else to focus on for a moment, until he could formulate a plan in his head on what to do about Marid and the executions. Daegal couldn't get away with mass murder. "Alexa didn't quite understand why I needed to come last night during the Initiation."

Torque's eyes widened slightly. "You're joking, right? What did she expect you to do, wait until you got back to her? No way would that have been physically possible."

"Well, I think specifically me coming on Leila's tits is what aggravated her. She, um, got a little rough with my dick." To say the least. He needed to instigate some major damage control before she was going to allow him back into their bed.

"You told her everything then? You are crazy." Torque cringed, as if feeling his pain. "I told you to keep quiet."

"I didn't actually tell her all the details at first. But she kept looking at me like she knew." No way could she have known what happened in Leila's bedchamber, but Alexa's eyes had held a spooky knowledge when he'd returned to her. Maybe he was simply reacting to his own guilt over the situation. Whichever, last night was definitely his final Initiation. He hadn't specifically promised not to come during the rite, but the way it happened had hurt Alexa's feelings. And that disturbed him. He'd never purposely hurt her.

"Women are experts at giving men that look, whether they know anything or not. So, I take it, you caved."

"Yeah, I caved." He wouldn't have felt right about keeping the truth from Alexa. The truth always came out eventually. Better she hear it from him than someone else.

"Well, you should be healed in a few hours, at least."

"Thank goodness for that. I just wish I could heal her hurt feelings as quickly." He hated when they argued. Loneliness filled his heart. Although less than twenty-four hours had passed, he already missed holding Alexa in his arms.

"She'll come around. Is she going to take this out on Leila? They had a good friendship building from what I understand."

"I don't know." He hoped not. Alexa didn't have that many friends on Xylon yet. And given their group dynamic, if Leila and Alexa didn't get along, that would cause a lot of strain on a lot of friendships. "Her hormones are out of whack with this pregnancy. The one thing our healing won't fix, since lack of the proper hormone levels would harm the babies. I have no idea how she's going to react from moment to moment."

"Remind me never to get Branded."

"You can't hold out forever, Torque. Your time will come. I recommend you choose. Otherwise, the Council will choose for you. You don't want to end up with someone you can't stomach. Branding is not reversible."

Torque grunted. "I'll think about it. Besides, they can't physically force me to Brand someone."

"Don't be so sure. I'm trying to get the regulations changed. We've both seen the Council push beyond a person's free will to do what they feel is best for Xylon and this system."

"True." Torque frowned. "They're not pushing for Alexa to multi-mate, are they?"

Braden's heart clenched at the thought. And he saw the concern in his brother's eyes. "Not yet. If they do, we're out of this system, regardless of my responsibilities. I won't let that happen to her."

"You could choose her mates."

Had his brother lost his mind? Braden couldn't believe what he'd just heard. "After what happened with Mother, how can you even suggest that?"

Torque shrugged. "I'm trying to figure out what's best for everyone, without another tragedy occurring."

His eyes revealed a deep hurt that Braden understood only too well. He clapped a hand on Torque's shoulder and squeezed before stepping back. "I don't want to think about it unless the problem actually occurs. I have other problems to worry about right now. Like the Marid mission, the safety of Xylon, and Alexa's current feelings."

The truth was he'd already thought too much about the Council's stand on multi-mating, and the horror that reality might cause for Alexa. Even though he was in charge of the military sector of Xylon, The Lair, he didn't dictate Xylon Law. The Council, as a whole, controlled their society and its workings.

"If there's a problem because of Leila's Initiation, have Erik talk to Alexa. They're pretty close, from what I hear. He might be able to calm her down and make her understand." A slow grin spread across Torque's face, transforming the look of hurt in his eyes to one of mischief.

Braden wasn't sure if Torque was trying to lighten the conversation or push him further to the edge of his control. "What are you getting at now?"

"Well, I just thought since Erik is a frequent visitor to your bedchamber—"

"Damn it, Torque! You know those rumors of threesomes among us aren't true. I've told you that before." He wasn't sure how those stories got started. If he ever found the person who originated the tale, he'd throttle them. The fact that Erik and Alexa were good friends certainly didn't help stem the rumors. Once things settled down, he needed to do something to change whatever perception existed. With Alexa's super breeder status, any rumors of her being fucked by another man just fueled the idea of forcing super breeders to multi-mate, whether their choice or not.

"Are you saying never?"

With a sigh, Braden hit a button, putting The Lair's emergency personnel on standby status. "I'm saying, take care of what I asked, then get me a report."

Torque laughed. "Well, that's one way to avoid answering the question, brother. All right. I'm on it."

* * * * *

Erik looked out the front portal. A wall of dirt greeted him. Too close. They'd missed hitting a hundred-foot mountain by only twenty feet. "Is everyone all right?"

Leila stirred beside him. "Ow. I banged my head a little on the side control panel. But I'll live. Are you all right? Kam, you?"

"Yeah, I'm good," Kam said.

"I'm all right." Erik's heart pounded in alarm, as he brushed away some blood from Leila's temple. When he saw she wasn't seriously injured, he relaxed. "Doesn't look too bad. You'll heal quickly." When she blushed, he leaned forward and kissed her lightly on the lips, knowing she was thinking about last night. He smiled. He couldn't help himself. But also knowing he had to see to his duties, he turned in his seat. "Kam, what's our status?"

"Communications, weapons, tracking...they're all offline."

"Repairable?"

"Yeah, eventually, but not without replacement parts. We have some on the ship, but not everything that we need."

"We can still take off, right?"

"Sure, but without tracking, it doesn't do us a lot of good. We'd be navigating blind, with only what we can see out the portals. And we can't send a distress message."

"If we have no choice, I'll take it. Any idea of how far off course we are from where we were supposed to land?" Evidently, they weren't going to make their meeting with Halah. Not on time anyhow.

"Five hundred miles, as an estimate."

"Shit." This didn't bode well. He hated missions that started this way. They couldn't walk the distance — too far.

"What do we do?" Leila asked.

"Stay put. Let them think they destroyed us. Halah will do a sweep. That's standard Warrior procedure. She may have defected, but I'd bet my ass she still follows her training. If she doesn't come across us by nightfall, we'll discuss starting out on foot. Though, I don't think it's a good idea, unless we have no other options. It's definitely too dangerous during the day." Outside The Dome, their life forms would be picked up by every patrol within tracking distance. After a mountain path and a few hills, the land between here and The Dome lay mostly flat. No cover existed for them to retreat to, if on foot and attacked.

They couldn't even use their transport-connectors to infiltrate The Dome. They'd need three of The Dome's connectors and a clear channel. Even if they could get inside with their own transports, alarms would go off everywhere, because they would register as Xylon, and a breach of Marid security. Even if used out here in the open to rendezvous with Halah, the Egesa would zero in on the power source within seconds.

"They're going to check on us when they spot the orbiter in one piece," Kam said.

Erik closed their portals and sealed them in. "If anyone comes across us before Halah does, we may have no choice but to kill them. Hopefully, it won't come to that. But it'll be easier to defend ourselves from inside here, than out in the open."

"I'm not so sure about that. Here, we're just sitting ducks, as my sister calls it. Not a good visual."

"Agreed," Leila said. "We should hide in the hills."

Erik shook his head. "We might miss Halah, or run into worse trouble with whatever lives up in those mountains. We're not supplied for wilderness survival. We're staying put for now. Sometimes the best place to hide is in plain sight. Besides,

Braden and I had a little something extra installed for defense before we took off, inspired by Halah herself."

"And until then?" Kam asked.

"I'll engage the scrambler, so the orbiter gives us partial protection from tracking devices. They'll still pick up the ship, but our life forms will register as indeterminate. They might pass us by and send a salvage team instead, or maybe send nobody at all if they consider salvage low priority. Either way, we should be able to buy enough time until Halah gets to us, as long as this isn't a setup."

"What if it is a setup?" Leila asked.

"Then we take off and get out of here, navigation online or not. I'd rather take my chances in space. Once outside their security net, Xylon will pick us up on the main tracker and send help. They know the ship's private code. They'll be able to scan the orbiter and link it to us. Down here, we're totally on our own."

* * * * *

"Where the hell are they?" Halah stomped around the open ground where she was supposed to rendezvous with the Warriors. She crushed a Mucous Spider under her boot, and green liquid squirted out. Nasty insect. Deadly, too. Once bitten, the venom caused paralysis and eventually death, if untreated, even for someone able to self-heal. The poison worked too fast. In certain areas, Marid was overrun with the ugly, purplish creatures.

She looked up at the sky, then checked her handheld tracking device. Nothing.

What if they'd been destroyed? That would put a kink in her plans, to say the least. Braden might not make a second deal so quickly.

Sometimes she felt her search for Josella was useless. She'd been looking for so long now. And nobody seemed willing to help, unless forced into it. She stiffened her spine. Well, she'd always had to rely on herself. She would continue to do so.

Her guard escort approached with a vid-cell in his hand. "There's been a report of a crashed orbiter about five hundred miles from here. My guess is that it's them."

"Xylon?"

"Unmarked. But the odds are good, in my estimation. The timing is too coincidental."

"Oh, for... Can't they do anything right? They're going to get themselves captured and executed, if they haven't already. Why aren't I picking up the ship?"

He studied her tracker. "Looks like some electrical interference. You, maybe?"

"Never happened before." She lowered the power settings in her jacket. Nothing on the monitor changed. "No. I don't think so." She looked up. "Sky is clear. Must be this blasted machine. I've heard rumors of various electronic malfunctions lately. Stupid, second-rate equipment, no doubt. Any reports of survivors?"

"Not yet. The orbiter just went down."

"Well, I think you're probably right. That has to be them. Dak! Can we get there before the recovery team?" If someone captured them before her, things would get dicey. Without her running interference, their identities would be uncovered a lot sooner. And depending on where they were sent, the whole mission might be jeopardized.

"An Egesa Patrol is already on their way," the first guard informed her.

Dak turned from the back of their rover, where he'd been checking settings. "No way. We've got a tank leak. We'll have to proceed at half speed or turn back and get another rover."

Halah hung her head. What else could go wrong? She climbed aboard the open-topped rover. "Let's go. We're continuing on. We can't afford to turn back now. If the Egesa get them, I'll figure out something once we rendezvous."

* * * * *

Kam woke to a mewling noise. He'd lain down in the back to nap on a pullout table that doubled as a cot of sorts, if one wasn't particular. He hoped the time would move faster if he slept. He hated to wait around. Cringing, he stretched out his back. The makeshift bed felt harder than a rock against his spine.

He wiped the sweat from his brow. With each passing minute, the orbiter grew hotter inside. They'd turned off the coolant, as well as most of the other systems, to appear un-operational and dead.

So far, only one patrol had come across them.

When the Egesa had tried to pry open the door, they'd been struck with a large, electrical current, charring them to bits. Their bodies, or what remained of them, now littered the ground.

When the Egesa team didn't check in, more would arrive. Halah had better find them soon, and approach the orbiter cautiously, or she'd be cooked meat, too.

From the information he'd read about her in the file Braden had provided, she was a smart woman and trained to control electrical currents. He knew a little about her power from personal experience. She'd zapped him good on Earth.

As long as she didn't get careless, she should be all right. Besides, he'd be watching for her. He checked his wrist sensor. Still, all clear.

Damn lucky for them the electrical system even worked after the hits they had sustained. And it worked correctly. They all could have ended up burnt to a crisp, if it had malfunctioned, or they could have wound up enslaved by those disgusting creatures if the current hadn't engaged at all.

Too many Egesa for them to fight off by hand had surrounded the ship. Luckily, all of them lingered near enough to the outer hull to get fried. If another patrol came along, he wasn't so certain of their fate.

Only limited electrical current remained. The automatic regeneration system had sustained damage during the attack in orbit. They needed to conserve enough power to take off and blast their way back out of the shielded atmosphere. Lasers still worked from what he could tell. But their more powerful weapons were useless. The odds of them surviving with Egesa patrols everywhere seemed slim to him. But he trusted Erik's judgment. The man usually kept a trick or two in reserve to use in desperate situations.

A groan drew his attention toward the front of the craft. Damn. Leila stood with her back toward him, her long hair cascading down her naked body, ending just above her nicely rounded ass. Her hands grasped a low-hanging pipe above her head. No, wait. Her wrists were tied to the pipe. Double damn. Near her feet, clothing littered the deck.

Shirtless, Erik stood in front of her.

Kam couldn't see anything else from his angle until Erik stepped to the side and turned Leila, unknowingly exposing her profile to him. Her tits jutted forward, and her hard nipples captured his attention.

Erik's hand slowly trailed down the front of her body. "Will you submit?"

"Y-yes."

"Good." He smiled, his hand moving back up her body. "Do you have any idea how really beautiful you are?"

She looked down, not responding.

"Look at me, Leila." He lifted her chin with his finger, until her eyes rose and met his. "Do you feel beautiful?"

Kam barely heard her whispered response.

"When you look at me, I do."

He couldn't imagine what she'd endured all these years with her scars. Relief swept through him, and he felt so glad they had helped her heal, because he found her a beautiful woman. Inside and out.

Erik's hands eased up to massage her raised arms. "Are you all right tied like this?"

"Yes. It's…sexy."

"Yes, it is. And so are you." His hand glided under her hair and down her back to smack her ass. Once, twice. The sharp sound echoed in the orbiter.

"Oh!"

Kam bit the inside of his cheek to keep from groaning. Why did they have to torture him like this? He'd lived too long without a woman of his own.

"You like that?"

"Yes, Erik, yes."

"Very good. I plan to do it to you often."

Kam couldn't drag his eyes from her as Erik spanked her again. Her ass jiggled, and he could see her skin growing pink even from his vantage point.

Leila moaned. "Erik?"

"Hmm?" He caressed her ass.

"Why do males like to spank?"

A grin tugged at his lips. "Why do females like to be spanked?"

Kam swallowed the laugh that threatened to spill from his mouth. The perfect way to avoid answering one question was to ask another. He waited for Leila's response.

"Not all like it," she said.

"And not all males spank."

"But you do…and the others."

"And you like it. It makes you hot." His fingers grazed her pussy. "And wet."

She blushed, but didn't lower her gaze.

Kam was curious to hear Erik's answer. He, personally, had never spanked a woman during sex. He had swatted a butt or two in his time, but only in fun. He preferred to do other things

166

to a female's ass for sexual gratification. But he knew Erik and Torque liked to spank. Braden, he wasn't sure about. Leila was the only woman he had ever seen Braden spank. If Braden spanked Alexa, he didn't know.

Erik simply chuckled. "Let's just leave the explanations alone for now. All that matters is your pleasure." He stepped in front of her and tugged open his uniform pants.

Kam noticed that Leila's breathing increased. She moistened her lips, and opened and closed her fingers around the pipe she was tied to.

Erik stepped forward and his mouth came down on hers. He kissed her deeply.

Pulling back, he tugged off his boots, and lowered his pants. He kicked his uniform and boots aside, then stood in front of her, stroking his dick. "You ready?" When she nodded, he grabbed one of her legs, draped it over his hip, and eased into her pussy.

"Oh, Erik!"

His hips pumped forward, softly and slowly.

"More, Erik."

He increased his thrusts a little at a time, until he was plunging into her with quick and determined force. "Like this?"

"Yes!"

Kam rolled onto his back, and threw his arm across his eyes. He rubbed himself lightly through his uniform. Their sexual escapade made his dick feel harder than steel, but no way was he jacking off here.

He felt like telling them to give it a rest, but he knew how they felt about each other. Neither of them had ever fully admitted the depths of their feelings aloud, but his mood sensor picked up their emotions with no problems. As if he needed a machine to tell him what he saw with his own eyes.

Leila moaned. "I'm coming, I'm coming."

Lowering his arm, Kam turned his head to see her body shaking in Erik's embrace. She looked so gorgeous when she came—her skin flushed, her eyes sparkled. He loved to watch a woman climax. Erik whispered something in her ear, thrusting into her gently now, pumping, and then rotating his hips.

"Yes, yes," she said in response.

Erik groaned deep in his throat, and he came, too. "Oh, Leila! Yeah, baby!" His body trembled, then relaxed.

They both stood silently in each other's arms. Erik reached up and untied her from the pipe. "From now on you have sex with nobody but me. Understand?"

"Hmm." She practically purred, her nails grazing his chest.

At the sensual sound, Kam's dick hardened even more. He needed a woman and some good, sloppy sex. Leila sucking him off had been great, but he needed his cock inside a warm and wet pussy, and hers was no longer available.

Leila clung to Erik, her arms heavy and her body sated. She couldn't bring herself to admit to him how much she cared. Not yet. This wasn't the time or the place to discuss intimate things, though she wasn't opposed to a quick joining...or two.

Erik was a fantastic lover. He still hadn't told her his most carnal need. She'd asked after Kam had moved to the back of the orbiter. But Erik had just said, *when we're alone.* She'd thought he might tell her while they fucked. Instead, he'd whispered hot, erotic things to her while stroking her pussy. She'd never climaxed so quickly. She glanced to the side.

She figured, by now, Kam must be awake. Even knowing he'd probably seen them didn't sway her. She couldn't move away from Erik. His hands felt too good roaming her body. Besides, something about being watched excited her. She kissed Erik's throat, eliciting a moan from him.

He sat on the edge of the control panel and pulled her close. His thumb rubbed her nipple, getting it hard. He tugged on the bud. "You like that?"

"You know I do. Suck it." She loved the touch of his mouth on her skin.

His lips closed around the nipple, and he drew gently on her flesh.

She stroked his hair. "That feels so good." While holding him close, his sucking seemed more tender than erotic. Also calming, in a strange way. She caressed his cheek, and her eyes closed, enjoying the moment.

Suddenly, a hand smacked her ass, breaking the mood. "Get dressed," Kam said, moving to his control chair. "Someone's approaching the ship. Five hundred yards out. I'm picking up their blips on my sensor."

Leila's eyes popped open. Somehow, her ass had become a focal point with these men, which was one of the reasons she'd asked Erik about spanking. She didn't know whether to feel amused or aggravated. She'd love to ask Alexa if Braden was equally ass-obsessed. He'd spanked her during her re-initiation and finger-fucked her hole, too. But was *her* ass the attraction, or all women's asses?

Erik released her nipple and sighed. "Great timing."

"Could have been worse," she told him with a chuckle, rubbing her butt.

"True." He reached up and stroked her hair. "Stay alert."

She nodded, knowing he was concerned for her safety. She felt the same about his safety. Her nerves kicked up a notch.

Neither of them moved away from each other. She needed more time. From the look in Erik's eyes, she knew he felt the same. She traced his lips with her finger. She couldn't wait until this mission was over, and they were safely back in The Lair.

"Unless you want Halah and company to find you two naked, I suggest you move right now and get your uniforms on," Kam told them. "Quickly, please."

This time they moved.

"Are you sure it's Halah?" Erik asked, slipping into his pants.

"I'm only picking up three signals on my sensor, too small for a patrol. And we're too far out, I think, for it to be anyone else."

"I didn't know your machine picked up readings from that distance." Erik fastened his shirt.

"I've been making modifications."

Leila quickly cleaned herself up and dressed. She moved behind Kam's chair and studied the readings on his handheld sensor. "What do you think?"

"Definitely a woman and two men. No Egesa."

Erik pulled out his weapon. "Get your disruptor ready, Kam."

"Give me one, too," Leila said, eagerness as well as anxiety laced her voice. Beads of sweat trickled down her back.

"You know that's not happening. You're a Class 3."

"So, screw the regulations. This is a serious situation." He couldn't leave her defenseless.

"Exactly. I don't want you getting yourself killed. You're not properly trained yet. I think Kam and I can handle three armed intruders."

"Erik, I need something. I feel totally vulnerable here." The regulations made no sense to her. She needed to protect herself. Although not yet certified, she was receiving instruction in and practice with a variety of weapons almost daily in her training sessions.

He stared at her a moment, then he nodded. "All right." He reached behind his back and pulled out a Pain Inducer from his belt. "Here. Take this, but you didn't get it from me."

"Understood." The weapon only worked at close range. To emit an electrical zap, the Pain Inducer needed to make direct contact with bare skin. She'd used one before, more than once, in real-life situations, regulations permitting or not, so she felt comfortable with how the weapon operated.

"Everyone get behind whatever you can, as well as you can. Try not to make yourself a target. When I say so, Leila, you open the door. If it's not Halah out there, Kam, don't immediately shoot in case she sent someone in her place, but be prepared. You ready, Leila?"

"I'm ready." As she reached toward the control, her hand shook. Inwardly, she steeled her nerves, chastising herself for the show of weakness.

"Open the door."

She hit the button and the hatch slid open.

A man, armed with a similar-looking disruptor weapon, stepped from the entry ramp into view. When he saw them, he stopped in his tracks.

Leila's heart pounded. So, the moment of truth had arrived. Was this man here to help them or kill them?

Chapter Eight

Halah's boots clanked on the steel ramp, sounding loud to her ears, even after enduring the irritating noise of the rover's engine. She stepped inside the orbiter, coming up beside Dak, and glanced around the interior. Definitely Xylon, from the layout.

Erik and Leila eased into view. Halah recognized them immediately. Those puny panels they'd partially hidden behind wouldn't have provided much protection if she were the enemy.

These Warriors proved almost more trouble than she cared to deal with. If any other way existed... She hated relying on others to get what she needed.

"Well, well, well, if it isn't my little, lost slaves. We thought you were the ones who crashed out here. Looks like a banquet of overcooked Egesa fillets out on the ground. What did you do to them? Doesn't appear to be flamethrower burns. Too many are dead for that to have caused their demise, unless you have an armed unit of Warriors hiding in here somewhere."

"A little electrical surprise. Something you can appreciate, I'm sure," Kam said, stepping out from behind a larger, side control panel.

Halah's gaze immediately fell upon Kam, and her heart raced. *Him.* Braden did send him on the mission as she'd hoped. Focused on the Healer and the other Warrior, she'd missed him completely. Looking into his eyes, she felt almost giddy, which was too silly to admit, even to herself. So, she dismissed the feeling. For now. "Ingenious. I commend you. What happened to our rendezvous plans?"

"Four interceptors jumped our butts," Erik said, not lowering his weapon. "Instead of one, like you reported."

"Really?" Halah cocked an eyebrow at him. "I guess the Egesa stepped up their patrols."

"Apparently," Kam said.

His eyes held a wary look. He didn't trust her. Good. She liked cautious, smart men. More challenging. Actually, she'd known about the patrols. She'd feared that Braden wouldn't send a team into a heavily patrolled area. So she'd done what she had to do. She'd lied. Though she assumed Braden probably knew about her deception, or at least suspected. He wouldn't be much of a leader otherwise. The fact that he'd agreed to send the team anyhow showed his desperation, or arrogance. She wasn't sure which. "Hand over your weapons and take off your jackets after you rip out the power supply to your personal shields. I don't want the surges picked up by any patrols."

Her guard stepped on board.

"Secure their belongings," Halah ordered him.

The man took their possessions as they reluctantly held out their weapons and jackets. Uncertainty shone in their eyes. She didn't blame them. Being unarmed, while on a dangerous mission would make her feel insecure, too.

"Not that I don't trust you," she announced with a false smile, "but I'll need to search each of you for hidden weapons." Trust was an act of faith she couldn't afford.

She stepped over to Leila first. The Healer stood about three inches shorter than she, but Leila possessed attitude. She saw it in the woman's eyes. Someday, with continued training, Leila would make a formidable Warrior.

"She's a Class 3," Erik said. "No weapons."

"I'll search her anyway, if you don't mind." Halah shrugged. "Even if you do mind." No way were these Warriors clean. She crouched behind Leila and felt around the woman's boots. Rising slowly, she fluttered her hands over and between Leila's legs. Halah cupped her pussy.

Leila jerked and tried to elbow her away.

"Easy." She laughed. "I'm just being thorough." She knew the teasing tone of her voice irritated the Healer and couldn't help pushing her even more. "We don't have time for…fun. Maybe later."

"Don't count on it."

Halah grinned. Leila had probably never touched another woman sexually in her life. Halah preferred men also, but dabbled from time to time, mostly in threesomes. She felt around Leila's waist and lifted a Pain Inducer from the inside fold in the back of her pants. "So much for no weapons." She tossed the Inducer to Dak, then felt across Leila's breasts, chuckling when the woman tried, once more, to shove her back.

Satisfied that Leila held no other weapons, she moved over to Erik. One finger stroked down his cheek. This one possessed little compassion for his enemies. She saw it in his eyes, heard it in his voice, felt it by the energy he exuded. He held his body poised for attack at all times. "You almost killed me on Earth with that energy ball."

He pulled his head back. "I remember. You zapped me. Hurt like hell." One side of his mouth quirked up. "I should have gutted you."

His attitude grated on her. Halah smacked his cheek. "Try anything like that again, and you die." Nobody hurt her without retaliation. She'd only zapped him because he'd engaged her in hand-to-hand combat. That was his fault, not hers.

"You bitch!" Leila stepped forward, but Kam pulled her back.

Erik never moved, only blinked when she struck him.

Knowing he was the most dangerous of the three, Halah kept her eyes fixed on him. She nodded toward Leila. "The Healer is feisty. I hate feisty women."

"And I hate traitors. Male or female. We saw you in a cell on the ship where we were captured during that Earth mission. The Egesa beat you. And you still give Marid your loyalty. That's fucking crazy."

Halah stepped behind Erik. "Yeah, that's right. I'm crazy. Don't forget it." Maybe they'd be more wary of her, if they thought her unbalanced. She crouched and felt around his boots. Her fingers slipped inside his right boot, and she pulled out a knife. "What have we here?" Most Warriors carried a backup weapon or two, so she wasn't really surprised. She stood up and circled him, holding up the retractable blade. She cocked an eyebrow.

He shrugged.

She twirled the knife in her hand, extracting the blade from its sheath. "Hmm, not bad." Halah flipped the blade closed and handed off the weapon to Dak. She finished her search of Erik, then moved on to Kam. Her heart thudded as she stared into his eyes. "We meet again."

"So, it seems."

She looked him over. "You don't appear permanently damaged in any way." Even in this semi-tense situation, her thoughts went from business to personal in record time. She'd forgotten just how handsome and sexy he was. His light blue eyes complemented his dusty blond hair perfectly. He stood tall and strong. She wondered what he looked like naked. She felt her temperature rise. *Soon.* "I must be losing my touch."

"I'm sure if you'd wanted to truly damage me, you would have done so."

She laughed, enjoying their exchange. "True." She had more training than he did and used to be proud of her Class 1 status. She stepped behind him and knelt down to search his boots. Her fingers moved up his calves and thighs. Hard and strong. Her pussy began to throb. He would have great thrusting power, she imagined.

An image of him pumping into her from behind, with a look of intense passion in his eyes, entered her head. She shook off the vision. That wouldn't happen—too emotionally and physically dangerous, but she *would* straddle him. She stood, and her hand slipped between his legs and cupped his cock. Oh, very nice. She couldn't wait to tie him to her bed and fuck the hell out of him. It had been a long time since she'd ridden a Warrior. "Feels like you've got a pretty big weapon in there." She massaged him slowly.

He jerked at her touch, before bringing himself under control. "Depends on your definition of weapon."

"Were you having a little three-way party before I arrived?"

Kam briefly glanced at Erik and Leila.

She wouldn't be opposed to a threesome, if he participated as one of the three. Though, she'd prefer a one-on-one fuck. "Maybe we'll have a party later. Just you and me," she whispered in his ear, flicking her tongue against his flesh.

A barely audible moan escaped his lips, and his cock hardened.

At his reaction, her pulse jumped. He wasn't immune to her. Perfect. But right now, other priorities loomed. He was clean. No hidden weapons. That somewhat disappointed her. He played by the rules. She preferred to associate with men who didn't play by the rules. That way, she never heard any speeches about doing the right thing, being a better person, and the rest of that moral shit. Morals were a luxury she couldn't entertain these days. She did what she had to do to survive. No matter what.

She stepped in front of them. "I brought slave attire for you all to wear. You'll need to get rid of your uniforms. And get rid of that thing," she told Kam, pointing to the sensor strapped to his wrist. "Hide everything in one of the orbiter's storage units. When we enter The Dome, all of you keep your heads down. If you're recognized, either by one of the Egesa or Assassins passing by, a Dome resident, or by someone watching one of the monitors, there won't be anything I can do to help you. All breeders are presently being killed."

"What?" The tone of Leila's voice rose in obvious distress. "Why?"

"I don't know." She wasn't about to tell them about the breeder sterilization failure. The Egesa could still sterilize pre-initiated breeders through The Dome's Initiation Rite, but once someone went through The Lair's Initiation Rite, the new sterilization formula wasn't permanent. And the formula didn't affect Branded breeders at all. "Are you Branded?" she asked Leila.

Leila glanced at Erik. "No." She looked back at Halah. "As your slave, I shouldn't have to worry about sterilization, should I? None of us are mated, so we're not in a breeder-release cycle."

Which meant they weren't presently fertile, Halah knew. Still, Leila looked panicked, as did the others. She could fuck with the Healer's mind, but she decided against it. "As long as you're not recognized, you'll be all right." Even if she was recognized, they wouldn't bother with sterilization now, since she was initiated and protected. Because she wasn't Branded though, she wouldn't be protected against sexual assault from the Egesa. The chemicals in the perspiration of a Branded breeder were poisonous to the Egesa. Without those chemicals, if she fell into the hands of those creatures, they'd fuck her to death, literally.

These Warriors' trust of her to keep them all safe made her increasingly uncomfortable. Even guilty. Somehow, she couldn't completely shake her old Xylon training and sense of responsibility.

Leila let out the tight breath she was holding. "Good. Now, how are we going to get through processing? As soon as they scan our bodies, we'll be identified as breeders."

"I've made arrangements. My quarters are a safe zone. Once there, you'll have access to my computer to retrieve what you need, if you can break into the database system."

"I'll handle that," Kam replied.

"I require my medical equipment to test the formula's viability."

"Not possible," she told Leila. "Xylon equipment or circuits of any sort will trigger an alarm inside The Dome. You'll have to use whatever the Med Lab has available. Now, give me the information on my sister." Once she had that, she could get off this rock as soon as she obtained clearance.

"Afraid not," Erik said. "After we get what we came for and are back here in our orbiter and armed, then you get the information. Otherwise, I doubt we'd make it off Marid alive."

Well, she couldn't say she was surprised by his response. She'd given it a shot. "I take it you're the one in charge of this mission." She already knew that due to the markings on his jacket. He held highest rank, a higher Class 1 status than she. But she felt like goading him. She hated being in a position that forced her to blackmail Warriors to get their help. They should have helped her years ago, when her loyalty to The Lair still burned strong.

"That's right."

"Erik Rhodes?" Again, she knew from her previous mission. She'd read all their files, and along with her encounter with them on Earth, she had a good feeling for each of their personalities. They didn't need to know how much information she had on them though. Erik would be the hardest to control. She noticed how he kept looking over at Leila, making sure she was all right. He cared about the Healer, and more than just as a Xylon Warrior. She would use that to her advantage, if necessary.

He nodded, acknowledging her inquiry about his name.

"We will do it your way. But don't push me." She turned and grabbed the clothing from the guard's hands. "Change into these." She tossed the outfits at each of them, more like scraps in her opinion. The thin, flesh-colored material didn't hide much. She wouldn't want to wear one, but looked forward to seeing Kam outfitted in the sexy attire.

"Why don't you give us each a Dome transport-connector, and the coordinates to your quarters?" Leila asked. "Nobody even has to know we're here."

"They already know you're here, genius."

Leila frowned. "I just thought—"

"Well, don't. I don't trust you. Any of you." The woman must think she's stupid. "Once given access, who knows where you'd end up. If you're discovered inside The Dome, without going through processing, you'll be executed. We're doing this my way or not at all. My ass is on the line too, you know."

"Let's get going then," Erik said.

Leila fingered the clothing, and a frown crossed her face. "Where's the top?"

"Slaves don't wear tops. Not even the females." Halah kept her eyes on Erik, who seemed agitated by the news.

"Since when?" he asked.

Halah shrugged. Let them deal with it. Baring her tits wouldn't hurt the woman any. "No boots either. And if you're wearing your regulation underclothes, get rid of those. I don't want any more attention drawn to you three than necessary."

"Can we have some privacy?" Leila asked, her gaze roaming over the smiling guards, who eyed her lustily.

"If you're the modest sort, get over it." Halah smacked Dak's arm and gave Bron a heated look to wipe the grin off the men's faces. "You're going to be parading around half-naked, and that's the reality of the situation. Now change." She needed to get them inside The Dome before their window of safe opportunity passed.

* * * * *

Rave stroked Gabriella's bare breast. "You sure you can distract Daegal long enough for Halah to get the Warriors through?" Their plans were finally coming together. Men had ruled Marid long enough. Now she and Gabriella would get the chance to flex some female muscle.

"No problem. Odds are he won't be watching anyway. He doesn't personally monitor the slave processing too often anymore, but better not to take a chance. I'll adjust all the body scanners not to detect breeders for twenty-four hours. Any longer than that, and the maintenance crew will discover the tampering. You'll handle the Top Commander?"

"I'll take care of him. Leila will be a great benefit to us. Her medical mind and knowledge is far superior to the Healers we presently have on Marid. She might be able to take the sterilization formula and perfect it, for the men this time. That'll put them all at our mercy."

"How will we force her compliance?"

"I don't know yet. We need to find her weakness. Everyone has one. I'll come up with something." The day she couldn't outwit Leila Abdera, she'd eat Egesa cock. She had watched Gabriella do it once, and turned nauseous when the woman had actually swallowed the male's brown cum. Disgusting. Gabriella wasn't a breeder, so she hadn't been Branded by Daegal when he took her as his mate—playmate was a better description, but she'd never say that to Gabriella. As such, Gabriella fucked who or what she wanted, whenever she wanted.

"Who else will be with Leila?" Gabriella glanced up at a monitor. She grabbed a remote control beside the bed and switched the screen to display the slave processing area.

"I don't know. Halah wasn't told. One Class 1 Warrior for certain. That's Lair regulations. Probably one other Warrior, at least. An orbiter of the size they'll most likely be traveling in can comfortably hold up to five, but only needs three to pilot, navigate, and handle weapons control."

"The rest who accompany her will need to die, unless you perceive a use for any of them."

"It's in the process of being arranged." She needed to cover several possibilities. She didn't know exactly what the Warriors had planned, so she wanted to set up various traps to make sure they didn't slip through Marid's security and get away.

"Halah, too."

"Halah, too. She'll get everything she deserves. We can't trust her. She'd double-cross her best friend, if it got her what she wanted." Not that the woman had any friends, other than those two losers who always trailed after her with their tongues hanging out.

"Agreed. Everything is moving along on schedule. Once Daegal is dead, I will be in charge, and we'll have enough power to not only control Marid, but to begin plans for control of this whole system. We'll finally get everything we want."

Rave still didn't quite understand how the overthrow was going to work. She stretched under the sheet. "What about the Top Commander? He will challenge you for control."

"No, he won't." Gabriella switched the monitor view to the transportation area.

Rave smiled. She always loved Gabriella's deviousness. "What do you have in mind? You can't kill him. We need him to control the Egesa, at least temporarily."

"I won't have to kill him. He will do everything I say. He's not well, like Daegal. Certainly, you've noticed."

"Of course. But it's nothing permanent, is it?" Maybe Gabriella was giving him some sort of nonpoisonous drug to control him. That would be handy. Gabriella had access to all sorts of special herbs and drugs. From where, Rave didn't precisely know. She'd found an off-planet source of some significant magnitude, and the drugs bypassed their normal bodily protection. But that's all she knew about it. "Some of the other Commanders will challenge you, if the Top Commander doesn't or can't. A woman, untrained, taking over The Dome will be met with resistance. Now, if I take over—"

"Never happen, Rave. Forget it." Gabriella switched the monitor to the Med Lab.

"What are you searching for?"

"Just checking things out, do you mind?" Gabriella's stern look softened and she set the remote aside. She held up her hand, and her voice lowered. "Now don't ask me any more questions in this. The less you know the better." Gabriella arched her back, offering her breast.

Rave lowered her head and sucked the nipple into her mouth. She didn't like it when Gabriella kept secrets. Secrets made her nervous and made her suspect she wasn't as secure in her position as she thought.

She wondered if Gabriella and the Top Commander had forged an alliance strong enough for him to switch his loyalty from Daegal to her. If not, and he wasn't being drugged, then she must know something incriminating or personal about the man that he didn't want revealed. Maybe his name. Rave snorted. Nobody even knew that. She needed to figure this out for her own good. Her hand slid between Gabriella's legs.

She'd get Dare and Shear to snoop around for her, see what they could find out.

* * * * *

Leila fingered the slave attire. At least the garment smelled clean. But that's about the only positive thing she could say.

With their backs to Halah and the guards, Kam and Erik changed into their pants. They then positioned themselves so that she could change behind them. Leila smiled her thanks, grateful for the partial privacy.

She pulled on the flesh-colored hide. The thin material barely covered her pussy and ass. Even though she hated the outfit, she couldn't deny how sexy Erik and Kam looked in the pants. Their muscular chests and tightly packed stomachs were shown off to perfection. The pants clung to their cocks, leaving little to the imagination.

Erik arranged her hair down over the front of her shoulders to cover her breasts. "Not only beautiful, but serviceable," he whispered in her ear. "Don't worry. Everything will be all right."

She nodded, but wasn't so sure about his words. The look in his eyes wasn't as calming as his voice. This mission had started out with problems and didn't seem to be improving as it progressed.

Leila noticed how Halah practically devoured Kam with her eyes. She wondered if he noticed. A protective feeling toward Kam struck. As one of her best friends, she didn't want him used or hurt by anyone, especially a former Warrior who wasn't trustworthy, in her opinion.

"Let's head out," Halah said. "If we go through processing during the busy time of the day, we'll be less conspicuous."

They left the orbiter and all loaded into the rover. Three in front and three in back. Leila reached next to her and clutched Erik's hand. She felt safer whenever he touched her.

Erik squeezed her fingers. His warmth seeped into her skin, heating her frigid grip. She smiled up at him, and he winked back.

As the rover headed toward The Dome, the terrain passed by too slowly. They couldn't be traveling at full speed. Leila wanted to fly. Moving over the land, with the breeze in her face, she noticed the air felt drier than on Xylon. Her skin hated this. She already felt itchy. And the scenery didn't touch her heart. She preferred the forests of Xylon to the few mountains and flat lands of Marid.

Over the next hill, Dak pulled the rover to a quick stop, jerking everyone forward.

"Why are we stopping?" Halah asked. "Is it the tank leak?"

Tank leak. Leila shifted uncomfortably. That must be why they were traveling at a slower rate.

"No. An Egesa Patrol is about to come through the mountain pass. See the signals?"

Egesa... Leila's heart pounded.

"Wonderful." Halah glanced back at them. "Keep your heads down, and your mouths shut, no matter what. Don't even think about running. They'll be carrying pulse rifles. Those things will cut you in two. They're not going to be thrilled to find baked comrades nearby, so expect trouble."

Like Dak said, a patrol of at least twenty Egesa came through the pass and into the valley. Some in rovers, some in heavy transports.

Leila's stomach tightened. She hated those evil, smelly creatures. The Egesa weren't too bright though. Halah could probably talk them safely past.

The unit stopped not far from them. Halah got out of the rover, and a large, male Egesa emerged from one of the transports. The Commander, Leila suspected. Rays from the low-hanging sun reflected off his bald head. His yellow eyes swept the area.

"Identify," he rasped out to Halah, focusing those eerie orbs on her.

"Halah Shirota. I claim salvage on the downed orbiter located several miles to the south in the DustFire Flats. These three from on board are my slaves, as is my right, according to Dome Law."

He grunted.

"Unfortunately, due to a malfunction of the damaged orbiter, an Egesa Patrol was electrocuted when they attempted to enter the ship."

"She didn't have to tell them," Erik complained in a harsh whisper.

"If she didn't, they'd track us down after finding the bodies, and kill us, no questions asked," Dak said from the front. "This way, she controls the situation."

Growls and grunts came from the other Egesa standing nearby. They hefted their weapons. Leila felt Erik and Kam stiffen. The Egesa Commander stared at them, sitting in the back of the rover. Hatred shone in his eyes.

"We take as prisoners. Our right."

"Only if they killed your comrades. They didn't. Like I said, their deaths resulted from a ship malfunction. The electrical system became damaged during flight. Your patrol found them before they fixed the problem. The patrol refused to retreat when warned. For your trouble, you salvage the ship. I have no use for that."

"Damn, woman," Erik whispered again. "We're going to need the ship and our weapons and equipment."

"We take female. Split salvage. Fair."

Leila clutched Erik's hand tighter. Halah's lies sounded convincing to her, but she didn't think the Egesa Commander believed her words or even cared.

"Don't worry," Erik tried to assure her. "I won't let them take you."

"How are you going to stop them?" When he didn't answer, she knew they were in trouble. Her head pounded so hard she winced. She'd heard horror stories of how the Egesa treated females alien to their own species.

Halah visibly stiffened. Dak and the other guard slowly got out of the rover, their weapons drawn.

"You can get slaves from the slave arena. You don't need her."

"As can you, Halah. We take. Torture and fuck in memory of comrades."

Halah stepped back a little, holding her disruptor at the ready. "No."

Kam leaned forward. "Twenty or more, against six. And three of us are unarmed. I don't like the odds."

"Our weapons have to be in this rover somewhere," Erik said.

"Little good that does us, since we don't know where," Kam replied. "We can't search for them."

A smaller Egesa limped up to the Commander and grunted something in their guttural language. He pointed to the display of the vid-cell in his hand.

The Commander nodded. He waved an arm to the troops. "Come! No salvage authority. You lose, Halah. Take female slave," he ordered his men. "Kill others."

"No," Leila moaned, her gaze shifting. His long nails captured her attention. She shuddered. Those claws would easily rip through tender flesh. She searched for some means of escape. But no escape existed. They were trapped.

Damn it. Halah wondered if Rave had set this up. The woman could capture Leila and rid herself of the rest of them in one swoop. Though she didn't think Rave would take such a chance. Making deals with the Egesa often backfired, unless made by Marid's top leaders. Whatever the truth, she wasn't defeated so easily. As long as everyone kept calm...

Two Egesa grabbed Leila from behind, one by the arm and one by the hair. They pulled her out of the seat, over the low back of the rover.

"Ow! Let go." She tried to elbow them off her, but their strength far outweighed hers. They growled and pushed her forward. She stumbled, falling to her knees.

Erik and Kam jumped out of the transport.

"No!" Halah warned them. Damn male Warriors. She knew they wouldn't be able to stay out of the fray.

Erik punched one guard in the jaw, sending him tumbling backward. Kam slugged the other in the stomach, and the Egesa fell like a brick, even though he wore a belly shield. Halah smiled. Impressive. She motioned Leila back toward their vehicle.

"Fire!" The Egesa Commander ordered.

A pulse beam flew past Halah's head. "Shit!" She engaged her disruptor and zigzagged toward the rover, dodging their fire.

Everyone dove behind the personal transport as laser, pulse, and disruptor shots flew.

Halah's guard fell from a shot to his side. He groaned, alive but suffering. Dak fired back, then pulled Bron to safety. "If they hit the tank while it's leaking, we're dead. The protective shield won't be enough to contain the blast. It'll blow like a bomb."

Halah grumbled under her breath. She didn't want to do this, but had known it a possibility once Dak told her of the approaching Egesa. "Challenge!" she shouted.

"What are you doing?" Dak whispered harshly.

"The only thing that's going to get us out of here alive." With a little luck. Well, more like a lot of luck.

The firing stopped.

Halah stood up, her weapon raised harmlessly in the air. Her heart pounded an uneven beat in her chest.

Kam grabbed at her.

She kicked him away. "Stay out of it." Was he trying to protect her or get them all fried? Anger toward the Warriors battled with a strange sense of compassion deep inside her.

"You challenge for female?" the Egesa Commander asked.

"Yes, I challenge." She forced her voice to come out strong and steady, even though that's not how she felt.

"What's happening?" Leila whispered.

"Halah is going to fight the Commander for ownership of you," Dak told her. "If he accepts the challenge, that is."

"Why should he?" Kam asked. "He's got us outgunned. This is crazy."

"They live for hand-to-hand challenges. It's a point of honor."

"Even against a female?" Erik asked.

"The Egesa don't discriminate."

"Drop weapon," the Commander ordered.

Halah dropped her disruptor. She walked around the rover to face the Commander. She needed to push her position and try to gain the best advantage for victory. "If I win, we go in peace."

"If I win, we take female, and kill rest. Including you."

Sweat formed on Halah's brow. His terms lacked acceptability, to say the least. "If you win, you take female, and let us go." If Leila needed to be sacrificed, she'd figure out some other way to accommodate Rave and still convince the others to give her the information she sought. If *she* died, Josella would be all alone. That wasn't an option.

"You challenged me. I decide. My rules. We fight now. No weapons. No shields."

From his stance and the look on his face, she knew he wasn't going to change his mind. Reluctantly, she nodded her acceptance of his terms. No other choice existed for her now.

"She can't win without using her electrical powers," Kam said to Dak.

"Don't be so sure."

"Is this a death challenge?" Erik asked.

"It can be," Dak replied. "Or until one of them surrenders."

"Shut up," Halah warned, turning her head toward them. "You're distracting me with your chatter." She needed to remain focused.

Halah removed her jacket and power supply, while the Egesa Commander removed his armor and laid down his weapons. If he lost, to maintain whatever honor he had left, he would keep his word. So would his troops. Combat was the only type of action the Egesa honored—or at least the Egesa who served as Marid Soldiers.

The Commander stood larger and stronger than the average Egesa. He wouldn't be easily defeated. Without her electrical surge powers, she was going to take a beating.

After many years of handling electrical currents, her body always retained some residual power, even without her power pack. If she used the power though, the other Egesa would kill her. The power probably wouldn't be enough to faze the Commander anyhow. The skin of the Egesa wore like tough animal hide. She needed to fight this challenge using only her hand-to-hand combat training.

A win would get her one step closer to finding Josella, and knowing that would hopefully give her enough strength to defeat the Commander. If she didn't win, they would all die, and Leila would endure a lifetime, however short, of horror at the hands of these creatures. As a woman, she felt at least some compassion for the Healer.

"We begin," the Commander announced.

Slowly, they circled each other. Halah looked for an opening. Egesa weren't very agile. She had that advantage.

The Commander lunged forward with more speed than she expected from him and grabbed her around the neck. His fingers tightened, gradually and with purpose.

Halah's windpipe immediately became compromised.

"Let me go," she heard Kam say, as she gasped for air. He sounded far off, though she knew they all watched from just behind the rover.

She brought her arms up sharply on the inside of the Egesa's, trying to break his hold. His fingers didn't budge. She pounded her boot down on his. No reaction. Purposely, she went limp, collapsing in his grip. Her body weight, though slight, put him off balance. They both went down, and she flipped him over her head, forcing his release.

Rubbing her throat and coughing, she scrambled to her feet. The Commander rolled to the side and pushed himself upright. She wouldn't underestimate him again.

While he still seemed a bit dazed, she kicked out at his stomach—a sensitive area, more so without his armor. He howled and stumbled backward. If she wanted to defeat him, she needed to do it fast. He'd have more endurance and could easily outlast her. She twirled and kicked his jaw, a direct hit.

He grabbed her boot and flung her to the ground.

She landed with a hard thud, and the air rushed out of her. "Ohh…" Her ribs felt bruised, though she didn't think any broke.

"Die, bitch." He raised his stud-soled boot to stomp on her face.

"Roll!" someone yelled.

She rolled into him, against his other leg. He fell like a boulder onto his stomach. She scrambled onto his back and held on. She couldn't choke him. His neck was thicker than her thigh. She needed to take a different path. With all her strength, she gouged at his eyes.

Growling, he got to his feet and tried to shake her off. She held tight with her legs hooked around his waist.

When she punctured his sockets, he wailed and clawed at her legs. Her pants ripped, and his long nails contacted bare skin.

Halah screamed. She bit her lip to stop her cries. She couldn't let him know he'd hurt her. She pressed her fingers harder into his eyes. He flailed back and forth, ripping at her hands. Her skin tore under his attack, sending waves of agony through her.

Finally, she had to let go. She fell to the ground, dislocating her shoulder when she hit. Blinding pain shot through her. She feared she wouldn't be able to get back up. And even if she did, her fighting ability would be severely limited. Still, she refused to surrender.

The Commander whirled toward her, his eyes gone.

Halah couldn't do anything but stare at the black, empty sockets.

He took a step forward and fell flat on his face.

Waiting for movement, Halah held her breath. When she saw none, she relaxed, not completely, but enough to think more clearly. She forced herself to her feet, staggering more than a little. She held her injured arm and tried to ignore the blood covering her body. Her own blood. Breathing heavily, but steadily, she raised her boot to rest on the Commander's back. "I claim victory," she said to the troops.

The other Egesa backed off. Reluctance showed in their eyes, however they honored the challenge.

Halah limped over to grab her jacket, power supply, and disruptor with her good arm. "Get in the rover," she told everyone.

Kam tried to help her in.

She shrugged him off. "Don't make me look weak. Get us out of here, Dak."

After they settled in their seats, Dak gunned the rover. They sped through the mountain pass and topped the next hill, putting distance between themselves and the Egesa. The rest of the way to The Dome lay flat and should be quickly covered, even with a tank leak.

"Thank you," Leila said from the back.

"Yeah. Sure." What was she supposed to say? Halah never felt comfortable with gratitude. They hit a bump, and the jostling almost caused her to pass out.

"You're hurt, Halah," Erik told her. "Let Leila tend to you."

"With what? She doesn't have any equipment." Halah glanced at Bron, unconscious beside her. He didn't look good. No blood stained his clothing. He must have been hit by one of the new pulse-beam weapons, which caused internal injuries without any external signs of damage. "Now shut up and let me be."

A hand touched her good shoulder. She jerked, then relaxed when she realized who'd touched her and why. Kam. The Warrior way after a fight. A show of solidarity and a good job. Uncomfortable with the gesture, she shrugged him off.

"At least let Leila reset your shoulder, Halah," Kam said.

Dak stopped the rover. "He's right."

"Damn it! Fine," Halah ground out. "Anything to shut all of you up." She couldn't take the pain much longer anyway. "Do it. Quickly."

* * * * *

Torque entered the Command Center and approached Braden. Finally, good news. "Pitch checked in. He and our sisters have Josella secured. The orbiter sustained some damage, but should be in full working order within twenty-four hours or less. There's a storm in the area. They'll need to wait it out and flush their external systems before they take off. I told them to stay put on the Sand Moon until we issue the all clear."

"How dangerous will it be there for them?"

Torque let out a heavy breath. His stint on the Sand Moon, when he'd been banished from Xylon for refusing to become a Dispenser, among other things, had burned a permanent memory of violence and pain on his psyche. "It's not a stroll through Xylon Square, but they should be all right for the short term. While the storm is raging, none of the gangs will attack. The crew is well-trained and well-supplied. With three armed Warriors together, if they do encounter trouble, they're at least equipped for defense. They'll check in with us every few hours so we know their status, and so they know ours."

"Any additional information on military movements from The Dome?"

"They're not shut down at this point, so I don't think anything is imminent. But we are seeing an increase in Egesa patrols. They'll register our shutdown, so it's only a matter of time before they do the same." Marid often attacked on a small scale. He knew a larger attack loomed somewhere on the horizon.

"The increase in patrols could be because of our team infiltrating their air space, if the orbiter was picked up."

"Maybe, but I think they're planning something big. They're trying to be subtle about it, hoping to catch us off-guard. I feel it."

Braden nodded. "All right, step up our own patrols. No non-Xylon ships are to be cleared for landing. No exceptions. Divert to Tamara or Sunevia. And increase the foot patrols on the surface, just in case."

"You think Assassins are already here?" Probably a stupid question. No way could Xylon identify and keep them all off-planet.

"They always have a few plants, like we do. I want our people on the lookout for anyone who appears out of place, Assassins or other spies. Let's see if we can flush them out for questioning."

"All right. I'll take care of things."

"I want to meet with the team leaders at—"

An alarm blared.

"What now?" Torque winced at the loud, squawking sound.

Braden checked the security board. "Damn! We've got a breach in the Med Lab. Alexa's due there for a checkup." He glanced at a timer on the wall. "Right now. Shit!"

Torque's heart raced. Alexa... He and Braden both grabbed their disruptors and their transport-connectors.

"Let's go," Braden ordered.

"On your heels, brother."

Chapter Nine

Alexa staggered and reached out for the nearest wall. She connected with empty air instead, not near enough to grab onto anything.

Despite the lack of support, she somehow managed to keep her feet under her and steadied her body. She'd been in the process of transporting back to her quarters after her medical checkup, when she got dizzy. She didn't remember anything after that.

"What happened?" Her hand automatically went to her slightly rounded stomach.

She looked around, not recognizing her surroundings. She stood in a completely white room with no furniture. Disconcerting, as if she'd landed in some sort of limbo.

Her mind reeled, and her thoughts seemed strangely muddled. She wasn't even certain how much time had passed since she'd left the Med Lab. She didn't have a timer with her. "Hello?"

No one answered.

Maybe she'd gotten the transport code wrong. No, that didn't make sense. The location was preprogrammed into the handheld. Had she hit the wrong button?

She looked at her transport-connector and tried to relocate. None of the buttons worked. "Darn it." She wished she had her vid-cell with her. Normally, she carried it, but today she'd left the connector recharging in her quarters.

Damn thing only needed recharging once every five hundred hours. The timing couldn't have been worse.

Of course, she hadn't expected anything to go wrong. She wasn't planning to be gone for more than an hour. She should have known better and recharged the cell last night. Braden would not be happy. But really…in The Lair, what could go wrong?

"More than I realized, apparently."

She took a deep breath, attempting to stay calm and focused. Panic wouldn't do her or the babies any good.

A panel on the side opposite her slid open, and she saw black beyond the opening. "I take it that's a hint," she said to no one in particular. She rubbed her stomach, wondering what to do. "Well, anything has to be better than staying here and doing nothing." She chewed at her bottom lip a moment, then sighed. "Probably."

She started forward, walking carefully, not knowing what to expect. The floor blended with the walls and made her feel unstable on her feet. She peered out the opening, but couldn't see anything.

Maybe she'd just take a step or two outside, in case she was able to see something once on the other side. Her eyes might only need to adjust to the change in lighting. The glare in her current surroundings almost hurt her eyes from the brightness.

She could always backtrack if she needed. Simply sitting around and doing nothing held no appeal. Besides, nowhere to sit existed in this strange room, except for the floor. Her stomach hadn't grown that large yet, but still, she didn't do floors well. So… "Here we go."

Holding her stomach, she stepped through the opening and into empty space.

* * * * *

Braden and Torque materialized inside the Med Lab. A six-man security team was already there, along with the confused and nervous medical staff, and the area erupted into chaos.

"Report?" Braden asked the ranking officer, as he scanned the area for Alexa. He didn't see her, only staff rushing back and forth, and Warriors barking orders to other personnel.

The Warrior in front of him stood at attention as he spoke. "No external breach, sir. The breach in the Lab came from an internal source." His eyes flickered with uncertainty. "We think."

"What do you mean, you think? Explain." A bad feeling gripped him. "Shut up!" he yelled to the others in the area. He couldn't hear.

Torque crowded close to listen to the Warrior's report.

"The Healer on duty said Alexa dematerialized out right after her checkup. That's when the alarm went off. We can't find an entry breach, so we suspect she transported out of The Lair, which caused the system alarm to go off due to the shutdown. We've been unable to contact her."

Concern kicked up his heart rate. "Keep on it," Braden ordered the soldier. The only thing that kept him from losing control was the knowledge that he had tools at his disposal to find her.

"Why would Alexa do that?" Torque asked, after the other Warrior stepped away. "Was she that upset with you, Braden? Now we're going to have to open at least one security channel in The Lair to get her back in."

"She wouldn't do that." Braden grabbed his vid-cell and punched in her locater code. Nothing. He frowned. He engaged the Locater in his brain that all Branded breeder-mates possessed for finding their mate. The Locater was part of the brain chip Xylons had implanted shortly after birth. The internal circuits for mate location became activated upon Branding. He shook his head. Impossible.

"Where is she?" Torque asked him.

"I-I can't locate her." His voice shook. Now panic held him captive. His fingers clenched and unclenched, and his knees felt weak. This was not happening.

"What? That's not possible, Braden. The only time a breeder-mate can't locate is if the other one is —"

"Dead." He shook his head again. He wouldn't accept that. If she'd used the transport-connector incorrectly, the atmospheric pressure would kill her. But she knew what to watch out for. He'd taught her well. She wouldn't make such a mistake. Unless some sort of malfunction occurred during materialization...

Torque grabbed his arm. "Let's go up to the Control Center. We'll try to connect with the main tracker. Maybe she's out of range for the handheld somehow."

"My internal tracker has no range."

"Supposedly. Our implanted chips oftentimes develop a temporary glitch. The science behind them is not completely perfected yet. You know that. One of yours might not be engaged properly. We can track her transport-connector. The computer will register its location. Lots of possibilities still exist, Braden. Let's not give up hope yet."

Braden nodded, unable to say another word. His throat had closed up tight. He needed to believe. He *did* believe. Alexa was not dead. He'd feel it in his heart, if she were.

* * * * *

The rover pulled up to The Dome's Transport Center. Kam glanced around the area, which looked mostly deserted, with just a few Egesa working, and not many transports docked. He'd expected more activity.

Dak got the three of them out of the back, then unloaded the injured guard from the front, hefting the man over his shoulder. "I'll check in later." Without waiting for a response from Halah or anyone else, he disappeared through a set of double doors.

Halah climbed out of the rover. Her knees buckled.

"Whoops." Kam caught her and lifted her in his arms. His heart pounded in concern. She'd lost a lot of blood.

"Put me down." Her head lolled against his bare shoulder.

"You're hurt."

Leila looked over her injuries. "We need to stop the bleeding and get her something to halt infection. You need to eat too, Halah. You're so thin. Can you self-heal?"

"Of course. After some patching up, I'll be all right. My shoulder's already feeling better. But we have to get you three processed first."

Kam admired her strength. She presented the appearance of one tough lady. He wondered about the woman inside. Was she as tough deep down, or did she possess a soft heart buried under all that strength?

Several Egesa surrounded them.

Erik turned toward the group. "She's hurt."

They grumbled and whispered among themselves.

"Forget them," Halah instructed, her voice sounding tired. "They're not going to help. Put me down." She tapped Kam's chest. "We have to go through processing. Once in my quarters, your Healer can fix me up. I have supplies."

"You can't walk," Kam said. She'd fall flat on her face before she made it two feet.

"Well, for all our sakes, you'd better hope that I can. If I'm not fit to control my slaves, you'll all go into The Pen, the slave arena, and eventually the Egesa will auction you off. I might not be able to get you back. Now, put me down."

Kam gently set her on her feet, but he kept his hand on her uninjured arm, supporting her. "Your wounds will attract attention."

"Not if I keep to my feet. Everyone will assume I just suffered a training injury, which happens all the time here. It'll take a few hours before the Egesa patrol returns with the charred bodies of their comrades, and the truth comes out. Help me get the blood cleaned off. No one will be the wiser."

"More will gush out," Erik told her. "You thigh is torn up pretty bad."

"I'll wrap the wounds, until they can be treated properly," Leila said. "It'll do for the short term."

Erik glanced at the Egesa staring at them. "We're already attracting attention."

"Don't mind them," Halah said. "They're half-brainers— not right in the head. You can tell by the eyes. A darker yellow. No threat." Baring her teeth, she made a sound between a feline hiss and a canine growl.

The Egesa scurried off.

"Nice trick," Kam said, with a laugh.

"Let's move behind those supply barrels before anyone else notices us." Erik herded them across the transport center. "You're dripping blood." He grabbed a rag from a work area. "I'll clean up what I can as we go along."

Kam watched for trouble, as they helped her limp to the safer location.

Halah grimaced. Every muscle and bone in her body hurt. "Hurry."

"This is not sanitary," Leila responded in a huff, wrapping her thigh.

"It'll be fine." After Leila patched her up with some additional rags Erik collected, Halah felt good to go. Although she remained in pain, she could make it. She had to. Her body, already starting to self-heal, but with a way still to go, required rest soon. They couldn't dawdle. "This way."

A little unsteady on her feet, she led them out of the transport center, through a narrow corridor, and into a large, crowded room. The noise hurt her ears, and her head pounded painfully.

Egesa guards stood everywhere with pulse rifles in hand or slung over their shoulders. Others dressed in Marid uniforms or civilian clothing. Slaves, evident by their attire, followed their owners around the room.

She directed her three "captives" to one of the long tables in the room where they stood in line with others. Despite her jacket, she shivered at the cool air pumping out of the vents. Her injuries affected more than just her strength. Once she healed completely, her body temperature should regulate properly again.

"Are all these people slaves?" Kam whispered to her, rubbing her uninjured arm.

"That's right. Don't touch me here." An unprocessed slave touching an owner in public could get the whip as punishment.

"Disgusting," Leila said.

"I never realized the problem was this bad." Erik moved closer to Leila.

Kam dropped his hand to his side. "Where are they all coming from?"

"Recruited from various planets and systems. Even Tamara." She wondered how Kam would take the news of slaves from his mother's home planet. He'd probably want to save them all. She knew his type. A hero of the people.

Kam glanced at her, and his eyes narrowed. "You know a lot about me."

She shrugged. "Know thy enemy."

"I'm not your enemy, Halah."

The look in his eyes actually seemed sincere. Too bad. She couldn't take the chance of lowering her guard. "So you say." At this point, she considered everyone either a current enemy or a probable, future enemy. Life proved safer that way.

Their turn arrived, and they stepped to the front of the line. Halah met the seated man's stare without flinching. *Here we go.*

"How many?" he asked, paying her little attention.

"Three."

He looked over her captives. "Two males and a female?"

"That's right."

"Mine workers, medical research, sex service, personal attendance, or return for auction?" He recited the list as if he'd said it a hundred times today already.

"Personal attendance — all three."

"Your name?"

"Halah Shirota."

"ID number?"

"HS-48-114."

He checked her records. "You're cleared for up to four slaves. These are your first, correct?"

"Yes."

"Their names?"

She hesitated, but only a moment. She hoped he didn't notice. "Leila, Erik, and Kam." She pointed out each of them. In case this whole thing backfired on her, she had to tell as much of the truth as she could. She wouldn't be able to claim ignorance of their identities, because of her prior Earth mission to locate them.

"Last names?"

"They didn't tell me." She knew from their files, but this man didn't know that. If questioned later, she could claim he didn't ask...or something. She could fool most of her adversaries, as long as no one who personally knew her history discovered the deception.

"Origin?" When she didn't immediately answer again, the man looked up from his computer screen. His eyes narrowed. "Xylon Warriors?"

No matter their clothing, they held themselves like Warriors. She'd bluff. "They arrived in an unmarked orbiter, not a Xylon civilian or Warrior-tagged vessel." Again, she told the truth, though made it sound a bit misleading. Xylons were highly sought after, and Warrior slaves were considered a prize. Nobody would lie about such a capture. He'd have no reason to check further. They didn't need that much time to finish this mission. Hopefully, she'd be off-planet by the time their deception became known.

Without full names, the three wouldn't pop up on the computer as *wanted* by Dome Authorities upon data entry. That would buy them extra time. The Dome consolidated records at the end of each extended work cycle. Once that occurred, their identities would be matched up, but they'd all definitely be out of here by then. If they wanted to live, and regain their freedom, they had no other choice but to guarantee departure before the consolidation, whether they'd accomplished the mission or not.

"Step to the side for tagging and a body and retina scan." He handed Halah a coded card.

Leila, Erik, and Kam each received a wristband coded with their information, and retina scans were taken. Then, one by one, they stepped into a box-shaped body scanner. Hopefully, Rave had taken care of things as promised or alarms would sound like crazy due to their breeder status.

"They're clear," she was told. "Do you want them collared?"

"No. It's not necessary. They're more docile than they look." If collared, they'd be almost completely under The Dome's control. Pain was sent through the collars to punish or contain an unruly slave, as well as monitoring whereabouts and physical health. The only way to disengage a collar was from the main control room. She didn't have access to that, nor did she know how to operate the system.

"You understand one public infraction and the collar becomes mandatory."

"Yes, I know."

"Very well. You can go. Next!"

Halah breathed a sigh of relief. She led them out of the room and into a large courtyard. Egesa, Dome workers, and owners with slaves headed to various destinations.

Between the emotional and physical strain, Halah felt nauseous. They needed to get to her quarters soon, before she collapsed. Unfortunately, they'd have to walk. Slaves weren't allowed to use transport-connectors. Not that she'd trust them with a connector, as she'd said earlier. But it certainly would make the journey easier.

Erik looked around. "I didn't realize so much of The Dome was aboveground. Our intelligence hasn't kept up with Daegal's development plans."

"They've expanded The Dome over the past few months. Many areas are still under construction. The main control areas and all high-level quarters are still underground. Some other facilities and quarters, as well. The transport center we came through is actually a secondary facility, which is why it wasn't very busy. The main transports are still kept underground until needed, then they're brought up through the transport lift, much like in The Lair. Now, follow me, and don't cause any problems, especially in public. If you're fitted with a collar, you will remain here on a permanent basis, because I won't be able to unlock you."

"Torque knows how to unlock the collars," Leila said. "He did it on the Egesa ship where we were held."

"Well," Halah sighed, her frustration level rising. "This Torque person isn't here, is he? So, do as I say." Moving out of the center court to a shaded area, she took out her vid-cell and called Dak. No way could she walk the distance to her quarters. He'd have to pick them up.

* * * * *

Daegal pulled his wrap closed and sat in front of his panel of monitors. He longed for the days when he used to take a hands-on approach to running The Dome. Now, with his physical problems, he rarely left his quarters.

Most days, Gabriella kept him satisfied with her exceptional lust. He felt ten years younger every time he fucked her. At least his prowess hadn't dampened with his other weaknesses.

But something was afoot. He felt it. Her sexual talents aside, he knew she'd already betrayed him once, and he suspected her of doing so again on an even larger scale. He wasn't as gullible as she'd like to believe.

For some time now, she'd been poisoning his food, and drugging the Top Commander's. He'd noticed from the first taste, his senses still ultra-keen. Soon after, they had both started ingesting a special counteragent that prevented the poison's absorption—provided by his personal Healer—and would continue to do so, until he figured out her plans and decided how to take care of her.

Neither of them needed to feign sickness, because their decrease in power and growing pain from their already existing medical problems fooled her into thinking her actions were the cause. The conniving bitch. He'd never confided the whole truth of his illness to her. Nor had he ever revealed the Top Commander's illness at all, since the man still seemed fairly able-bodied and in control of himself. That decision now worked to his advantage. Their decrease in health would appear to her as caused by her poison. She'd regret her actions. A particularly nasty surprise would befall her very soon. Nobody betrayed him.

After a quick knock, and without waiting for entry permission, the Top Commander rushed into his quarters. "Good. You're here. Sorry to interrupt. We have trouble." He glanced down at Daegal's lack of clothes. "Hmm. Just a guess, but have you spent the day fucking Gabriella?"

"Why?" Strange thing to ask.

"Rave jumped me and wouldn't let me out of bed, until just a while ago. She was quite aggressive about it. More so than usual. Looks like Gabriella did the same to you."

Ah, so the plot turned even more intriguing. "Interesting. Most likely, they didn't want us to see something that occurred today. Reset the monitors to track their movements more closely." Not long ago, he'd watched them fucking on video. Mildly entertaining. And they'd also met several times on "business", according to Gabriella, though she never related any details. "Given Gabriella's deception lately, I think it's safe to assume those two are working together and planning something."

"Agreed. I'll take care of the monitoring. Do you want to review the day's vid-disks to see if we can spot anything?"

"That would take forever, since we wouldn't know which area to view. This whole planet is monitored. Put some trusted men on it instead."

"Will do."

"Wait, let me check Gabriella's recent browsing." He typed in some commands at his control panel. "It looks like she's been viewing the slave processing area, the upper transport center, and Med Lab more than any others. Concentrate on those areas first."

"All right."

"What did you bust in for?" The man had come here for a reason, before they'd gotten distracted by Gabriella and Rave's nefarious activities. "You said something about trouble." Just what they didn't need more of.

"I'm getting in reports of Egesa collapsing all over the place and dying just as suddenly."

His heart lurched. He needed the Egesa. "Everywhere?"

"Just in The Dome right now."

Daegal wondered if Gabriella had poisoned their food source as well. "Have all food sources checked. How has this hurt us so far? And what's your assessment long range?"

"I've received some reports of slave uprisings in the mines. Nowhere else yet. Our plans for Xylon are still set. No off-moon Egesa have been affected that I can verify. I'm dispersing Assassins where I can, to maintain control. The Lair has shut down. They probably picked up our troop movements, and they may have made a deal with Gabriella to arrange the poisoning. They're wily bastards. If all the Egesa perish, we won't be able to maintain defense of the moon."

"Call those who are off-moon back, except for the ones on the Xylon mission."

"Shouldn't the mission be delayed? If there's a strong retaliation, we won't be able to defeat them."

"For now, just have our patrols stand by. I'll make a final decision after I know the extent of the problem."

* * * * *

Kam helped Halah into her quarters. "Easy." She looked pale and ready to pass out. She'd already stumbled twice since they left the rover topside. She refused to allow herself to be carried.

Erik and Leila entered behind them, followed by Dak. "You need me to stay, Halah?" Dak asked.

"No, I'll be fine with them. Go back and watch over Bron. I don't trust Marid's Healers to take care of him without some supervision."

Kam studied her face. She immediately masked the concern in her eyes, as if embarrassed to show she cared.

She carefully sat on a beige lounger and leaned back. As Dak left, she waved toward a door. "Leila and Erik, the slave area is over there. That's where you two will stay."

"What about Kam?" Leila asked.

"He stays with me."

Kam stood frozen in place, shocked at her statement. He'd noticed her interest in him, but hadn't expected her to take him into her bedchamber. He didn't say anything to dissuade her though. This turn of events might be to their advantage.

If he shared her bed, he could watch Halah's actions more closely and make sure she didn't try to betray them to Daegal. He didn't like to think about her switching loyalties, but knew they needed to practice caution where she was concerned. Beyond that, the idea of possible sex with her wasn't an unpleasant one.

Leila's voice came out tight. "I need to change your bandages to something more sterile. And I'd like to apply a salve to fight infection."

"Fine. Medical supplies are in that cabinet by the laundry processor."

Kam and Erik exchanged a quick glance. Erik hid his thoughts, but Leila obviously disapproved of the arrangements. Her whole demeanor screamed her feelings. Kam couldn't signal anything to Erik because of Halah's Class 1 Warrior training. She knew what the signals meant. They'd have to talk later. He looked down at Halah instead, while Leila hovered over her, checking her wounds. "We need to wrap up this mission quickly. Can I get on your computer?"

"Go ahead."

"Is it password-protected?"

"No, but the information you're seeking will be."

"I'll handle it." Torque was better at cracking code, but he'd manage. He knew what information they already had and what they still needed on Daegal and The Dome. If he found the data, Marid wouldn't stand a chance against the more technologically advanced Xylon. Even with former Warriors in their camp, they'd been unable to progress at the same rate as The Lair.

* * * * *

Braden hung his head as tears burned his eyes. He took a deep breath, refusing to show his emotions while in the Control Center with other Warriors milling around.

Torque continued to flip switches and type in command codes. "Are you sure that is Alexa's correct tracking code?"

"Yes. You can double-check the code in the database." He couldn't handle this. He felt like shouting, tearing up the room, running until he collapsed from exhaustion.

His mate. Alexa. His love. His children. Gone.

"Damn it!" Torque hit the control board. "Nothing. I can't even track her transport-connector. It's like that particular handheld never existed. This doesn't make any sense. I've run a diagnostic twice, and I can't find any errors in the system."

So, that was that. The main tracker hadn't been operational for long, and apparently bugs still existed. No other explanation seemed feasible. With a heavy heart, Braden turned from the data screens and headed out of the room.

"Braden? Where are you going?"

He didn't answer. He couldn't, even if he had known where he was going, which he didn't. He just hoped Torque let him go. He couldn't face anyone right now. He needed time alone to think.

"I'll keep looking, Braden."

Home. That's where he'd go, where he could feel Alexa's presence and see her soft touches. He stepped out into the corridor. Empty. Good. Torque didn't follow, and no one else stopped him.

Again, he tried to locate Alexa through the connection between their implanted brain chips. He concentrated as hard as he could.

Empty. Black. Dead. A scream welled up inside him, but he contained his pain. If he broke down now, he'd certainly lose his sanity for all time.

A body. He needed to see her body. Without that, he would never believe she was truly gone and always wonder if she was waiting for him to come for her.

He needed to make plans for an extensive search. He'd do it alone if need be, if the Council refused to release a search party.

Stopping in mid-stride, he turned and smashed his fist into the wall. He didn't care about the pain. Without Alexa, he didn't care about anything.

* * * * *

Leila joined Erik in the slave area and sat down with him among a pile of dingy pillows. Strangely, she didn't feel the exhaustion she'd expected. "You look relaxed, given the situation."

"Looks are deceiving. How's Halah?"

"She'll be all right. Kam is still on her computer, searching for the information we need. Are these quarters safe?" She glanced around, wondering if they were being monitored.

"I couldn't find any monitors or listening devices, but then I don't have any special equipment to locate anything that might be well-hidden."

"Do you think we can trust her?" She'd already decided Halah unworthy of trust, but she wanted Erik's opinion.

"No. She's a traitor. I'll never trust her, and you shouldn't either."

"Agreed. What's next?"

"We'll need to contact Braden, when we can. Let him know our status. And check up on Halah's sister to make sure she's in place."

"Halah is not going to let us do that. If the transmission is picked up by Marid Control—"

"She has to know a secure way to do it. She contacted Braden with no problems."

"Well, true." She glanced toward the door. "Have you noticed the interest she's taken in Kam?"

"Difficult not to." He turned her chin back toward him and smiled. "Jealous?"

Though Erik smiled, she saw the serious question in his eyes. "Concerned. I don't want him hurt. She wants to use him."

"I think he's smart enough to figure her out. Maybe he can keep her in line. And I don't think he'll mind a little suck and fuck if she jumps him." Erik chuckled, dropping his hand from her chin to a pillow.

"I'm not amused. She almost electrocuted him on Earth." She worried about Kam and wondered if he needed another shot for his headaches. He hadn't said anything, but then she doubted he would until the mission ended, no matter his pain.

"Me, too. She delivers a powerful zap."

Her hands fluttered over his arms and chest. Fear over what could have happened to him gripped her. "She's dangerous, Erik."

"Don't worry." He grasped her hand and kissed the palm. "She won't hurt him. We need the sterilization formula and a safe way out of here. She needs the information on her sister. It's a perfect arrangement. So, for now, you might as well relax."

"I just want this over with."

"I know, but we won't be able to get into the Med Lab undetected until the early hours of the morning at best. And Kam may need a few days to retrieve the information from the computer, depending on the security."

Leila sighed. "I know you're right. But how am I supposed to relax?"

"Oh, I can think of a few ways."

* * * * *

Kam turned off Halah's computer. He'd copied the information he'd retrieved onto a disk. Where he was going to hide it, he wasn't sure. A slave couldn't walk around toting a data disk. For now, he just set it next to the computer screen.

The data was almost too easy to find and unlock. Suspicion nagged at him. He shook his head, dismissing the feeling, and attributing his uneasiness to a mission he wanted ended before all hell broke loose. If the information he'd found proved accurate, they'd be able to destroy The Dome and everyone in it.

His thoughts immediately went to the poor slaves...and Halah. Something would need to be done to save the innocents before any destructive measures were taken. Braden had no idea of the volume of slaves actually held here. None of them did.

Since he'd found the information they needed so soon, they'd be able to leave Marid earlier than anticipated, if Leila retrieved the formula quickly. He hoped Braden had Josella secured.

He glanced over at Halah, stretched out on the lounger. She'd barely nibbled on the hunk of bread Leila had found for her in the food preserver earlier. She really should be in bed right now. He stood up and walked over to her. "Do you want me to help you into your bedchamber?"

Her eyes met his. "Yes."

Her immediate response surprised him, not only her acceptance of help, but her soft tone. He thought she must be in more pain than she'd admitted. Instead of helping her to her feet, he reached down and picked her up in his arms. Her eyes revealed momentary surprise, but then she accepted his actions and relaxed. "Which way?"

"That door." She pointed opposite the slave area.

Good placement. The distance would aid them, if they needed to sneak out on her. He entered her bedchamber, expecting what he didn't know, but not what he found. Everything looked stark, generic, no color at all. Almost sad, was the description that came to mind. And he saw no personal items displayed or sitting around.

"What's wrong?" she asked him.

"Nothing." He laid her on the bed. He certainly wasn't going to say anything and possibly offend her. They still needed her help.

"Stay with me."

The words weren't a request, but a lightly veiled order. He recognized the tone and grinned. She sounded more like herself now, which was a good sign of healing. He sat beside her on the bed. "Are you in pain? Do you need some medication?" He rubbed his temple, not wanting her to go through what he did almost on a daily basis.

"I'm all right. Come morning, my wounds will most likely be completely healed." Her eyes narrowed. "You're in pain. Why?"

Her perception surprised him. He shook his head. "It's nothing." Leila didn't have the medicine he required for relief. No matter how bad he got, he'd need to wait until they returned to Xylon for treatment.

She reached up and stroked his temple. He felt a small shock and instantly jerked back.

"Sorry. Better?"

Kam rubbed the skin she'd touched, amazed at the decrease in pain. She'd sent a small electrical charge through him that somehow eased the throbbing. "What did you do to me?"

"A little perk of my electrical training. I discovered the ability years ago. It only works on certain kinds of pain. Consider that zap an apology for the one I gave you on Earth."

He wanted to question her further, but saw that she was tiring and knew other matters took precedence right now. "Leila should search the Med Lab for the formula tonight." He felt guilty pushing her, but they needed to get out of there and back to Xylon. The longer they stayed, the more uncomfortable he felt. If they could leave within twenty-four hours, all the better.

"I'll take her early in the morning when the least amount of staff are on duty."

"How are we going to get off Marid, now that our orbiter has been salvaged?"

"That's your problem."

Kam glanced down at her and cocked an eyebrow. A difficult woman with complex emotions, for sure. He wished he had his wrist sensor to read her true feelings.

She frowned at him. "Fine. I'll arrange it. I'll have Dak place another orbiter on reserve. Can you or Erik pilot an Egesa orbiter?"

"Yes. All three of us can. You're coming with us, right? Braden will most likely bring Josella to Xylon."

"Wait." She sat up straight, cringing. "Most likely? You don't know where my sister is?"

"Careful. Don't reopen those wounds. We don't know Josella's exact location. Not until we check in with Braden. He felt safer doing it that way. We'll contact him before we leave here. You have a secure way?"

"Yes." She relaxed back against the pillows. "But I'm taking my own ship, wherever she is. Even if she's on Xylon, I'll follow you. Don't betray me, Kam. If you do, you'll regret it."

Careful to avoid her injuries, he caressed the back of her hand. "I won't, Halah."

"Somehow, this isn't how I pictured us in bed together," she whispered, her words slurred. She curled her fingers into his palm, then reached over and massaged his cock. Her fingers relaxed against him, and her eyes drifted closed.

"Maybe one of these days," he mumbled, moving her hand back to her lap.

His gaze roamed her body. She was too skinny, but had nicely rounded breasts and hips. And extra-long legs. Her hair was shorter than he usually liked on a woman, barely down to her shoulders, but the black strands shone in the light. He let his fingers touch the beautiful tresses. Silky and soft to the touch, too. Her mouth, now relaxed and with no tension surrounding it, revealed full, kissable lips. Her skin looked like cream.

Though he knew she wasn't up to sex, desire still shot through him. His dick stirred in his pants. "Damn."

* * * * *

As he stood at the door, Daegal looked down at Gabriella, now resting and still tied to the bed after their latest fucking session. He brushed his fingers along his flaccid dick. Yep, the woman was one hot whore. Such a shame she wasn't a loyal bitch. He strolled into the living area and over to his screens.

The video of Halah bringing the Warriors through processing had been found. If he hadn't suspected something odd, it would have taken a lot longer to detect their presence. And he'd found where Gabriella had tampered with the body scanners, too.

She helped sneak the Warriors in for some reason. He didn't believe she was working for The Lair though. Gabriella kept her own agenda.

He'd also heard about Halah's challenge of the Egesa Commander. One of his best soldiers. Word of the loss spread quickly through the ranks. The Egesa was probably weakened by the poisoning in the food. The Top Commander confirmed the find not long ago. The idea of Halah defeating the Commander with her skills alone was ludicrous.

Why the Warriors had come here, he didn't yet know. But he could guess. Information. He often sent his own people to Xylon for the same reason. The fact that they'd brought a Healer with them made him think their interest involved the sterilization formula. They couldn't possibly know about its ineffectiveness yet.

Well, let them look for the formula. Let them find it even. They weren't getting off Marid. At least, not alive. He'd see to that. As long as the truth about the formula didn't get out, Xylon would fear his control of all future generations. If he found a way for himself to survive…

He glanced back toward the bedchamber. Gabriella obviously wanted him dead. But why? Certainly, she didn't have command aspirations, as the Top Commander had suggested when he'd reported the poison found. If he died, Marid would plunge into anarchy. Whatever her plans, he'd decided not to wait. The opportunity for payback tonight proved too deliciously perfect to pass up.

As more information poured in, he watched his screens. Rows of numbers popped up on one monitor. He frowned. Even though food sources were now locked down, the death rate of the Egesa continued to climb. If word got out, Xylon would attack while they held the advantage. He'd decided to call off his planned surprise invasion. Retaliation might place them in too vulnerable a position.

Right now, retaliation of another sort loomed in his mind. He strolled back to the bedchamber. "You awake, Gabriella?"

"Oh, yes. That was a great fuck. What's next for tonight?"

"I have a little surprise for you."

She stretched on the bed and smiled up at him. "I do so love your surprises. Tied or untied this time?"

"I'll leave you tied for this one."

"Oooh, good. What is it, my love?"

He remained by the door of the bedchamber and pulled a remote control from a pocket in his wrap. "Watch the box." He nodded toward a silver box on a long stand at the end of the bed, on the other side of the footboard.

As he pressed a button on the remote, Gabriella watched in fascination.

The top of the box eased open. For a moment nothing happened, then hundreds of Mucous Spiders rushed out of the box, crawled over the footboard, and onto the bed.

Gabriella screamed, her voice shrieking with her terror. "No! No! No!"

Daegal laughed. "Have fun, my dear." He closed the door, his only regret being he'd have to fumigate the room to get rid of the critters, then have a cleanup crew come in to remove them and Gabriella's body. The whole affair was going to make a mess. "Well, I wanted to redecorate anyway."

Now he needed to figure out what fate to bestow on Rave, who was part of this betrayal. She'd been a good Assassin for him. Too bad.

First though, he'd take care of Halah and confiscate her "slaves" for himself. He needed to interrogate them. They might know where Laszlo was hiding. And finding Laszlo had become imperative to his survival.

* * * * *

Erik settled in next to Leila on their makeshift bed. "They're asleep. The main door is rigged though, so we can't get out without setting off an alarm. I didn't see Halah set it, so either it's automatic, or Dak set it somehow when he left earlier. I might be able to crosswire the thing, but unless there's a reason, I'd rather not take a chance of accidentally setting it off. Her transport-connector is probably in her bedchamber. I couldn't find it. And I can't find any communication devices that are for anything other than on-planet. So, for now, we're stuck."

"Are they fucking in there?"

Erik barked out a laugh. "You're blunt these days." He still wondered if she were jealous. She seemed too concerned about Kam's sex life. "Not at the moment. Nor earlier, from what I could tell. Kam's still in his pants, and she's still in her clothes, too. And asleep, last I saw."

"She's probably not well enough to do anything anyhow."

"Probably. We have at least a good four hours before we can get into the Med Lab. We should try to sleep." He frowned as she glanced toward the door. "Stop worrying about Kam. He's a big boy. Now lie back and get some rest."

"Rest, hmm?" She smiled up at him, a glitter of mischief in her eyes. "Or…"

"Or what?"

"*We* could fuck." She flipped her hair behind her shoulders, exposing her bare breasts to him.

Erik about swallowed his tongue. His gaze caressed her bare skin, and his tiredness immediately disappeared. He raised his eyes to study her face. "Not that I'm complaining, Leila, but your complete turnaround about sex is something I'm not quite used to yet."

"It's your fault, you know." She smiled and rubbed little circles along his thigh. "And the others."

"Yes. I suppose it is." He smiled back and caressed her cheek, grateful that Leila was full Xylon. Her genetics gave her an advantage psychologically. He knew other women damaged by abuse, mental and/or physical, and not full Xylon, who weren't able to heal their psyches as quickly, if at all. He suspected Xylon genes combined with their self-healing elements weren't only helpful for physical wounds, but mental ones as well, even though no official studies had been conducted in that area that he knew of.

Her smile faded, and her eyes took on a serious glint. "I want to know your most carnal need, Erik. We're about as alone as we're going to get for quite some time. So, tell me."

With an equally serious demeanor, he leaned into her. "My most carnal need, Leila, is...you." He kissed her gently on the lips.

No words came out of her mouth, and she looked stunned.

Her wide-eyed gaze and silence worried him. Maybe he should have made up a lie instead of revealing the truth to her. Speaking his need aloud didn't sound as impressive as the thought of it in his head. He wondered about her mood right now, but feared asking. He felt too vulnerable from exposing himself. "Disappointed that it wasn't something erotically nasty?"

"How can I be?" Leila sniffled, tears forming in her eyes. She wrapped her arms around him.

Erik's heart expanded in his chest. He couldn't remember ever connecting to a woman as deeply as with Leila. She felt like a part of him. During the re-initiation he'd licked the back of her neck and told her "someday", wanting her to know his intent to Brand her. As soon as they returned to Xylon, he wanted to bind her to him forever. He swallowed hard. "Leila, will you permanently join with me?" Even though not the proper place or time, the question popped out before he could stop it.

She sat with a stunned look on her face. Her mouth opened, then closed, then opened again. "Yes," she gasped. "Oh, yes."

Joy like he'd never felt soared inside him. He hugged her to him, never wanting to let her go. "I want to make love to you,

Leila. Right now." He pulled back to gaze at her beautiful features, unable to get enough of her.

Tears shone in her eyes. "I'd like that, Erik," she whispered. "I-I'd love that."

"I love you, Leila." He gulped. He'd never said those words to a woman.

"I love you," she whispered, her voice catching in her throat.

He felt as if his whole life had new meaning. His hand covered one of her breasts. Knowing she'd agreed to be his added new intensity to his feelings. "So soft." When his thumb brushed across her already hardened nipple, she mewled. He loved her responsiveness. "Your skin is so sensitive, Leila."

"To your touch."

He smiled. To his touch. He leaned down and lapped at the nipple. Delicious. Her fingers slid through his hair, caressing his head, encouraging him. He ached for the feel of her hands on him always. He sucked the fleshy bud into his mouth.

"Mmm. Yes, Erik."

He pushed her down flat against the pillows, continuing to suck her. Leila arched her back, pushing her breast further into his mouth. He lightly nibbled on the hard peak, until he felt her tremble. He pulled the nipple gently with his teeth, then released it.

Leila sighed.

Erik's hand slid over her ribs and down her stomach. Again, he felt her tremble. Or maybe that was him, this time. He pulled off her barely there slave skirt. She lay naked beneath. Even though he'd seen her naked more than once, the first look always took his breath away.

He caressed her thighs. "You're the most beautiful woman I've even known, Leila. Inside and out." His dick hardened painfully. He unlaced the front of his slave attire and pushed off the tight pants.

As she looked at his dick, hard and ready to go, Leila licked her lips. Intentionally or not, the movement made him crazy.

"Too sexy, Leila. I'll lick your lips." He leaned down and traced her mouth with his tongue, then whispered, "You lick my dick."

Without any further encouragement, she scrambled to her knees in front of him.

Her eagerness made every muscle in his body tense in anticipation.

Leaning over him, her tongue eased out and licked the beads of clear liquid atop his penis.

At the touch of her tongue, Erik jerked. "Ah, yeah." He tangled his fingers in her hair, guiding her. "Lick the underside, baby."

She grazed her tongue up and down the underside of his cock. With a gentle touch, she flicked the sensitive skin on the backside of the bulbous head, making him groan.

He loved watching her tongue move over his dick. The incredible, moist feel shot through him like electricity. "You will do as I say. You will submit to me." He needed her submission.

She glanced up at him. "Yes, Erik. I will submit to you. And…"

"And?"

"You will submit to me."

He laughed and cupped her cheek. An interesting topic actually. He'd never submitted to a woman. Not totally. "Suck my dick, but don't make me come."

She cocked an eyebrow at him.

"We'll talk about my submission later."

Leila took him into her mouth and bobbed up and down. "Mmm."

Her enjoyment of the act almost sent him over the edge. He worked hard to maintain control. He didn't want to climax yet, nor did he want her to stop. "Suck it good, baby. Oh, yeah.

That's perfect. Suck." He needed to make this fuck phenomenal for her. Between only the two of them, with no audience, he didn't want her disappointed. "Ah...enough, for now." He gently pushed her back.

She smiled up at him. "I love the way you taste." She stroked his thigh.

He grabbed her hand before he embarrassed himself and came right then. "On your back." He barely got the words out. He wanted to dominate, control, make her come. He couldn't fight his carnal need of her, nor did he want to.

She laid back.

"Spread your legs."

Again, she did as he directed.

His heart pounded against his ribs, as he tried to keep himself from simply falling on her and fucking her like a wild animal. "Spread them wider. Bend your knees to the side."

Slowly, erotically, she widened her thighs.

He stared down at her pussy, open and weeping for him. He could almost taste her on his lips, on his tongue.

Suddenly, he understood. He might be leading her sexually, or think so, but he was most certainly just as much, if not more, at her sexual and emotional mercy. The realization hit him hard, and he knew that soon his control would shatter. He looked into her eyes. "They're going to hear us."

She glanced at the door, then back at him again.

"Are you sure you want this? Here? Now?" He needed to give her a last chance to stop their passion from escalating to the point of no return.

"Yes, Erik. I want this. I want *you*. Love me. Take my body. Fuck me until..."

"Until?"

Her eyes locked with his. "Until I can't come any more."

A tight breath stuck in his lungs. His desire for this woman ran hotter and more intense than he'd ever experienced.

Anything she wanted, he'd give her. He nodded, exhaling heavily. "Yes, Leila. I'll fuck you until…"

Chapter Ten

Erik bent over her pussy. He gently spread her moist folds, determined to give her an experience she'd never forget. He knew tonight would be singed into his memory for all time. He wanted her to share the same memory.

Her hand gently touched one of his, and her eyes revealed a tenderness that made his heart lurch in his chest. His need for her burned stronger than ever. His gaze shifted from her cinnamon eyes to her delicious pussy, and the scent of her sex teased his nostrils, exciting him even further. "Do you want my tongue in your pussy, Leila?"

Leila arched toward him. "Yes. Do it."

Her need matched his own. His heart pounded against his ribs, and his pulse raced in anticipation. Leaning lower, he feathered his tongue across her clit, then swirled his tongue in a slow circle. Her unique flavor exploded on his taste buds.

She gripped the pillows on either side of her hips, her fingers clenching the fabric tightly.

With a gentle touch, he flicked his tongue against her clitoris. He wanted to build her pleasure a little at a time until she exploded.

"Ah, suck it. Please…"

He sucked the bud into his mouth and drew on the sensitive flesh.

"Oh, Erik."

Erik slid his palms beneath her ass and raised her pelvis for better access. He sucked, slowly and steadily, giving her what she wanted and needed, taking from her what he wanted and needed.

"Yes, Erik. More!"

When he felt her muscles tighten, he eased his lips from around her clit, purposely halting her pending climax.

"No, don't stop." She whimpered. "I need to come."

He caressed her thighs, enjoying the flush on her body. "Not yet, baby. Touch yourself. I want to watch."

A sexy smile eased onto Leila's face. She reached between her legs, and her fingers teased her clit. A small moan rose from deep within her. Her eyes fluttered closed, and she bit her bottom lip.

Erik swallowed hard, moving his hand up and down his cock. So hot. He'd watched her pleasure herself before, during the re-initiation. But this time, she did it all for him. "Now suck your fingers."

Opening her eyes, Leila brought her moist fingers to her lips and sucked her juices. Her sensual gaze never left his.

His voice caught in his throat. "Good?" he barely managed to get out.

With a look of delicious ecstasy in her eyes, she nodded.

He smiled at her, amazed at his fortune of having her in his life. "I agree." He lowered himself on top of her and held his cock at the entrance to her pussy. He hesitated. Control. He needed to maintain control. He eased forward and slid inside her one slow, thick inch at a time.

"Oh! Such delightful torture." She wrapped her legs around him and pulled him further into her body.

He pumped his cock, pushing all the way in, then pulling almost completely out of her. As his passion grew, he realized her love for him had truly saved his lonely soul. He didn't think so much emotion between lovers possible. He covered her lips with his, sliding his tongue into her mouth, tasting and teasing her.

With her internal muscles, she squeezed his cock.

He pulled his mouth from hers. "Damn, Leila," he gasped.

She squeezed his cock again, clamping her legs tighter around his hips. Her nails grazed the muscles in his chest, and she pinched his nipples.

"Ah!" He jerked. All gentleness and control evaporated. His hips pounded against her. He rammed his cock hard and fast into her pussy. He couldn't stop. And he couldn't go any slower or easier on her. She'd gotten him too hot with her actions. A loud groan escaped his throat.

Matching his rhythm, she undulated her hips, giving as good as she got. "Yes, Erik! Fuck me!"

With a growl, he grabbed her arms and shoved them above her head. He captured both her wrists with one hand and held tight. His hips continued to pump her hard. He tugged on one of her nipples, licked it, then tugged again. "You like that?"

"Yes, harder."

"Tug harder or fuck you harder?"

"Both!"

At her words, he felt his climax near to bursting. "You're killing me, Leila." He tried to focus on something else to delay the inevitable, but Leila kept distracting him with her hip thrusts, sexy mewls, and internal cock strokes. "Ah, hell." He nibbled on one of her nipples, then the other, scraping his teeth along her fleshy buds, harder, rougher, until she orgasmed.

"Erik!" Her climax shook her so strongly that she almost bucked him off. "Oh, Erik. Don't stop. I-I'm still coming. Oh!"

He continued to thrust hard. "Yeah!" He caressed her tits, squeezing and massaging the round flesh, and flicking his thumbs across her nipples.

Even though he'd released her wrists, she kept her arms above her. "Oh, Erik. I'm coming again!"

"Oh, yes. I feel it!" Her vagina gripped his penis. He fucked her wildly, his cum ready to shoot into her. How he was holding out for so long, he didn't know. His whole body trembled.

Leila continued to come. Many of Xylon's women were multi-orgasmic. She definitely possessed the ability. She screamed, and he felt a particularly strong climax shake her.

Her orgasms, with her pussy pulling at his dick, proved too much. He thrust as deeply as he could get and spilled his seed inside her. "Leila! Ah, yeah!" He shot cum that seemed to go on forever. The pleasure pulled a shout from him, and he shook violently, almost passing out from the sheer ecstasy of the experience.

Leila stroked his back until he collapsed on top of her. She kissed him gently. "I think you fucked me until... Just like you promised," she whispered.

All he could do was nod.

* * * * *

"So?" Daegal asked the Top Commander. "Where is Rave?" Once he took care of her and Halah, his female problems would be extinguished. Then he could concentrate on finding Laszlo, solving all their health problems, and destroying Xylon once and for all.

"I don't know. She's disappeared."

He stepped closer, forcing the Commander back a step. "Disappeared? We had her monitored." Was he totally surrounded by incompetence and deception?

"I know. Last we tracked her, she was going into Dare's quarters. Then she, Dare, and Shear disappeared. Maybe they found out about Gabriella."

"How? Her body hasn't even been removed yet."

The Commander shrugged. "Rave has a lot of connections. Who did you get the spiders from?"

Worry tugged at Daegal. Maybe this network of deception was larger than he thought. "I sent down an order for a group of slaves to collect them for me after I first found out about Gabriella's betrayal with our food. They couldn't possibly know I used them tonight."

"You sure about that? Did you place them in the bedchamber yourself?"

No, he'd told one of the female servants via vid-cell to do it, while he'd attended to business in his office. "Damn women. Can't trust a one of them. What about our hidden surveillance inside Dare's quarters?"

"Malfunctioning, apparently. All we're getting is static."

"Where are all of these malfunctions coming from?" Too many abnormalities kept occurring for simple coincidence. His suspicions, due to the vastness of the problems, led him to believe Laszlo held a hand in this somewhere.

"We haven't found the source yet."

"Did you check the transport-connector records? Maybe they relocated."

"Yes. Nothing."

"What about the transport center? Did they somehow leave the moon without our knowledge?"

"No unaccounted ships show up in the system."

"Did you search Dare's quarters for hidden rooms or escape passages?" He felt his temperature rising with his frustration.

"Yes. Again, nothing."

"That's impossible. They have to be somewhere. They didn't just disintegrate into thin air." He couldn't believe those three had managed to outwit them.

The Commander paced, in obvious thought. "There's a possibility they masked the usage of their transport-connectors."

"How?" Daegal blocked his path.

The Top Commander met his eyes. "Rave told me once that Halah managed to bypass the tracker routes while on Earth, to escape capture, when the Warriors held her. They may have shared information."

"Why would Halah share anything with Rave? And how is it that Halah figured out how to do that, when we don't know how? If she doesn't use the tracker channels, how does she find a clear route for transport materialization? That's ridiculously dangerous. Did you question Halah about the information after Rave told you?"

"No. I thought Rave made up the story. The idea seemed preposterous at the time. Still does."

Daegal sighed. He was getting tired of these former Xylon Warriors who came to The Dome, pretending to be loyal, but never really switching alliances or sharing information that Marid desperately needed. Their databases held mega-memory of personal information on current and former Warriors, but technically they fell far behind Xylon in their knowledge.

"Maybe Rave did speak the truth, after all. At least that would account for her disappearance. I screwed up by not following through. Xylon is more advanced, as is their Warrior Training. And Halah is an electronics genius, from what I understand."

"Halah is a pain in the ass, is what she is. Monitor her closely. I want to know her every move."

"Yes, sir."

* * * * *

Kam stood at the door to the slave area. "Leila," he called out lightly. "Wake up. Time to go."

A little at a time, Leila stirred. Carefully, she rose from the pillows.

Kam could tell she was trying not to wake Erik. Just as well, since he couldn't accompany her.

Earlier, he and Halah had heard them making love. Impossible not to. Halah wanted to watch, but he'd convinced her otherwise. Erik and Leila deserved their privacy. Besides, he wouldn't have been able to keep his hands off Halah if they'd watched what sounded like one hot fuck.

He waited while Leila pulled on her slave attire and adjusted her hair to cover her breasts. Sexy. He ached for relief.

Once they returned to The Lair, he needed to attend a Joining Party just to clear his head and bodily urges, even though he normally didn't care for the Warrior gatherings.

Leila walked up to him. She glanced over her shoulder at Erik, then returned her gaze to his. "I'm ready," she whispered.

He led her into the living quarters, where Halah was clipping items to her belt. "You have to go alone with Halah. She can explain your presence, if you get stopped and questioned. Erik and I would attract too much attention and be harder to justify."

Leila nodded.

"Let's go," Halah said. She looked over at Kam. "By the way, the door is rigged, so don't get any ideas about sneaking out of here. It's fitted with a tamper-alert beeper whose signal connects to my vid-cell. If you try to crosswire the pad, I'll know and materialize back here before you can trip the system."

"Understood." He'd already seen the engaged alarm pad earlier and wondered if Erik might be able to bypass the codes.

"How are you feeling?" Leila asked her. "Do you want me to check the bandages before we go?"

"No. I'm fine. We need to get you in and out, and all of us off Marid before we're discovered. I've been unable to connect with one of my contacts. Something's wrong."

"Serious?" Kam asked, concern building inside him.

"I don't know. But I have an uncomfortable feeling about this mission."

"You're not the only one," Leila replied, worry evident in her eyes.

"Let's get this over with. Come on."

After Leila and Halah stepped through the door, and the panel slid closed behind them, Kam saw the alarm reengage. He sat in front of the computer and fingered the disk he'd copied earlier. *Too easy.* The thought kept running through his head.

"Hey," Erik said from the other side of the room.

Kam turned and watched him enter from the slave area, rubbing his eyes.

"What's going on?" Erik glanced around the room.

"Halah and Leila just left for the lab."

"What?" He looked toward the door. "Why didn't you wake me?"

"You couldn't go with them, Erik."

Erik frowned, then after a moment visibly relaxed. "Yeah, I suppose not. Either one of us would look too suspicious out with her at this time of night. Or is it early morning now?" He yawned. "What are you doing?"

"Thinking we need to contact Braden. I was going to approach Halah after we had the sterilization formula in hand, but I think we need to be ready to go once that happens."

"Agreed. Where would she hide a communication device? To reach Xylon and connect with Laszlo's board, she'd need a powerful system, and in a private place, somewhere easily accessible to her, and where no one would overhear her, even if she had company, so she could communicate in an emergency, if necessary."

The both stared at each other. "Her bedchamber," they said at the same time.

"Let's look," Erik said.

They both entered her room and glanced around the interior. Erik picked up a round throw pillow from a chair, then set it back down. "Strange room."

"You noticed."

"Everything's gray. How could I not notice? Depressing. That woman possesses a scary psyche, in my opinion."

Kam thought "troubled" more accurately described Halah, but he didn't comment aloud. "How do you want to approach this?"

"Well, a control panel has to exist somewhere. You take that side, and I'll take this side."

* * * * *

Leila looked down each corridor they passed. Because of her slave status, they'd walked, but at least she got a good look at more of The Dome, which might prove useful to Xylon in the future. Everything she saw she tried to file away in her memory.

She couldn't believe how deserted the area seemed. Maybe a large number of soldiers and workers didn't really exist in The Dome as they liked their enemies to believe. Interesting.

Halah led her into the deserted Med Lab. "If we're caught and questioned, we're here to get help for my wounds. And you, as my slave, simply escorted me, because I'm still not walking all that well."

"Sounds reasonable." She glanced around. Totally empty. The area held an eerie feel, very unlike her comfortable and caring setup of the Med Lab in The Lair. "Isn't anyone at all on staff at this time? What if an emergency comes in?"

"There's an emergency button. The formula will be under security. I'll need to disable the system." She made her way over to an area with lots of shelves and cabinets, all labeled. "This is where they keep the pills and shots. The more sensitive formulas are locked up." She pointed to a large white unit in the corner.

"Refrigeration?"

"Partial, from what I understand." Halah opened the alarm pad. She pulled some tools from her belt and went to work. "Keep an eye out. I can explain our presence, but I can't explain tampering with the system."

"Isn't this place monitored?" She glanced around for vid-equipment and spotted a monitor in the far corner.

"I hacked into the computer system, and disabled all the monitors in this area before we left my quarters. It'll register on the main board, and they'll send a crew to check out the malfunction. But we'll be gone by the time they get here. Hopefully."

Halah's knowledge and abilities impressed her. "How did you learn so much about the workings of The Dome?"

"I made it a priority. Knowledge is power. An old, universal saying, but true nevertheless." She closed the pad and punched in some numbers. The door clicked open. "We're in."

Halah opened the door and motioned for her to enter. "Find what you need and get out fast. I'll stay by the door and watch for anyone passing by."

* * * * *

"Found it," Erik said, popping out of the bathing room. "I can't believe it's in her bath. Good cover. It's behind one of the tiled walls. I'll place a transmission to Braden." Finally, things were looking up on this mission.

Kam joined him in the bathing room. "How'd you find it?"

"These set of four tiles are a slightly different color. Very subtle. Almost looks like some damage occurred and the tiles ended up replaced. I pressed in on them, and these other tiles here slid back."

"Slick. Can you work the board?"

"Yep. Just like Xylon. Halah must have designed and set it up herself. I wonder how she knew about Laszlo's communication board and which channel to use to connect. Braden never did say. We just discovered the device ourselves not long ago. I'd love to question her about that." He flipped some switches, engaged the scrambling feature, then found the proper channel. Erik frowned.

"What's wrong?"

"Braden's not responding to Laszlo's channel. He should have it networked in to his vid-cell. I'll see if I can contact the main control area. I'll have to use voice transmission." He switched the channel. "This is Class 1 Warrior, Erik Rhodes, contacting Xylon Control. Do you read?"

After some static, a voice came out loud and clear. "Rhodes! This is Torque. What the hell are you doing on this channel? You were supposed to—"

"Scramble your transmission, Torque." The communication should be secure, but he didn't want to take any chances.

"All right. Done. What's going on?"

"We're inside The Dome. We have the information on Daegal. Leila is at the Med Lab looking for the formula now. Where's Braden?"

"He's...unavailable at the moment."

Unavailable? Erik looked over at Kam. Something was wrong. By his hesitant response, Torque obviously didn't want to explain over the airwaves, and they didn't have time to ask a lot of questions that didn't directly relate to the mission. Nor was it a good idea to lose focus right now by concentrating on whatever problem had developed in The Lair. His need to return to Xylon quickly escalated though. "Do you have Josella?"

"There's a hitch. We had her contained, but she escaped. I just got the word from Pitch. They're looking for her, though so far, nothing."

"Why would she run?"

"Hell if I know. When I had the chance to get off the Sand Moon, I took it. No telling what's going through that female's mind."

"What am I supposed to tell Halah?" He hadn't planned on this turn of events.

"It's your call."

Erik thought a moment. "All right. We'll tell her we have Josella on the Sand Moon. We just won't tell her that we don't have her precisely located or secured until the last second."

"We're going to betray her trust," Kam muttered, weariness lacing his voice.

"We don't have a choice, Kam. If we tell her now, she'll turn us over to the Egesa." His responsibility consisted of getting what they had come for and making sure everyone returned safely. He intended to do that job.

"We've registered some suspicious troop movements on Marid," Torque transmitted. "They seem to have pulled back from whatever they were doing, but I don't like it. Get out of there as soon as you can."

"Exactly our plans. We'll be coming in on a Marid orbiter." He looked to Kam for confirmation. At his nod, Erik continued, "Ours was damaged and has been salvaged and probably gutted by now."

"Understood. We're closed down to non-Xylon flights, but I'll have our trackers watch out for you. Transmit your identification code on our emergency channel as you approach orbit."

"Will do."

* * * * *

"Got it," Leila told Halah. "Marid's equipment is archaic, but this looks to be the formula. The compound contains the basic elements common to our protection fluids." The solution had better test correctly. A mistake was not acceptable. A second mission to The Dome would prove too dangerous to arrange right now.

"It's not their protection formula, is it?"

"I don't think so. A component to break down the main ingredient is present. I'll need Lair equipment and time to study the compound better. But I can't find anything else of interest in here, so I'm fairly certain this is it."

"Does the formula require refrigeration?"

"No, we lucked out."

"All right, let's get out of here. Let me have the vial."

"You?" Suspicion immediately took hold.

"Where were you planning to hide it?"

Hmm. "Good point. Here." Even though she knew it best to give the vial to Halah, since she had no place to carry it herself, she still handed over the formula reluctantly.

Halah slid the vial into her belt. They closed the unit, and she reset the alarm pad. "We're ready to go."

A sound of boots along the corridor stopped them.

"They're here to check the malfunction," Halah whispered. "Sounds like two of them."

Her heart racing, Leila moved to dart out of the room.

Halah grabbed her and pushed her against the wall. She planted a kiss right on her lips.

Leila froze, so stunned by Halah's actions she couldn't react.

When Halah brushed aside her hair and squeezed her bare breast, male laughter floated to her ears.

Halah stepped back, false surprise on her face. "Isn't there any place private these days?" she barked at the men who stood there grinning at them.

"Try your quarters," one of them suggested.

"That's so boring. I'm looking for a sexual kick. Something different. Certainly, you understand." She grabbed Leila's hand and grinned sexily at the men as they passed.

Their loud laughs followed them down the corridor.

As soon as they got out of range, Leila pulled away from Halah and wiped her mouth with the back of her hand. "That was disgusting. What happened to the 'seeking help for your wounds' plan?"

"Oh, you probably loved it." Halah chuckled. "Besides, it worked well. They didn't even think to question us. So, don't complain."

* * * * *

Erik studied Dak as he paced back and forth, while they waited for the women to return. The man had appeared in Halah's quarters without them noticing or without him tripping the alarm Halah had rigged up. He must have materialized in, which meant he and Halah were closer than he'd thought for her to allow him access to her entry code.

Dak told them that two ships were ready to go—one for him and Halah and one for the rest of them. Erik couldn't wait to get out of The Dome and off Marid, though he and Kam harbored a bit of concern about the data Kam had retrieved from the computer. Kam had told him how easily he'd broken the passwords. This whole thing might be a setup. But at this point, instead of giving Kam more time to poke around The Dome's system, he simply wanted to get the formula and get out of there. The formula itself was more important than the information on Daegal and The Dome, in his opinion.

Even if they found what they needed to destroy The Dome, they'd need to clear out the slaves, and remove any deadly bacteria that might spread into the atmosphere, not to mention a whole host of other pre-destruction operations. And if any of Marid's scientists ended up escaping, or were off-moon at the time of destruction, they could re-create the sterilization formula. Xylon would find itself right back in the same situation as now, if they didn't have a counteragent ready to go, even with The Dome destroyed. The formula came first.

The door opened, and Halah and Leila stepped inside.

Erik instantly relaxed when he saw Leila and saw that she was all right. He noticed Halah didn't reset the alarm. He assumed that indicated success. "Did you get the formula?" he asked to make certain.

"We have it," Leila told him.

"Wonderful. Good job, you two."

"The ships are ready, Halah," Dak said.

"What about Bron?"

"He's not well enough to travel. He can't self-heal, and as such won't be walking for some time."

Erik couldn't help but notice how unhappy Halah looked at the news.

"We can't wait." She turned toward him. "I'll show you the communications board now, so you can contact Braden."

"Well…" He scratched his chin. "Actually, we already found it in your bath and made contact."

"You found it?" She frowned, and a look of irritation crossed her face. "How clever of you." The sarcasm dripped from her voice. "Where is Josella?"

"Not until we get ready to board the ships."

Halah huffed out a sigh of frustration. "Fine."

"Can we get some decent clothing before we leave?" He glanced at Leila, having asked the question mostly for her sake and comfort.

"You need to stay in the slave outfits, or you'll attract attention with those wristbands."

"Lovely." Leila stroked her hair over her bare breasts.

"Can't we cut off the bands?" Kam asked.

"An alarm on the main control board will sound if we do. You need to wait until you're back on Xylon, or at least out of Marid's orbit, or The Dome can track where the band was broken."

Erik held out his hand. "All right. Leila. Kam. Let me have the disk and the formula for safe keeping."

"Halah has the vial," Leila told him.

He turned toward the woman, his hand outstretched.

"Where are you going to hide them?" she asked with a raised eyebrow.

"I created a spot. Not that I don't trust you, of course."

"Of course." She handed him the formula, and Kam handed him the disk.

As the ranking Class 1 officer, he felt better holding onto the items himself. At least he knew they were safe. Erik pushed them down his pants into a small pouch. He'd fashioned the pouch from one of Halah's underclothes found in a drawer, while the women were gone. The vial and disk should be safe there, unless he got searched for some reason. Though he figured a slave probably wouldn't rate a search for contraband—not a slave who'd already gone through processing.

"Are we ready to go?" Halah asked.

"Ready," Leila and Kam answered together.

"Let's go," Erik said. "The faster the better."

* * * * *

"Report?" Daegal asked.

"Two ships register as placed on standby in the secondary transport center," the Top Commander told him. "They do have clearance. Looks like Rave arranged for one of them a while ago, before she disappeared. She obviously didn't take the ship, which means she set it up for someone else, or if she did want to use it for herself, she either never made it to the orbiter, or is still planning to sneak aboard at some point. The second one was cleared by control for an off-planet visit to Sunevia for Dak. Supposedly, for a visit to his home planet. But given his loyalty to Halah, I think that's their escape. I've sent an Assassin to question Bron. He's one of her cohorts and was recently hurt in the encounter with the Egesa Commander. He might know specifics. They all had to know their deception would eventually be discovered."

"What about the surveillance in Halah's quarters? I suppose that's not working." Daegal's patience wore very thin right now. Excuses made him irritable, and he'd heard enough lately to last a lifetime.

"Surveillance in her personal space never worked for long. We've sneaked into her quarters to fix the malfunction multiple times, and always within twenty-four hours, the hidden monitors went back down."

"That's because she kept finding the equipment, you idiot. Cancel their clearance."

The man typed in a few commands at the main control panel. "Done."

"Place guards around the ships. If Halah shows up, take her and anyone with her into custody. Same with Rave. You've been monitoring Halah's external activity, at least, as I asked?"

"Yes, of course. She and the Healer went out together and returned to her quarters just a few minutes ago. We don't know exactly where they went. We lost the transmission. I think they visited the Med Lab. The surveillance system went screwy around there about the same time. I'm waiting for a report from maintenance. A couple of men were dispatched to check out the equipment failure."

Daegal hung his head. He took a moment before speaking, needing a sense of calm to keep control of his voice. "When captured, I want them alive."

"That might prove difficult. They won't be easily subdued, if their plan is to escape in that ship. If they lift off, they die, Daegal. It's already arranged."

Daegal nodded. He preferred them alive. He needed information. But their deaths would shake The Lair to its foundation. Not a bad alternate plan. "Are the Warriors collared?"

The Commander punched a few buttons. "No. None of them. We won't be able to control them remotely."

"Are they armed?" He needed to change their slave procedures, so that all slaves were collared, whether their actions or planet of origin necessitated it or not.

"Unknown."

"Do we have a clear visual between Halah's quarters and the upper transport center?"

"Monitors are going out all over the place. We can partially monitor, but don't have complete control right now."

"Sabotage?"

"I don't see how."

"Well, find out how!" If Laszlo were behind the malfunctions, and they could track the path of origin, they'd have him. Capture wouldn't be far behind.

* * * * *

Erik glanced around warily. He, Leila, and Kam followed Halah and Dak as though they were on a leisurely stroll. The hair on the back of his neck tingled. Something wasn't right. He felt a trap. The area looked too deserted, as if purposely cleared. Halah and Dak's boots echoed in the corridors and stairways.

The click of video equipment as the machines followed their progress seemed more than normal monitoring. In situations like this, he didn't feel comfortable being unarmed.

They approached the transport center and stepped inside. Halah stopped abruptly and herded them behind some orbiter panels stacked in the back.

"What's going on?" Kam asked.

"Egesa troops are stationed outside of our orbiters. We've been discovered."

"Shit," Erik cursed. "I knew it. Get us some weapons."

Halah hesitated a moment, then nodded to Dak. "Arm them."

From an equipment bag on his back, Dak handed a disruptor to him and to Kam. "These are a new design and work a little differently than the disruptors on Xylon. You need to flip open this chamber here and keep your thumb pressed to the unlock mechanism on the handle while you fire."

"Thanks," Erik responded. No wonder they hadn't been able to use the Marid weapons on their previous mission. This new bit of intelligence would prove valuable for future missions. "Stay close," he told Leila, wishing a better way existed to protect her. "Do either of you have a shield for Leila?"

Halah shrugged off her jacket and held it out. "Put mine on. The shield is already engaged."

"I can't take your shield," Leila protested.

"Take it," Halah and Erik said to her at the same time.

"I'll be all right," Halah checked her weapon. "You have a plan?" she asked Erik.

"You still determined to take your own ship?" he asked her.

"Damn right."

"That's going to make it harder."

"We're all going to die anyway." She grinned.

Erik laughed. She was still a Class 1 Xylon Warrior, no matter what, willing to run headfirst into an impossible situation. "Fine. What's stored in those supply barrels we hid behind earlier? Fuel?"

"The ones on the left have fuel. The middle ones are cleaning fluid. The ones on the right contain water. You can keep them apart by the colors."

"All right. The ships are docked on the outer end, so we're going to blow this place. We'll shoot the barrels. When the Egesa run for cover, we make our way up the ships' ramps fast. We can take off amid the chaos. After that, it's every man—or woman—for himself, so stay out of my airspace."

"And you stay out of mine. My ship is the one on the left and contains the extra fuel I'll need. You take the other one. It's armed and will get you to Xylon."

"Everyone ready?"

"First things first, Warrior," Halah said.

"What's that?"

"Where's my sister? Give me the coordinates, or we're going nowhere."

"She's on the Sand Moon." At least that was the truth. He didn't like double-crossing her on this deal. But a bigger issue lay at hand.

"The Sand Moon? What's she doing on that savage rock?" Her eyes held a concerned and wary look.

"I don't know how she got there. But our main tracker found her. Braden dispatched three Warriors to locate and hold her, until further orders."

"Where on the Sand Moon?"

"Don't know. The Warriors lost her. Sorry, Halah." Erik fired his disruptor, as did Kam, and the barrels exploded.

"Bastards!" Halah screamed. She and Dak fired at the barrels, spilling soapy cleaning fluid along the transport deck.

The Egesa guards and workers ran for cover as fire shot into the air. They slipped and slid on the mixture of fluids.

Halah pointed her weapon right at Kam. Erik raised his disruptor toward her, but Kam batted it down.

"Go!" Kam yelled at him.

He hesitated, but then he and Leila rushed up the ramp of the orbiter on the right.

"Come on, Kam!" Erik ordered. He saw Halah lower her weapon, hurt visible in her eyes, even from a distance.

She and Dak rushed up the ramp of the other orbiter. Halah stumbled halfway up, her thigh not yet completely healed. Dak returned to help her the rest of the way.

Kam ran up the ramp to join him and Leila. Until Halah closed her ramp, Kam kept watch, firing at the Egesa at the same time.

"Close the ramp!" Leila shouted to him.

Erik slid into the pilot's seat, and Leila seated herself next to him. Kam raised the ramp and closed the hatch. He rushed to the control area. He sat behind them at weapons' control.

"Everyone acclimate yourselves quickly," Erik ordered. "We have no time for indecisiveness."

"Halah is taking off in her ship," Kam reported. "I've got her on the screen back here."

Erik engaged the engines. Another blast rocked the area. Fire engulfed the building.

"Get us out of here," Kam told him. "The roof's coming down."

Egesa guards continued to fire at them, despite the presence of the uncontained fuel.

"Here we go," Erik said.

The orbiter moved forward out of the transport center and lifted up into the sky. Ground guns fired at them the entire time, but only resulted in minor structural damage.

"Looks like Halah is in the upper atmosphere. And there she goes. She's in orbit." Leila studied the screens in front of her. "A patrol of at least six is already up there firing upon her. The ground patrols must have alerted them."

"We have to help her," Kam said.

"Are you nuts?" Erik maintained hand control, preferring to pilot himself, instead of turning their fate over to the nav-computer. "She's the perfect diversion. While they're busy with her, we can get out of here."

"Erik, we betrayed her trust. We can't let her die."

"Shit!" *Morals.* Erik maneuvered the ship up into Marid's upper atmosphere and then punched them into orbit. He located Halah on the screen and headed for her. "If this gets us killed—"

"Two interceptors are coming up behind us," Leila reported.

"Weapons are ready," Kam returned.

"Fire at will. There's Halah, up ahead." Erik adjusted his screen resolution. "She's got four on her tail."

"Get us closer," Kam said.

"I found a secure communications channel." Leila flipped on the frequency. "I think I can contact her without our transmission being tapped into."

"Do it," Erik told her.

"Halah, this is Leila. Please respond. We're coming to help. Hold on."

The channel crackled, then Halah's voice came out of the speakers. "You come up on me, you bitch, I'll kill you all myself. You betrayed me. You're all a bunch of fucking—"

Leila cut the transmission. "She doesn't sound too happy."

Erik laughed. "Good assessment. All right. We're in range, Kam."

"I need Leila back here to fire at the patrols on our tails, while I help Halah."

Leila glanced over at him.

"Go," he told her. She wasn't completely trained in ship-to-ship weaponry, but she knew enough. Even if she didn't hit anything, she'd cause enough of a distraction to buy them some time.

Leila scooted out of her seat and took the empty chair next to Kam. "All right. I'm ready."

Kam and Leila both fired weapons simultaneously.

"She's destroyed one herself," Erik reported. "At least Dak's aboard with her to help. That ship is too big for just two people to handle its operation. She probably planned for Bron to accompany them. She's in for a time of it."

The orbiter shook as they took a hit.

"No damage," Leila reported.

An interceptor following Halah erupted into a fireball.

Kam cheered. "Got one!"

"She's shot through the net." Erik adjusted the navigation controls. "I'm following."

"Another interceptor is incapacitated. Not sure if I got that one or if she did. This equipment is older than I am."

"We're through the inner security net," Erik told them. "We're coming up on the outer shield. Keep those patrols off her butt, so she can shoot through. We'll follow right behind."

The orbiter rocked. Leila bounced from the seat and landed on the deck. "Ow!"

Erik looked over his shoulder. "You all right?"

"Yes." She scrambled back into the chair and strapped herself in. "Stupid piece of equipment came loose."

"Destroyed another patrol ship," Kam informed them. "Only three left."

"She's through the shield." Erik increased their velocity. "Following. I'm engaging our private tracker code early in case any Xylon orbiters are in the area and can help us."

A laser hit the orbiter and smoke filled the back. "Shit, they got one of the fuel tanks," Erik said. "Shutting it down. We're still functional. Damn it, woman!"

"What's wrong?" Leila asked.

"Halah was the one who hit us."

"Just back away from her. Let her go," Kam said.

"Already done." Erik veered off toward Xylon as Halah continued toward the Sand Moon. "We've still got two interceptors on us. The other one is following Halah."

A pop echoed in the orbiter. Leila looked around. "What—? Did you hear that noise?"

"The two interceptors are now breaking away. Looks like they're headed back to Marid," Erik reported.

"Why would they do that? Is a Xylon patrol on their way?" Leila unclicked the strap holding her in the chair at weapons' control.

"Not that I'm picking up," Erik answered.

She looked toward the back, then sat in the chair next to him at the front of the craft. "Do you want me to check out that noise?"

"No, stay up here with me. Kam, check it out."

"On it." Kam got out of his seat and headed back to where the pop had sounded. He flipped open a panel. "Well…we've definitely got a problem here."

"Report," Erik ordered. The man sounded too casual. The hair on the back of his neck rose.

"There's a bomb on board."

Chapter Eleven

Erik checked the airspace. Assured no other enemies lurked nearby, he put the ship on autopilot. He and Leila made their way back to where Kam stood. All three of them stared at a small bomb planted in one of the side compartments. Small, but large enough to destroy the ship. The timer on the top indicated they had seven minutes before the device blew.

"Eject it," Leila said.

"The casing is bolted in," Kam replied. He popped open the rest of the panels. "We don't have the tools to get it loose. Just one small tool kit. We'll never get the bolts off with anything in there. How long until we land?"

"Nine minutes," Erik reported.

"Can you disarm the explosive?" Leila asked Erik.

He looked over the casing and wires. "I can disarm quite a few explosive devices, but I've never seen this exact type before. It's old and certainly not a Xylon or Marid design."

"I wonder if there's one on Halah's ship too," Kam said.

"And I wonder if she planted this one." Erik didn't want to believe her responsible, but she'd specifically told him which ship to take. "She might have set us up right from the beginning." The bomb, the too-easy to get data, no telling what that sterilization formula really contained—the whole thing put a bad taste in his mouth.

"I'll never believe that of Halah," Kam argued.

"Yeah, I know." Softhearted Kam. Kam believed in Halah, believed in Laszlo, believed in the goodness of people. Not him, he knew better.

"I'm going to try and contact her," Kam said.

"She's out of range for the Marid communication devices. They're fairly short range on these ships. We can't contact her." Leila patted his arm. "She's smart and resourceful. She'll be all right. And I don't believe she planted this bomb."

Erik didn't comment. He grabbed the small tool kit from the storage unit. "I'm going to have to try to disconnect the explosive." He looked at Leila and a deep, painful sorrow filled him. If he couldn't disarm the bomb in time…

"You can do it," Leila told him, her trust in him evident in her eyes.

"I'm going to see if we're close enough to contact Xylon," Kam said. "I'll let them know what's going on."

Erik looked over the bomb. Multiple wires, each a different color, connected the device. Two wires led inside the casing, and two terminals were located on the outside.

The timer continued to run down. Each tick grated along his nerves. He wiped a hand down his face. Whatever he did would be guesswork at best. And this wasn't a time for educated guesses. "Do you have Xylon?" he asked Kam. He needed advanced computer support.

"Yeah. Torque's on. The signal is weak though. We're still a little far out for this equipment."

"Give me a headset."

Leila handed him the equipment he requested. Her trembling fingers brushed his and fierce determination to save them grew and burned in his heart, urging him on. He put on the headset and adjusted the mic. "Hey, Torque. Kam filled you in, right?"

"Yeah, I'm filled in. This situation doesn't sound good, Erik. What can I do to help?"

"I'm not familiar with this type of bomb. I need computer research support."

"Describe the device."

"About six-by-six, casing is bright green. Four wires— black, white, red, and yellow. Wait." He brushed away some dust. "Code on the side is SB-11412."

"Searching the computer databases."

"Hurry." If Xylon possessed no data on this bomb…

"Hey, I got it. Bringing up the disarming procedure now. Damn. That model must be fifty years old. Be careful. It's Sunevian and unstable, from what I'm reading here."

What more bad news could they receive? Sunevian. Halah was half Sunevian. Erik didn't voice his concerns aloud. Leila and Kam looked worried enough without him adding more doom and gloom to the situation.

"All right. First, unscrew the right terminal."

Erik carefully followed Torque's direction. One wrong move and they were all no better than the dust he'd brushed off the casing. "Done." Sweat dripped down into his eyes. He swiped it away, feeling suddenly very closed in. All the air in the craft seemed to disappear. He purposely slowed his breathing and forced himself to stay calm.

"Now cut the yellow wire."

"Speak up! This transmission is shitty. Did you say yellow?"

"Yes, yellow."

Luckily, the small tool kit contained what he needed for the job. "Cut."

"Unscrew the left terminal. Then cut the white wire."

"Hang on. Damn thing is screwed tight." Someone stripped it when they put the bomb together, probably on purpose. Damn it! "All right. Got it. And the wire is cut."

"Remove the bottom screws and then open the casing."

Four screws lined the bottom. He loosened and removed each one. Gently, he lifted the casing, trying not to rattle anything inside. "Open."

"Remove the inner chamber. Don't bump it on anything. And make certain the wires don't pull loose."

"Removing." He carefully set it aside. The inner chamber connected the black and red wires with the timer.

When he glanced at Leila, she sent him a look of reassurance. "You're doing great."

"Now cut the red wire. The timer will stop."

"Cutting…" *Oh, shit*! "Um, Torque?" His heart pounded painfully.

"Yeah?"

He looked at Leila as he spoke. She didn't return his gaze. She stared at the bomb, her eyes widening. Erik cleared his throat. "The timer didn't stop."

After a moment of silence on the other end, Torque said, "What's the timer say?"

"Three minutes."

"How long?" Torque's voice rose among the static.

"Three!"

"Nearest transfer orbiter is four minutes away, Erik."

"What'll we do?" Leila turned toward him now, fear in her eyes. "Maybe cut the black wire?"

"Can we cut the black wire, Torque?"

"Not unless you want to die right now, instead of three minutes from now."

Erik stroked Leila's arm. She felt so cold. "Torque, what kind of bomb is this? How does it work?"

"Self-contained electrical trigger. Fairly archaic, compared to current, microchip models."

"Can the trigger itself be shorted out?"

"Probably, but since Kam said the bomb was bolted in, you can't get it to a secondary electrical source. And nothing that can be physically moved on the orbiter contains enough power to do it."

"Oh, yeah?" Erik reached inside the jacket Leila wore and ripped out Halah's electrical power source. With the tools, he opened up the black box and stripped the wires.

"What are you doing?" Kam asked, looking over his shoulder.

"I'll bet Halah keeps this thing juiced up to maximum." She'd better. Their options ran out after this.

"Hurry, Erik." Leila's gaze darted toward the timer.

Erik wrapped the wires around the trigger mechanism on the bomb. "Stand back." He engaged the power source. Sparks flew everywhere and they all jumped.

A column of black smoke rose from the bomb.

"Look!" Leila shouted. "The power surge didn't work. It's still ticking down."

The electronic readout showed three seconds, two, one... The timer stopped on zero.

Erik grabbed Leila. All three of them hit the floor.

Silence. No explosion.

"Did I miss something? Leila asked, her voice sounding more than a little shaky. "Are we dead?"

"I don't think so." Kam sat up and looked toward the bomb.

"The surge must have worked." Erik sent up a prayer of thanks.

A sudden, loud poof made them jerk. A fine mist drifted out of the bomb's inner chamber and filled the orbiter. They began to cough.

"Get the oxygen masks," Erik ordered. "That's poisonous gas coming out."

They scrambled to their feet.

Leila searched the compartments. "There are no masks."

"Erik," Torque said over the headset. "Are you still there?"

"Yeah. The bomb didn't go off. It's disabled, but gas is filling up the orbiter. We don't have any extra oxygen up here."

"We've got a transfer orbiter right off your starboard side. We'll get you off."

"Thanks, Torque. Kam, prepare for a mid-orbit transfer."

"Right." Kam moved in front of a control panel and flipped some switches. "Atmospheric hatch activated. Ventilation reversed to draw the gas up into the system. We should have enough air for the transfer, as long as we relocate fast."

Leila staggered, and Erik lifted her in his arms. "Hold on, sweetheart. Just a few more minutes. Breathe shallowly."

* * * * *

Back on Xylon, deep in The Lair, Erik, Kam, and Leila walked down the ramp of the rescue orbiter. Erik was amazed. The transport center looked filled with Warriors, there to greet them. A deafening cheer went up.

Erik searched for Braden in the crowd, but he didn't see his friend. His worry escalated.

Torque stepped out of the milling throng. "Welcome home." He clapped each of their shoulders, then glanced with interest at Leila's bare legs. He cocked an eyebrow.

"Slave outfits." She held Halah's jacket closed around her breasts.

"Ah, yes. Of course."

Erik clapped Torque's shoulder, grabbing his attention. "Good to be back. They got to us just in time. Thanks for your help."

"What happened with Halah?"

"Last we saw her, she was headed for the Sand Moon with a Marid interceptor on her tail. Did we ever get Josella back?"

"No. She's still missing. I called off the search for her after the transport orbiter picked all of you up. Pitch and my sisters are on their way back home now."

"Is there any way we can contact Halah or find out if she made it to the moon?" Kam asked.

"I'll see if her tracker code is in the computer. Though the device seems to have a glitch or two, so don't hold out hope of locating her." Torque turned back to Erik. "You have the formula and data?"

Erik hesitated. "Yeah. We brought back what we could." Whether what his pants contained turned out to be useful or not still needed to be determined. "Where's Braden?"

Everyone grew strangely quiet.

"All right, what's going on?" Something was obviously very wrong. He wanted to know the problem, right now. "Where's Braden?" he asked again, more forceful this time.

The Warriors surrounding them began to disperse, murmuring among themselves.

A worried look crossed Kam's face. "What happened? Is Alexa all right? The babies?"

Torque's eyes revealed his sadness. "We don't know. A lot's happened while you've been gone. Let's get you all some decent clothes and head to the Council Chamber. You all need to be briefed on the recent news, and the Council wants to debrief you on the Marid mission. We have some planning to do."

Epilogue

In her bedchamber, Erik held Leila in his arms. Given the present situation, neither of them felt right about a Branding ceremony at this time. But soon. He wasn't going to let her get away from him for long. He'd petitioned the Council for permission to permanently join with her. After they obtained that permission, they'd decide when to hold the rite.

"It'll work out," she told him, rubbing his chest and shifting under the covers.

Somehow she didn't sound all that convinced. He commanded The Lair now. Laszlo had disappeared. Alexa was gone. Braden was missing. He held Leila tighter, determined to protect her from everything that might ruin their happiness together. "It stops here," he whispered. "No more losses."

"What are we going to do about Braden and Alexa?" she asked him. "The Council is discussing plans, but by the time they decide on a mode of action, it might be too late."

"We're going to find them."

"But how?"

"We'll build a secondary booster for the tracker. And I want you to come up with a diagnostic for the brain chips. See if you can create one to fix glitches remotely."

"It'll take time."

"Put it on priority. Even above analyzing the sterilization formula."

"The Council won't like that."

"Stall them. I'm going to send out search teams." No way was he just letting this situation sit. He'd do everything in his power to get his friends back, if they still lived, or their bodies, if they didn't. His heart clenched at the disturbing thought.

"What if the Council won't sanction a search? They've never supported searches, when it takes too many Warriors from their posts. And since they have you to lead The Lair, they might not be so eager."

"Alexa's a super breeder. They'll want her back. And Braden has super breeder genes."

"That didn't seem to concern them when they banished Torque all those years ago. He has the same genes."

"Banished, yes. But they had access to him, if they needed him." His vid-cell beeped. He reached over to the table beside the bed. "Yeah?"

"This is Torque."

Erik clicked on the speaker so Leila could hear. "You have Council news?"

"Just came in over the computer. The Council has decided not enough evidence exists to warrant a search at this time. They think Alexa's disappearance is a simple domestic disturbance, and also say there's no proof of foul play in Braden's disappearance. They want to wait and see if they both show back up on their own before allocating Warriors for a search."

"Typical bureaucratic—"

"There's more, Erik."

"What?" The tone of Torque's voice worried him.

"Your request to permanently join with Leila has been denied."

Leila gasped.

Erik surged upright in the bed. "What? Why?"

"They say you two need to breed with off-planet, DNA-compatible mates, like Braden did, to strengthen and expand the gene pool."

"Erik—" Leila grabbed his arm, panic in her eyes.

He covered her hand with his. "The Council can kiss my ass. I want you to follow the orders I gave you earlier. Agreed?"

"Will do. I'm with you on this, Erik. And I'm sure Kam will be, too. He wants his sister found. And we all know you and Leila belong together."

Though still reeling from the news, knowing Warriors supported him kept Erik sane. "Good. We'll meet in the morning to set up our game plan. Keep this quiet. Bring Pitch and your sisters in on this, but no one else outside the circle."

"Consider it done."

Erik disconnected the cell.

"Erik—"

"Shh." He gathered Leila in his arms. Her trembling tugged at his heart. "Don't worry."

Leila hugged him. "I love you, Erik. I can't lose you."

"And I love you. I won't allow us to be separated. Ever."

"What are we going to do?"

Only one solution existed. Erik held her at arm's length. "Get on your stomach."

"Erik, now is hardly the time—" Her eyes widened. "You're going to Brand me without Council approval."

"That's right. It's the only way, Leila. Once my mark is placed, nothing and nobody can undo it." The Council had no right to deny their request to officially join. They were strong Warriors, would make strong Breeders, and produce exceptional children. Exactly what Xylon needed.

"They'll banish us!"

"With Braden missing, no way. Who's going to run The Lair? Even if they do, as long as we're together, I don't really care. Do you?"

Without hesitation, she shook her head. "No, not as long as we're together." Excitement leapt into her eyes. "We'll need two witnesses."

"Braden instigated that rule as a precaution, in case either party changed their mind. I'm in charge now, and I don't want other Warriors involved. Banishment would be mandatory for them if the Council refuses to budge on their decision about us."

"But you're already getting the others involved."

"In a military capacity only, and I intend to be very careful with their assignments, so no punishment comes to them." He needed to protect them all as much as possible. Their loyalty to him wouldn't be their downfall. He respected them too much to allow anything to ruin their lives.

He laced his fingers through Leila's and stared deeply into her gorgeous cinnamon eyes. "I want our ceremony private. After it's done, we'll continue to keep quiet about the Branding for as long as possible. With your hair so thick and long, the mark won't even be seen. You just have to be careful and always wear your hair down."

"I can place one of my skin patches over the Brand. No one will ever know."

Yes, perfect. This would work. "Excellent idea. That'll give me time to work things out with the Council, if I can. If not, we'll handle whatever comes our way together. Now, get on your stomach, baby. Let's do this."

Leila positioned herself flat on the bed, on her stomach, as he directed.

Erik pushed a pillow under her hips, hoping to make her more comfortable, and give him easier access to her body. He stroked her back. "I'm sorry this isn't more romantic for you."

She turned her head and smiled up at him. "I like the intimacy with just the two of us. That makes it romantic."

"You do want this, right, Leila?" She'd already said she loved him and wanted to join, but the possibility of banishment shouldn't be taken lightly. He didn't want to put her through the ceremony unless she was absolutely certain.

"Oh, yes, Erik. Please. I want to be a part of you for the rest of our lives, however we need to accomplish that. If the worst happens, I'll follow you anywhere fate sees fit to send us."

Erik relaxed, so grateful that he'd found Leila. He pushed her hair aside and licked the back of her neck. He felt her shudder in anticipation. His cock stirred, quickly growing hard. With a light touch, he glided his hand down her back and over her ass. "So soft." His fingers touched her pussy. "So wet."

She laid her head down on the pillow clutched it in her arms. "Make love to me, Erik. I need to feel you inside me and know that we're joined forever."

He positioned himself behind her and slowly eased his cock into her pussy. "Oh, yeah." Their bodies fit together perfectly.

Leila mewled and pushed back against him, raising her ass slightly. "All the way in, Erik. Please."

He pushed deep. Each time they came together, either physically or emotionally, his love for her grew stronger. He pulled back, then pushed forward again, gently penetrating her as deeply as possible.

"Oh, Erik. Yes!"

He held her hair aside and laved her neck. They both needed to come at the same time that he placed his mark with the implant in his mouth, or the Branding wouldn't work. He felt her vagina tighten around him and he knew she was close.

Also close to coming, he strengthened his resolve and held back, waiting for her, so he could time this perfectly. "I love you, Leila. No one has ever touched my heart like you do. Come for me, baby."

"Oh, yes. I'm coming, Erik!"

Her body trembled beneath him. Erik lowered his mouth to her neck and formed the Brand with his lips. He let go, losing control and climaxing along with her.

Ecstasy like he'd never felt rushed through his body. He heard Leila scream, and her voice felt like a part of him. Their bodies, minds, and souls merged as one. He had no idea the Branding ceremony held such power. His whole body shook.

Their joining became complete.

Leila collapsed, and he collapsed on top of her. It took several moments for both of them to catch their breaths. He checked the back of her neck. The round brand, with an intricate and unique design, marked Leila as his. She belonged to him now. They belonged to each other.

"Are you all right?" he asked softly.

She nodded and reached down to touch his hand.

He moved off her and gathered her into his arms. He felt her heart pounding in her chest, with the same rhythm as his. "Forever, my love."

"Forever." Her eyes closed, and she relaxed in his arms, drifting off to sleep.

Erik held her close to his heart. No matter the problems on Xylon, he and Leila were now joined as breeder-mates and nothing could ever tear them apart.

Enjoy this excerpt from
Diamond Studs
© Copyright Ruth D. Kerce, Diana Hunter,

Ruby Storm 2005

Diamond Assets
Ruth D. Kerce

"I saw Hunter Dunlap in the company sauna yesterday with only a skimpy towel on and nothing else. That man is a major hunk. If he even once glanced in my direction, with a modicum of interest, I'd jump his bones and stay strapped on like a bronc rider at a rodeo."

"Ooo, baby! Yee-ha!"

Ronni recognized the voices as belonging to two clerks in the lingerie sales division—Jess and whatever-the-other-was-named; she couldn't remember.

"I can't believe his wife ran off with his personal assistant. She had to be nuts to give up that man's body, not to mention all his money."

"I'm sure she got a wad of a settlement. Can you imagine how much he must be worth as co-owner of *Everlasting Love*?"

"If Ronni had worked for Hunter back then, it never would have happened."

"You said it. Who picks out her wardrobe anyway? She dresses like my spinster aunt. And those glasses…"

"Oh, they're the worst! She looks like an owl."

Tears misted Ronni's eyes, and her chest tightened. So what, if she dressed conservatively? This was a place of business, not the *Ho to Go* club. Before she heard any more trash about herself or her boss, she pushed her way out of the stall.

With flushed faces, and lips at least temporarily sealed, the two clerks rushed out the door.

They were right. She did look like an owl. She lowered her utilitarian glasses and perched them on the tip of her nose.

Maybe she *should* check into getting something more fashionable. Or redo her makeup. She had good skin. She could play that up. She needed to lose about ten pounds to show off her cheekbones better, but overall she was happy with who she was. She'd never be a ravishing beauty, but that was okay. She liked herself.

As she thought about her position in the company and her boss, she acknowledged that the two women had been right about something else. Hunter was a major hunk with a major body. Tall, fit, with just enough muscle to make any woman weak in the knees.

His eyes were what really drew her though. Deep brown like rich, thick chocolate. They showed a hint of mischief when he smiled, as if he held a wealth of sexual secrets that he'd love to share. Or maybe that was just wishful on her part.

She'd had many a fantasy about the man.

Diamond in the Snow
Diana Hunter

"Take them off. No, take them off right there. No sense in making a path of wet snow from here to wherever." She deliberately turned her back on him and busied herself with the cups, spooning in several tablespoons of the cocoa mix as he undressed.

Deciding to call her bluff, he stripped off his shirt and pants and then his briefs as well. But the air hitting his damp skin was cold and he shivered again.

"Throw me one of those hand towels, will you? I don't bite, you know."

His voice was almost in her ear. She jumped as he took the towel from her outstretched hand to dry his thighs. Grinning, he chose not to move from behind her, instead baiting her by remaining where he was.

She knew he was there…and that he must be naked. It had been a long time since she'd seen a naked man. And the memory of him in the snow, standing like a knight in armor, stirred her deeply and in places that had not been moved in quite a long time. Her head dipped as the smile deepened into a grin and she slowly turned around.

Briefly tempted to cover himself with the small scrap of cloth, he decided two could bluff. Throwing the towel to the corner, he straightened, completely naked in the center of his kitchen.

Carolyn's breath caught as she stared at the knight without his armor, still strong and invincible before her. Strength emanated from his broad chest, the powerful muscles at rest, yet still striking in their potency. No hair marred the perfection of smooth skin that glimmered in the candlelight, the line of his chest leading her eyes down past his narrow waist.

Paul felt himself respond to the appreciation and hunger in her eyes.

Wasn't that what she'd wanted? She had been the one to tell him to undress here in the kitchen. She was the one who couldn't stop teasing him. Every time she looked at him, her fascination with him multiplied.

Now his power dominated the room and threatened to overwhelm her.

Diamond in the Rough
Ruby Storm

Cupid flipped open a red, embossed folder on his desk. His blue eyes thoughtfully scanned the list of this year's human names of lonely, forlorn people who needed to discover love in their lives. It was his job to pair a human female and male, forward their names to the recruits, let the magic begin, and hope like hell it worked.

Tilting his head slightly to the side, he gazed over the thin wire rims of his bifocals and pursed his lips. The two before him, however, had Cupid somewhat apprehensive in regard to the poor humans who would be assigned to this rather young and over-exuberant team of fairies.

Realizing that their boss scrutinized them, Rosebud squared her slender shoulders, elbowed Larry to the side despite her petite stature, and took a dainty step forward. Darting her thick-lashed eyes sidelong, she cringed when Larry puffed up his cheeks and noticeably blew the edge of her wing from the side of his face where it poked one brown eye.

"Rosebud Kisses and Larry L'amour. I see this will be your first mission. Do you think you're ready?"

"Yes, sir!" the two shouted in unison.

"Rather enthusiastic, aren't you?"

"Yes, sir!"

Cupid winced. "You realize that if you accomplish the mission, you both will be granted your Gold Wings for permanent fairy status?" His hand shot up as the two before him opened their mouths again. "No need to answer. I see that you've both finished at the top of your classes. That's very good. The only thing left is to see how you work out in the field."

"We'll do a wonderful job, sir. When we're done, there will be one more couple on this earth madly in love."

One thick brow cocked over Cupid's eye. "Well, yes...we'll see about that." Studying the names scribbled across the paper, his fingers shuffled across the surface of his desk to grab a red pencil. He closed his eyes and let the tip of the pencil drop haphazardly to the paper. Peering beneath one eyelid, he drew a red heart around two names.

God help them – and I don't mean these two in front of me...

About the author:

Ruth D. Kerce got hooked on writing in the fifth grade when she won a short story contest—a romance, of course. And she's been writing romance ever since.

She writes several subgenres of romance—historical, contemporary, and futuristic. Her books are available online in many internet bookstores. Her short stories and articles are available on several websites. She has won or placed in writing contests and hopes to continue to write exciting tales for years to come.

Ruth welcomes mail from readers. You can write to her c/o Ellora's Cave Publishing at 1056 Home Avenue, Akron OH 44310-3502.

Why an electronic book?

We live in the Information Age—an exciting time in the history of human civilization in which technology rules supreme and continues to progress in leaps and bounds every minute of every hour of every day. For a multitude of reasons, more and more avid literary fans are opting to purchase e-books instead of paperbacks. The question to those not yet initiated to the world of electronic reading is simply: *why?*

1. *Price.* An electronic title at Ellora's Cave Publishing and Cerridwen Press runs anywhere from 40-75% less than the cover price of the <u>exact same title</u> in paperback format. Why? Cold mathematics. It is less expensive to publish an e-book than it is to publish a paperback, so the savings are passed along to the consumer.

2. *Space.* Running out of room to house your paperback books? That is one worry you will never have with electronic novels. For a low one-time cost, you can purchase a handheld computer designed specifically for e-reading purposes. Many e-readers are larger than the average handheld, giving you plenty of screen room. Better yet, hundreds of titles can be stored within your new library—a single microchip. (Please note that Ellora's Cave and Cerridwen Press does not endorse any specific brands. You can check our website at www.ellorascave.com or

www.cerridwenpress.com for customer recommendations we make available to new consumers.)

3. *Mobility.* Because your new library now consists of only a microchip, your entire cache of books can be taken with you wherever you go.

4. *Personal preferences are accounted for.* Are the words you are currently reading too small? Too large? Too...**ANNOYING**? Paperback books cannot be modified according to personal preferences, but e-books can.

5. *Instant gratification.* Is it the middle of the night and all the bookstores are closed? Are you tired of waiting days—sometimes weeks—for online and offline bookstores to ship the novels you bought? Ellora's Cave Publishing sells instantaneous downloads 24 hours a day, 7 days a week, 365 days a year. Our e-book delivery system is 100% automated, meaning your order is filled as soon as you pay for it.

Those are a few of the top reasons why electronic novels are displacing paperbacks for many an avid reader. As always, Ellora's Cave and Cerridwen Press welcomes your questions and comments. We invite you to email us at service@ellorascave.com, service@cerridwenpress.com or write to us directly at: 1056 Home Ave. Akron OH 44310-3502.

NEED A MORE EXCITING
WAY TO PLAN YOUR DAY?

ELLORA'S
CAVEMEN
2006 CALENDAR

COMING THIS FALL

THE
ELLORA'S CAVE
LIBRARY

Stay up to date with Ellora's Cave Titles
in Print with our Quarterly Catalog.

TO RECIEVE A CATALOG,
SEND AN EMAIL WITH YOUR NAME
AND MAILING ADDRESS TO:

CATALOG@ELLORASCAVE.COM

OR SEND A LETTER OR POSTCARD
WITH YOUR MAILING ADDRESS TO:
CATALOG REQUEST
C/O ELLORA'S CAVE PUBLISHING, INC.
1337 COMMERCE DRIVE #13
STOW, OH 44224

COMING TO A BOOKSTORE NEAR YOU!

ELLORA'S CAVE
2005

BEST SELLING AUTHORS TOUR

Discover for yourself why readers can't get enough of the multiple award-winning publisher Ellora's Cave. Whether you prefer e-books or paperbacks, be sure to visit EC on the web at www.ellorascave.com for an erotic reading experience that will leave you breathless.

www.ellorascave.com